44 Erotica Sex Stories of Anal Sex and Naughty Fantasy Beast Erotica

3 Books in 1

Book 1: Anal Adventures
Book 2: Fantastic Beast Sex
Book 3: Hot Mature Women Sex Stories

Victoria Gray

This book is a work of fiction. Any references to historical events, real people, or real places are used fictiously.

Forward

Hello and thank you for checking out my book. I wrote these erotic adventures to entertain others and I’ve them some great stories about anal sex. I hope you enjoy them!

Table of Contents

Book 1:

Anal Adventures

25 Hot Erotica Stories of Extreme Anal Sex

Victoria Gray

Mandy's First Experience

Mandy sighed, feeling like everything was going to the toilet. After a big breakup, her job driving her bad, and stress, the last thing she wanted to do was to deal with anyone. But, her best friend Jasmine insisted upon seeing a guy, so that's what she did, even though this normally wasn't her scene at all.

That's why Mandy was here, in the club with a bunch of random people. But none of them were catching her attention. That is, until a muscular man with sandy blonde hair and blue eyes caught her eye. She looked at him, and the look sealed the deal.

He marched over to her, smiling at her with a devilish grin.

"You alone?"

"Yeah. Recently broke up with my shitty ex. Could use a pick-me-up," she admitted.

"Want me to show you something different, but fun?" he inquired.

Mandy looked at him, slightly unsure as to what that meant. But, this was her first time experiencing freedom in forever, so she immediately said yes.

The man, who she learned shortly after was named Randy, took her hand, practically gliding her to the hotel across the street from the club. Soon, his lips were on her own, and Mandy immediately responded.

He was a good kisser, and the fact that he used tongue turned her on even more. She rutted her hips against his cock, feeling the bulging muscle against there. He smiled, pulled away and touching her hips.

"Eager are we?"

"Yes," she replied.

"There is one thing I'd like to ask of you, and that is...I want to try putting it in your ass," he said.

Put it in her ass? That seemed so bizarre.

"Are you sure? I've never done that before."

"I wouldn't mind trying it. If it's too much, I won't continue. But I'lll make sure you're prepared," he said.

Mandy was hesitant, but she soon agreed, and Randy pushed her onto the bed, kissing her passionately. He soon tore off her clothes, leaving her naked and flush. His hands moved up, touching the bud of the nipple, and she soon gasped, feeling her body jerk in response. He teased the edge of her bud, letting his hands dance over the area. His lips moved to the other bud, teasing it with his lips, and Mandy immediately groaned.

He moved down her body towards the folds of her pussy, spreading her apart and using his hands to both penetrate her and tease her clit. He was like a professional with this, surprising Mandy as he started to push his fingers into there, teasing her pussy with every single touch. He inserted one finger, and then the second, all while circling her clit with his thumb.

The sensations were almost too much. Not even her ex was this good. She tensed up, moaning out loud as she came hard, feeling her body squeeze his fingers and then relax.

"You good?" he asked.

"Yes."

"You want to try it still?" Randy inquired.

Mandy nodded, trusting this guy.

"You prepared me better than my ex ever did, so I'lll try it," she said.

He smiled, moving his index finger downwards, teasing her pucker. He reached towards his pocket, grabbing the lube and putting it on. With deft hands, he inserted the first finger, causing her to suddenly gasp at the intrusion.

It was a stretch, that's for sure, but he soon pushed the digit in deeper, causing her to gasp at the sensation of it. It felt so full, so nice, and while he inserted the fingers, he teased her clit with small touches. He was a natural at this, and as Mandy started to feel him put a third in, she realized he was met with little resistance.

She never thought doing it in the butt would feel so fucking good.

He started to dance his fingers in and out, penetrating her softly, and as she felt this, she began to tense up, feeling her body immediately respond in a positive manner to this. After the third finger was inside completely, she spoke.

"I want your cock," she said.

"Good to know. Want it missionary?" he asked.

"Y-yes," Mandy said.

She figured for her first time it would be good. He spread her apart, pulling his pants off to reveal his large, seven-inch cock. It was throbbing, and for a moment, Mandy wondered if she could get that inside her. But then, he gently pushed in, and soon it was all the way in.

It was a bit of a discomforting tightness, but then she grew used to it, moaning in pleasure at the sensations bestowed to her. He began to thrust, pushing in and out of her hole, and each one hit her in a different spot than being fucked in the pussy ever did. He pulled her hips up, pushing deep into her, and with deep, penetrative thrusts, she screamed.

His hand moved up to her clit, teasing her there, and soon he dipped two fingers into her pussy, fucking both of her holes. Mandy never felt so fucking full, and as she felt him push in deeper and deeper, she could feel the onset of her orgasm come over her.

When it did, she squeezed against him, causing him to groan and release inside her. She didn't expect him to do that, but it felt so amazing that she didn't want him to stop. When it was over, he pulled back, looking at her with a smile on his face.

"You enjoy that?"

"Yeah. I wouldn't mind doing that again," Mandy admitted.

He reached up, kissing her softly on the lips.

"Well if you ever need some butt fun, I'm always ready for that," he said.

Mandy nodded, taking that into consideration. It was a simple one-night stand, but it woke up something within Mandy that changed her forever.

She was a butt slut now, and she wanted nothing more than to be fucked in the ass again, especially be a thick, hard cock.

Spicing It Up

Angela wanted to try this. She heard from her friend Mia that anal is amazing, and with the right cock, she knew she was in for a treat.

That's why, when she felt the throes of pleasure from the stimulation her husband Paul provided to her, Angela knew for a fact that this was it. She felt enraptured in pleasure, and when Paul pulled back from her aching cunt, which was dripping in both saliva and her own juices, he pushed his hands to his mouth, wiping the contents and smiling.

"Was that good babe?"

"Yeah. Fucking amazing," Angela admitted with a blush.

He looked at her, and as he pointed to the toys, Angela nodded. She wanted to try this with Paul. He wasn't huge, but he also wasn't tiny, so he would fit pretty tightly within her. She did try masturbating once with her ass along with her vibrator, and it gave her some of the best orgasms of her life.

She felt his hands touch her pucker, just massaging the area there. Angela tensed, realizing how different, but also how nice this felt. He then slipped his hand back, grasping the lube and putting it onto his hands. Angela looked at Paul with an anticipatory glance, knowing full well that her husband wouldn't hurt her.

With ginger hands, he pushed the first digit in. Angela tensed, feeling the foreign sensation within her. She loved it, but at also at the same time didn't know what to think of it. He pushed his hands into her, fingering her ass with his digits, and she soon relaxed, moaning to the touch. Her body clenched up, and while he continued to tease her, his tongue moved between her legs, licking at her clit.

She relaxed, moaning at the sensations she was given. He soon added in a second digit, teasing the area there, and it was then when she began moaning in his ear, feeling everything start to change within, her whole body reacting to his touches in a manner that she wasn't used to. As he continued to finger her, moving the digits around, he touched the area against her body that sent jolts through her body. Angela cried out, and as she did so, Paul let his tongue move towards her clit, touching and teasing her.

"Fuck, fuck fuck!" she cried out, feeling the desperation and the need for more start to overtake her. She loved everything about this, and then, when she felt the aftereffects of her orgasm start to diminish, she looked at Paul, who smiled at her.
"You good?"
"Yeah. Better than good," she admitted.
He smiled, pushing her legs further apart. He pushed a third digit in, and Angela immediately felt the tightness against the ring of muscle. She felt her entire body grow tense, especially due to how stuffed up she was. He thrust his hands in and out of her, deeper and deeper, and Angela was struggling to keep her consciousness there. She could feel another orgasm come about, and when it all hit her, she tensed up, crying out loud and in pleasure as she came hard against his hands, shivering in delight.
He pulled back, smiling as he looked at her.
"Do you want to be on top?" he asked.
"Sure," she replied.
Angela felt nervous when it came to this, and soon, she moved her body so that her ass was right over his lubed cock. When she moved down on it, she immediately felt the ongoing tightness that came along with it, screaming out loud and in pleasure at the sensations of this. She then started to ride his cock, tensing up and moaning out loud at the sensations that were riding through her body. After a few more thrusts, she then felt him grasp her hips, pushing in and out of her hard.
Angela couldn't believe the sensations she was feeling through her body. It was strange, mostly because she never thought that she'd get a chance to experience pleasure in this way, but as he penetrated her, filling her up and also teasing her pussy with his fingers, Angela knew that the desperation for more touch, for more from her husband, the man that she loved, drove her mad.
"God I'm close," he said.
She looked at Paul, who had a look of desperation in his eyes. He seemed just as happy to have this happen as she did, his whole body reacting to her actions. After a few more thrusts, she then felt him tense against her, and she then noticed his hands as they moved up, penetrating her hard as he soon pushed his cock as deep into her as possible. With a groan, he came inside, and that's when Angela felt it.
The combination of him cumming inside and her own personal pleasure was too much, and she then cried out, tensing up as she soon released as well, feeling her orgasm completely overtake her.

She moved off his cock, the cum trickling out of her ass as a result of their efforts, and when she looked at it, she smiled.
"That was fun," she admitted.
"Sure was. I didn't hurt you or anything, right?" Paul asked, worry that he might've hurt his wife obvious in his eyes.
"No, you're totally fine. In fact, I think I found my new favorite thing to do in the bedroom," Angela said with a purr. She looked at Paul, who blushed as well, and soon she gave him a deep kiss that expressed her adoration.
"Good. I'm glad I didn't hurt you. I love you babe," he said.
"I love you too."
Angela curled up to Paul, ignoring the cum that was in her ass for now. She was happy, and she knew that this adventure was one that she would love to go on again and again, and she knew that she would enjoy it no matter what would come about in the future.

The Anal Surprise

Hannah trusted her boyfriend when he said he wanted to try something new with her, but she would be in control.
However, she didn't expect it to be anal. But, when his hands moved towards her thighs, touching them, she looked down at Rob, who smiled at her.
"Are you okay babe?" he asked.
"Yeah. I'm just nervous. I've never done this before," she said.
"Well, if you're worried, or if you're in pain period, we can always stop. I promise that I'lll never hurt you," he admitted.
Hannah looked at Rob, noticing how honest he was, and she soon nodded.
"Okay. I trust you on this. But, how are you going to...prepare me?" she asked.
"I bought a couple of toys for this," he said.
Hannah watched as he brought forth a bottle of lube, along with a butt plug that looked small enough. She blushed at the contents, but then, Rob started to spread her folds open, diving his tongue into her sweet pussy. He licked in all the right places, and soon, Hannah's hands moved straight to his hair, teasing it slightly, and as he did this, she began to gasp.
"Fuck, this is just too good!" she cried out.
"You know I want to make you feel good baby," he said to her.
She blushed, but then she started to lose herself in the pleasures of the moment. She began to feel his tongue circle her clit, teasing it there as he began to push the toy inside. She expected it to hurt, expected it to be painful for her, and she expected it to be too much and she would refuse, but it went in so perfectly that she enjoyed the unfamiliar tightness that went along with it.
Rob took his time, letting the plug sit all the way in as he went to town, dining on her ripe pussy, and Hannah started to tense up, gripping the sheets as she felt the onset of her orgasm start to come about. She then lifted her hips up, moaning as she felt her body release. Rob accepted the juices, letting his mouth take care of cleaning her up before he pulled back.
"Are you good?"
"Yeah. I am. I want to try more," she said.

Rob grabbed a bigger butt plug, and soon, he pulled out the smaller one, causing a gasp to emit from her mouth. He then pushed the larger one into there, and Hannah felt the stretch this time, but I wasn't anything too bad.
"You good?"
"Yeah babe. I like the feeling," she said.
Rob started to play with the butt plug, pushing it in and out, and that's when Hannah felt a strange trickle of pleasure. She didn't expect it to feel so good, but then as he started to penetrate her deeper, she soon began to feel the difference. She knew for a fact that this was indeed something she could get used to, and then, just a few mere minutes later, Rob then began to move a bigger butt plug into her.
She felt the stretch this time, her body initially at first shocked by all of this, but then later on, she felt the urge to accept this. She then started to moan, feeling the excitement from everything that was happening, and soon, Rob started to thrust the toy in and out. Hannah cried out, feeling a strange pleasure within her body as she soon came hard.
When Rob finished, he pulled the toy out, looking at Hannah's spent body.
"Want to try it with the real thing?" he offered.
Hannah knew that Rob was bigger than the toys, so it made her feel slightly apprehensive. But then, she nodded, gripping the bed as he spread her apart. He undid his pants, pulling his cock out and stroking it.
"Fuck, you look so good right here," he said.
"Thank you. I'm glad," she admitted.
Rob then spread her cheeks apart, easing into there. At first, Hannah cringed at the sudden feeling of tightness, unsure of whether or not she was fine with it. It was then when he pushed all the way in, causing her to tense up at the sensations of this, her body aching for more.
He pushed his cock all the way into her, immediately causing her to let out a moan of pleasure, her entire body losing control at the sudden fullness. She then watched rob spread her pussy open, pushing a small vibrator into there.
"For real?" she asked.
"Yes. I want you to feel good," he said.
Hannah was so happy that Rob cared about her pleasure, and soon, he started to push the toy all the way in, turning it on and watching as she screamed out, the feeling of both her holes being penetrated

being the most amazing thing ever. He soon started to thrust hard, but Hannah didn't care, because her entire body was at the mercy of all of the stimulation that she managed to feel at this point. She knew for a fact that rob was too good, and she knew that he was ready to make her feel good. It was then that, after a couple more thrusts, she felt her entire body tense up, her pussy completely dripping in pleasure, and she soon came hard. She felt her whole body completely lose itself, and she noticed that Rob came shortly after, but she didn't even feel it because she was so wrapped up in the pleasure that she felt.

Rob then pulled out, and Hannah simply laid there, completely spent from the feeling that she experienced. This was her first time experiencing this type of sex, and she knew that it woke something up within her.

The need to do it more and more.

She looked at Rob, smiling weakly, and it was then when she realized that Rob enjoyed it too, and they probably would end up doing this again sometime in the future.

The Neighbor's Love for Butt

When Nikki started messing around with her neighbor Caleb, she realized that the sex was out of this world. He knew how to make Nikki cum buckets, and it was something that not even her ex Toby could do. She didn't even need to use a toy or anything, because Caleb would touch her in all the right places, and she would become a melted puddle of pleasure.

But then, as she looked at Caleb this time, with the toy in his hands, she immediately grew nervous.

"You want to put that...in my butt?" she asked.

"Yeah. I wanted to try it for a while, but I didn't want to just spring this on you, because I didn't want to oops it into the back door, you know," he said with a smirk.

Nikki hesitated. She heard that this would hurt. But she looked at Caleb, and she knew that he was gentle enough with her that she could trust him.

"O-okay, but is it cool if I get into position? And I want you to take it slow," she said.

"That's fine dear. Trust me, I know that it's not something you're used to, but I promise that I'lll make sure that you're comfortable," he said.

Nikki trusted him, and that's something she couldn't always say about others. She got on the bed with her ass up, and as she felt Caleb spread her legs, teasing the very edge of her thighs, she felt her body become a melted puddle of pleasure. She moaned, experiencing the pleasure that came forth with this, and soon, he started to spread her apart, pressing a small bullet vibrator right into her pussy lips. Nikki cried out, tensing up as she felt the vibrations start to swim through her body.

This felt too good. How could this feel so good?

She then felt his hands spread her ass cheeks apart, his hands teasing her pucker with small dancelike touches. She tensed up, letting her body immediately respond to his actions, and soon, he grasped a bottle of something. She imagined it was lube, and after he uncapped it and spread the contents onto his fingers and the toy, she immediately tensed up.

He gingerly pushed a finger into there, spreading her apart with the small touch. It was tight, but Nikki loved it, and she soon began to moan as the neighbor thrust his fingers in and out of her a little bit faster, making his motions almost a bit rough in a sense. She began to moan at the sensations that were given to her, the sudden tightness a bit of a shock to her, but then as he pushed the second finger into there, she soon began to moan even more, tensing up as she felt him push his fingers in a penetrative manner deep into her. She loved this, and soon, he began to move his fingers in and out, faster and faster, and it was then when she felt his hand tease the toy inside her pussy. She immediately felt her body tense up, feeling the excitement grow within, and when he pushed the toy up slightly, she cried out, feeling the throes of her orgasm as it took over her. When she relaxed, she soon watched as he pushed back, and when Nikki stared at the neighbor, he smiled at her before he pulled back, smirking.

He took the toy out, causing Nikki to cry out, the pleasure and feeling of emptiness beginning to take over her. He then spread her cheeks apart, and then, the sound of the uncapping of lube was heard, and she soon looked over.

He stroked his cock, smiling at her as she blushed. Nikki was excited for this man to take her first time, her anal virginity, and when he pushed the dip against her hungry hole, she shivered.

"Fuck," she said to him.

"You like that babe?"

"Yeah. it's good," she replied, flushing red.

He then started to push himself into her, and the sudden tightness overwhelmed her, and soon, she started to cry out. It was then when he pulled her back so that she could control the speed of his cock going in, and then with small thrusts, Nikki got the rest of his aching dick into her ripe pussy. She shivered, feeling her body tense up with shock at the sensations that she felt. She then started to move slightly, pressing down against him, but then he bucked his hips up, suddenly moving towards her, and when he did, she screamed out.

"Fuck!"

"You okay?"

"Yes, do that again!"

Nikki felt the desperation grow within her, and she soon watched as he began to move his hips up and down against her, his body aching with need. He started to press up and down against her, pushing faster and faster against her, and she soon cried out as he slammed his cock against her body. She felt it all the way in her body, and when he pushed the entire length of his cock into her, and he pushed the toy that he had against her clit, she screamed out, suddenly feeling her body cum hard.

She felt his cock pull out, covering her ass with his cum. She shivered as she felt the spurts of cum against there, and when he finally finished up, he pulled away, smiling at her.

Nikki felt like she experienced a heavenly sensation, her body wanting more, but her mind completely exhausted. She fell down onto the bed, falling asleep shortly after. Caleb was soon right next to her, and when she cuddled up to his larger body, she felt happy and satisfied. She would love to try anal again, and she knew that Caleb enjoyed it just as much as she did as well. They'd both try to plan another experience such as this, and Nikki knew for sure he was as desperate as she was for more, so much more than she expected to feel.

The housewife's Love For Anal

Carrie loved anal, and when she saw the face of exertion that her younger neighbor had it made her shiver. He pushed his cock against the edge of her pucker, teasing her there, and when she felt the slight ache of the burn when he probed her like this, she groaned.

"Fuck," she said.

"You good?" Derrick asked. That was the name of the younger neighbor, and he was a total looker. With sandy blonde hair, blue eyes, and tall frame with bulging muscles, Carrie loved it whenever they had their romps together after she sent off her daughter Abby to school. Usually it involved just fucking and having a bit of fun, nothing serious because she didn't want to worry about that, but when Derrick offered to try anal the first time, she was initially hesitant, but then as he spread her apart, pushing his cock into her the first time, she knew that she made the right choice.

It was heavenly to feel his dick inside there, and while it was originally something that made Carrie shiver at first, and question whether or not she wanted this, but as she continued to feel the cock slowly sink in, filling her up completely, it made her want to enjoy more and more. It was then when he started to fuck her mercilessly into the sheets and while Carrie never thought that she'd love anal like this, she knew that with Derrick, she could enjoy this now.

And here she was, with the thick cock right near her entrance, slowly sinking in, and as he continued to more in with every single inch, she started to take a deep breath, relaxing her muscles as he pushed all the way into her.

She shivered as she began to feel him completely fill her up, and it was then when she started to feel everything tense up and then relax, she knew that this was the experience that she wanted, the one that she desired more than anything else.

He groaned as he filled Carrie up, and Carrie knew for a fact that he was enjoying this just as much as she was. He soon pushed all the way in, and when he pushed his cock deep into her, sheathing himself deeply against her ass, she felt everything penetrate deeply.

After being asked by Derrick if she was cool, and the response of a resounding yes, he soon started to thrust into her, immediately pushing deep into her and fucking her relentlessly. She pushed her ass up, meeting his cock with the heavy thrusts, and when he pushed all the way in, she felt the familiar tightness, one that she knew and loved.

"Fuck yes! Give me more of your fucking cock!" Carrie cried out, her entire body losing control as she felt it go deeper and deeper. She could practically feel her insides being completely filled by his dick, and when she realized that she was already getting close, she relished in it.

But of course, Derrick wanted to give her some extra attention too. With deft hands, he moved towards her pussy, fingering her deep with his digits and rolling a thumb against there. Immediately, Carrie felt her entire body get kicked into overdrive. Despite having her daughter, Carrie was still extremely sensitive down there, and as she felt him start to penetrate her harder and harder, she felt her body begin to lose control, the only thing happening being the screams of pleasure that exuded from her mouth.

When she came hard, she felt like everything was a blur. She loved how her orgasms felt whenever she got fucked in the ass. They were deeper more penetrative, and they hit every single part of her being, her entire body losing control of it all, and everything becoming a blur.

After she relaxed, she felt him start to push deeper and deeper into her, and Carrie was mesmerized by the sthate of his body. He was desperate, with sheens of sweat on his face, and then, after a few more thrusts, he cried out, groaning in pleasure as he soon came deep within her, his cum hitting every inch of her being, and filling the walls of her tight, hot ass.

When he pulled out, he sat back, looking at Carrie with a happy smile.

"You good?"

"Yes dear. I'm definitely happy with the results this time around. You've definitely gotten better," she said.

"That's because I have such a good teacher. I mean, you're so good, and you teach me how to really make you happy. I mean, you're the first woman I've truly been able to pleasure, and it makes me happy knowing this," he admitted.

When she heard this, she felt both happy, but also a little bit surprised by it all. She looked at him, and he soon spoke.

"I want to keep doing this with you. I mean, I know that you have the daughter, and yeah she's getting older, but I don't want to lose

you Carrie. You're like, the best person I've met, and I like doing this," he said.
Carrie smiled, pulling him close and stroking his cock, smirking at the look that he had on his face.
"Well, you don't have to worry about me leaving, because I have no plans to. Now come on, let's go for another round," she told Derrick with a purr.
And it was then when the younger man followed the MILF's lead, letting her stroke his cock to hardness again. Carrie took control, as she loved to do, and when she was able to blow him again, and from there have him fuck her again in both her pussy and ass, she loved every moment of it. This was something that she didn't regret doing, and she realized over time that it was something that she didn't regret at all in her life.

Forest Anal Adventures

For Gina, the one thing that she didn't expect her boyfriend Luke to do was push her up against a tree in the middle of a forest and make out with her. But they were alone, and public sex was totally a thing for her, but she didn't expect it out here, in the middle of the forest during the day.

But that didn't stop Gina from kissing, and as Luke kissed her back, grinding his cock against her, she got this idea. Gina had recently become fascinated with anal, even to the point of doing it with Luke a little bit. It was awkward, that's for sure, but they always managed to have a lot of fun with it, and Gina never complained.

They never did it out in public though, and when Gina pulled away, she looked at her boyfriend with a smoldering smile, desperation obvious on her face.

"I want you to fuck my ass till I can't move," she said to him.

Those words were enough to sir Luke on, for he pushed her against the tree, furiously making out with her for what seemed to be forever before his hands slipped to her pussy, teasing her through the confines of her pants. Gina moaned, feeling the heat start to grow, and the aching throb within her body.

He continued to tease for a minute until he pulled away, moving his hands to the waistband of her pants. With a swift motion, he slipped them off, pushing his face into her pussy, and his hands towards her pucker. Gina didn't know when he managed to put on lube, but soon a probing finger was in there. She immediately reacted to the touch, moaning in pleasure as she felt him penetrate her ass as he continued to eat her out. Gina tried to stay quiet, but the little motions were more than enough for her, and in her mind, she felt like she was experiencing a little taste of heaven.

"Fuck, fuck!" she screamed out loud, trying to hold herself back. He continued to eat her out, teasing every inch of her folds and her body reacting to his own sweet touches. It was heavenly, and then, after a few more moments, she felt a second finger enter into her.

She wanted his cock. She immediately pulled back, slamming her body against the tree, ass out and ready for him.

"Please, just cut the crap will you? I want you to fuck my ass," she moaned, her hips wiggling to help punctuate the need for him.

Luke didn't need to be told twice. He soon spread her cheeks apart, grasping the very tiny bottle of lube he had on himself for moments like this, and he poured the contents straight onto his cock, groaning at the sudden feeling that this gave to him. He looked at Gina, who had a flushed face, her hips out, and her ass looking hungry for action. He immediately pushed the tip inside, sliding his hard member straight into her, causing her to immediately moan in response.

"Holy fuck!" she screamed out loud, immediately tensing up at the sudden feeling. But then, just as quick as it was to happen, she soon felt him press all the way in, filling her pussy up with the sweet tightness.

She immediately shuddered, feeling everything change within her. It felt so right, so perfect, and then, as he started to push in and out of her ass, the tightness overwhelming, she felt it hit all of the right angles. She loved anal, and the fact that she was here, pushed straight up against a tree, being fucked mercilessly by the man that she loved, immediately turned her on even more, and the only thing heard from her was a cacophony of moans.

She noticed Luke's hands right by her pussy, fingering her wet cunt and pushing two fingers into there while he slammed his cock straight into her. The sudden force of the push, and the tightness and fullness of her hole as he pushed all the way in, turned her on even more, and then, after a few brief moments, she felt him push in deeper and deeper, pistoning his cock in and out of her. She immediately moaned in pleasure, her entire body feeling the effects of it all, and then, when he pushed a finger inside of her pussy, curling it up to that bundle of nerves that she knew and loved, she screamed out loud, and it was then when everything changed.

With a shudder, she came hard, feeling the throes of her orgasm completely decimate her. When she finally finished, she felt Luke punctuate two more deep thrusts straight into her, and then, after the third, he groaned, immediately pushing himself all the way in and shuddering at the tightness that came along with her orgasm. She felt her entire body lose control, and that's when Gina realized that Luke indeed finished all the way inside her. He pulled back, putting his cock away as Gina pulled her pants up.

"Well that was a bit of fun," she said.

"Sure was. I think we definitely were a bit loud though," he said.

She heard the sound of footsteps nearby, and Gina knew immediately that someone did hear them. She smiled to herself, feeling both accomplished yet fearful at the realization of this. They both grasped one another's hands, each of them getting away from the scene of where they were.

It was an adventurous romp, and Gina would totally do it again. Next time though, they'd have to make sure that they didn't have anyone else nearby, and they'd have to pay attention to the sounds that were being made.

But, Gina and Luke smiled to one another, and despite the fact that there was a lot of cum in Gina's ass, she'd do this again, and she knew that Luke would certainly do the same thing.

Anal Art Inspiration

Carli struggled to paint the rest of her picture. She needed some inspiration, something that would help her keep on going, a reason for continuing on this pathway.

What she didn't expect, was for Darren to call her, saying that he would come over to the studio to help.

Darren was her current fling, almost to the point of boyfriend level. They were implicitly together, but they never announced it on social media or any shit, but when he came inside, they both hugged one another tightly, making out shortly after. Tongues began to move in perfect synchronization with one another, and then, as Carli pulled away, she looked at him with a huff.

"I need inspiration," she said.

"What kind?"

"I don't know, I just feel that all of my art is...boring. I feel like I need to spice this up. I've been painting erotically, but I want to try something new," she admitted.

Carli blushed as Darren looked her over, smirking in excitement. His hand moved up towards her ass, holding it there in his hands and cupping it. She gasped, feeling the sudden excitement and need for whatever was about to come next.

"I mean...I could show you something new," he said.

Carli was familiar with what he was talking about. Anal. She noticed that Darren was very into the idea of anal sex, but she never really was interested. That is until now. She did practice with a plug a couple of times before today, but something seemed different this time. She felt that their connection was stronger, and as she moved towards the touch, she smirked.

"I wouldn't mind that," she said.

"Good. I'lll make it worth your while then," he said.

He pushed her onto the art bench, and soon, his hands moved towards her pants, pulling them down and off her body. Carli gasped at the sudden feeling of this, realizing just what was going on. His hands moved skillfully, like an artist at the canvas, against her pussy, teasing her with small, needy touches. Immediately, Carli moaned, feeling her entire body move against Darren's hands. His hands were skillful, and as he tore her art smock off her body, he pressed his hands to an erect nipple, sucking on this slightly. Carli gasped, feeling everything change within her, and as she began to feel him move his tongue against there, she began to immediately tense up, moaning out loud at his motions. She then watched as he pulled back, smiling at her before he soon pushed his hands towards her ass.

"I brought something for this moment," he said.

It was lube. She could smell it, a strong strawberry flavor that was chill and perfect. He then pushed the first finger into there, letting his hands move towards her pussy, teasing her in both of her holes. Carli gasped, immediately feeling everything change. This was so perfect, so nice, and as she felt him continue these actions, her body ached for more. Her pussy throbbed for more of his touch, and as he continued to do this, she knew for a fact that he was enjoying this just as much as she was.

"You good babe?" he asked.

"Yes. I want your cock though," she said.

"Good. How do you want it?" he asked.

She looked over near the bench that was by the canvas that she was working on.

"Over there. Take me from behind," she uttered.

Darren didn't need to be told twice. He soon raced over, pushing her against the bench, grasping her hips, and soon his cock sank into her. She groaned, suddenly shocked by the intrusion, but then her ass got used to it as he sank into her, gasping in pleasure at the sensations that he felt.

She immediately moaned as he filled her ass up with his cock. He thrust in deep, letting his hands play with her nipples from behind. The tweaking sensations, along with the feeling of his cock, drove her mad, and as she felt each of these sensations, she looked over at Darren, who was grinning at her with a dark glance.

"This feels...so good," she told him.

"Anything for you princess," he told her with a purr.

He soon fucked her harder and harder, thrusting in so deep that she felt like her entire body was being driven mad by all of this. He soon fucked her faster and faster, shoving a couple of fingers into her wet cunt, thrusting in deep. With each and every single penetrative action, Carli felt like she was losing her mind, and then after a few more thrusts he pushed all the way in, making her tense up, cry out loud, and then cum hard.

The sudden feeling of this drove her mad. She then tensed up, immediately gasping as she finished against him. His cock then pushed all the way in, and with one final groan, he came hard inside of her. The two of them finished up, and when it was all said and done, Darren pulled back. He turned to give her a kiss, and soon, he spoke.

"You good babe?" he asked.

"Yeah. I'm definitely happy with this," she told him.

"Well, if you ever need more inspiration in the future, you just let me know," he told her with a teasing smile.

She nodded, feeling happy with the way everything was. She got back to her canvas after they kissed goodbye, and she had the art inspiration that she needed. Soon, her fingers worked in a dizzying way, moving about as she continued to smile. She thought about how intimate that action was, and she finally got fucked in her studio, something she so desperately wanted. Carli wouldn't mind trying this once again, and she wouldn't mind trying anal again and again in this studio.

The Stepmother's Love for Anal

Destiny loved anal, but her ex-husband never did it. Of course, when she couldn't get it from him, she immediately went to her stepson, who was now not even a member of the family. Destiny married into the family for one reason, and one reason only: cold, hard cash. That meant that she now had a wonderful settlement, but she hated her love life with her ex. The truth was, they never did more than vanilla bullshit, and when Destiny said that she wanted to try anal, he was adamantly against it.

But, her stepson Frankie certainly loved it.

As she felt him kiss down her body, she soon shivered. She had the money now, but she also got the stepson. The truth was, Frankie and his father ended up having a huge fight, and the soon parted ways. Sure enough, he asked to come stay with her for a bit, since he was only 20 and needed to get on his feet. Destiny was fine with that, and they both agreed they wanted to continue this little shindig.

As he continued to tease her nipples with his tongue and fingers, she reached up, grasping a tuft full of blonde hair. That was another thing, her ex didn't have hair, and when she heard the groan from the other man's mouth, she felt a sense of excitement and need. She soon began to tug on the hair more and more, causing him to let out a series of moans and groans. She smiled to herself, watching as he continued to move down towards her thick pussy, teasing the folds there.

"Fuck, you're so good," she said.

Frankie simply smiled and pushed a lubed finger into her. When did he lube up his finger, she didn't fucking know, but she didn't care as she felt the stretch against her body, the sudden need for more, so much fucking more, starting to drive her completely fucking mad. His motions were very exact, and as he continued to move his fingers in and out of her pucker, teasing her clit with his tongue, she felt as if her entire body was at the mercy of this man, completely enthralled by the way he did this. His actions were skilled, way more skilled than the average man, and when she felt him add a second finger, diving his tongue in to tease that bundle of nerves within her, she immediately tensed up, screaming out loud, and the throes of her orgasm started to erupt. Of course, he licked all of this up with a fervency even she was surprised about, and when he pulled back, licking his lips in satisfaction, he looked at her with a smoldering glance, need obvious in his eyes.

"Fuck my ass," she said.

"Damn, you're desperate today Destiny," Frankie said.

"Because you're the best fuck I've got. You're so much better than your dad. He doesn't know how to treat a girl right in the bedroom," Destiny said.

That was met with a grunt of approval before he turned Destiny around, smacking her thick butt and causing her to let out a moan of satisfaction.

"You like that don't you?"

"Yes I fucking do," she told him.

"Well, there is more where that came from," he said.

Doggy style was the preferred method of choice for anal for Destiny, because he got in deep, and the penetration was amazing. As he pushed himself all the way in, destiny let out a groan of satisfaction, feeling his cock push all the way into her, filling her up. It was such a familiar feeling, and as he started to push himself in and out of her with the smallest of thrusts, Destiny lost her shit. She screamed out, tensing up with every single thrust, and soon, she felt him push in and out of her like a piston. Every single pistoned movement drove her mad, and when he started to push in deeper, his hands moved towards her clit, rubbing her with a fervency she never thought she'd get to enjoy. Destiny was grunting and groaning, only able to make those sounds and not much else.

"Yes, please fuck me. Please completely destroy my ass!" she cried out.

"You know I'lll do that for you baby," Frankie said.

He pulled her around, pressing his lips to her own in a passionate, needy kiss. As he did that, he pushed in deeper, his thrusts hitting that one spot, and that, combined with the clitoral stimulation was more than enough for destiny.

She screamed out, sounds that she normally didn't do in the past due to the fact that she needed to be quiet about this, but the fact that her ex husband isn't in the picture anymore allowed her to make the wanton noises she desired. She felt her entire body tighten, pleasure a big part of everything that was going through her head right now, and she soon came hard.

She then felt a couple more penetrative thrusts, and then, there was a groan. She looked up at Franky, and as he came, a look of

complete satisfaction was present on his face. He looked at her, and soon, she smiled back.
"You good?"
"Oh I'm very good, you're certainly better than your father ever was, that's for sure," she said.
"Yeah, I'm glad about that. I heard he's getting remarried. Are you upset about that?"
Destiny laughed to herself, hearing how pathetic this guy was.
"Wow, so he kicks me to the corner and then goes for some other girl? What a fucking idiot. Not my problem though," she told him.
He laughed, looking at Destiny with an approving smile.
"Yeah, I don't blame you. he's definitely an idiot. But you have someone better now, right?"
"Course babe. Love you."
It was weird how that all happened, but destiny loved that she had a man ready to give her the anal pounding she wanted, and the fun that she desired.

Josh's First Time

Josh didn't expect his girlfriend Faye to agree to this, but as she sat there, naked and beautiful with her pussy spread, and her tiny little hole, he blushed.
"So how do you want to do this?" he asked.
"I wouldn't mind riding. I heard it hurts the least," she said.
Josh flushed at those words, listening to them and nodding.
"I can do that," he said.
Josh then spread her apart, already noticing how wet she was from when he ate her out and fucked her a little bit earlier. He almost came during then, but he wanted to try it in her ass. He soon pushed a finger in, pressing her legs up so that her hole was right there. He watched as the pucker resisted for a minute, but then as he pushed it in deeper and deeper, she then let out a small cry.
"Fuck," she said.
"I'm not hurting you, right?" he inquired.
"No, you're good. it's just...different that's all," she admitted.
Josh pushed the finger in deep, penetrating her, and as he looked over at her, he noticed that she was at first a bit pained, but then she relaxed. He pushed a second finger into her, letting his other hand that was free play with her nipples, and as he watched her, he noticed the need for more as she started to stare at him.
"Fuck," she said.
"You good there princess?" he asked.
"Yeah, I'm good," she said to him.
"Great. I'm going to continue."
Josh knew that he needed to take it slow, and as he pushed the second digit into Faye, earning a small moan of approval from her, he smiled, knowing that she went from disliking this, to enjoying the sensations. He began to thrust his fingers in and out of her, starting with the smallest of touches and then going a bit faster. After he was able to push a third finger in, he began to lick her clit, touching her there slightly as he continued the onslaught against her body.
"Holy shit," she muttered, tensing up at his words. He smiled, continually moving his fingers in a very dainty, but also in a way that made her feel good, manner. He watched as she went from

being against every action to keening her body so that she could enjoy it. It was after the third finger that he felt she was ready.
He soon pushed his fingers out, earning a gasp from her, and soon, he started to move his hands towards the bottle of lube. With a shaky hand, he rubbed the contents on himself, and she soon looked at him.
Josh sat back, watching as Faye moved right over his cock, the hungry hole practically begging for him to completely push into. With a sigh, he did, and soon, he was all the way inside her tight pucker.
The sudden, overwhelming feeling of her hole taking him in drove Josh mad. He immediately felt the urge to slam down and fuck the shit out of her, but instead, he let her move her body up and down with small jerks, moaning in pleasure at the sensations that she felt. He looked up at her, and she gave him a reassuring smile.
"I'm good," she said.
"Great. I'm glad babe," he said.
She started moving a bit faster and faster, and as he watched her do this, he felt his own cock start to grow needier. He wanted to move her faster, but he wanted to make sure that she didn't get hurt. So he sat there, watching the show as she continued this, and it was then that, after a few more thrusts, she relaxed, looking at him.
"I want you to try," she said.
"What do you mean?" he inquired.
"I want you to...try pushing inside me. Fucking me. I want you to go harder," she told him with a flushed face.
This was the first time Josh saw his girlfriend so needy, and as he pulled back, he nodded at her.
"Well, I can definitely do that," he said with a smile.
She smiled back with a happy grin, and he soon grasped her hips, plunging his cock in deeper and deeper and controlling the thrusts. This was better than he imagined! It was tight, so goddamn tight it drove him mad, and as he started to move himself up and down against her, watching with rapt eyes as she responded to his actions, he felt the urge to do more, so much more. He continued to thrust into her with a faster pace than he imagined he would get to try, and it was then when she started to move with him. Together, they thrust together, and it surprised Josh that she was getting off to this so readily. But then, after a few more thrusts, she soon tensed up, and Josh watched as she cried out loud, tensing up quite a bit as she soon came against him.

That was enough for Josh to let out a groan of pleasure, letting his body move against hers, and soon, as he pushed in, he moaned, emptying himself into her. It felt so right, so perfect, and then, after a few more thrusts, he pulled back and smiled at her.

"You good?" he asked.

"That was just...wow," she admitted, blushing madly.

"I take it that it's a good wow then," he teased.

"Yeah, a very good wow. I'd do it again if I could," she admitted.

Josh felt a strange sense of happiness as he heard those words. He knew for a fact that he would get a chance to do this again, and when he was here with her, he felt like he was enjoying this far more than he imagined he would get to.

It was the perfect moment, the opportunity he'd been waiting for, and he knew that with Faye by his side, happy to be fucked like this, he knew he'd get to do it again.

Anal on the Beach

"Are you sure you want to do this?" Danica asked, her naked backside looking perfect in the sand.

Ray knew though that this was the opportunity of a lifetime. Here they were, on a nude beach together that allowed for intimate activities, and he had a dream to take his girlfriend's anal virginity here. Danica had been practicing, as how she told him through sexts, but he never took it until the time was right.

"Yeah babe. I want to," he told her.

The blush on her face said it all, but Danica wasn't going to complain. Soon, she smacked her butt in a teasing manner, looking at him on all fours while she was on the towel.

"Then come here, take my ass," she replied, her voice a needy, smoldering tone that set Ray on fire.

His cock was aching, hard as a rock, and when he moved closer, letting his hands touch her fluffy, huge ass, he played with her pucker, realizing that she was partially prepared. He looked at her, and then she flushed.

"I was getting ready for this moment," she admitted.

"Then I guess that makes two of us," he teased as he pushed a finger in gently. The first two fingers went in with no problems, but Ray wanted to try something else.

He wanted to rim her.

He never got to do that before, but seeing the perfect little ass, the need in her eyes, and the way that her pucker was practically begging for him made him spread her cheeks, tongue diving straight into her ass to play with it. She immediately gasped at the strange and foreign feeling, and Ray wondered if she might say something. But then, she didn't, and Ray took this as a sign that she wanted more, and that's what he did.

His tongue dove in deep, teasing her ass, and when he saw her relax, moaning at the actions that he bestowed to her, he knew that he was at least doing something right. He continued to dine on her fine booty until she pulled back, flushing red.

"That's fine," she said.

"You good?" he asked.

"Yeah it's nice but...I really want your cock," she said.

Her naked backside was begging for it. Ray looked around, realizing that they were all alone. He could feel the breeze, smell the ocean, and look at his beautiful girlfriend as he did this. He shifted his body, taking his cock that was hard as a rock out of his swim trunks, and soon, he pressed into her.

The sound that came out of her mouth was that of a garbled scream, but also that of a moan of pleasure. He soon started to press in deeper, pushing all the way in to the hilt. He was balls deep in her ass, and he loved the feeling of it. He began to press against her, fucking her slowly at first to get a feeling for this, but then, she turned around, a look of desperation present in her eyes.

"Don't just fuck around here, fuck my ass so hard I'm seeing stars," she demanded.

He never expected to hear those words, but they were an impetus for him, and soon, he began to thrust in deeper and deeper, loving the delicious sounds that he heard, his body craving more from this beautiful woman. He started to fuck her faster and faster, getting in deep and penetrating her as such. She cried out, the excitement in her body, and the need in her eyes saying everything. He started to grab her hips, pushing all the way in and feeling her react to how deep his cock was getting.

He did look up at Danica a couple of times, but she seemed perfectly passive. As they continued to fuck though, she reached around, grabbing one of Ray's hands and putting it against her pussy.

"Rub me, I'm getting close," she said.

Those were the words that made Ray act immediately in instinct, pressing his hands there and rubbing her tight pussy with his fingers. He started to fuck her harder and harder, letting his cock push in deep, and it was then when she started to cry out, each and every single thrust driving her to the brink of insanity. Ray knew that if there was anyone around, they would've heard them, but they were all alone, and he knew for a fact that nobody cared what they did on the beach.

"I'm fucking close," he said.

"I am too."

After a few more thrusts, he reached inside, touching the bundle of nerves there. She screamed out, suddenly shaking at the feelings that she got, and it was then that, after a few more thrusts, she soon came hard. The tightness and the constriction was enough to drive Ray to the brink of insanity as well, and it was then when he pulled out, his cum spraying all over her ass.

He felt satisfied, his whole body shaking with delight. When he finished, he laid down on the sand, his shorts covered with both sand and a little bit of cum. When he looked at Danica, who seemed spent, he smiled.

"Did you know that?"

"Yes. It was the best thing. I want to have sex on the beach way more often now," she said with a smile on her face.

Ray took that as a good sign, and when he reached in to give her a kiss, he beamed right back.

"Well, I guess that makes two of us then. I think it's safe to say that we are definitely going to come back here and do this again."

that was an amazing first time anal experience for both of them, and when Ray realized what he just did, he knew that he wanted to do it again and again with this woman, for it was the best thing he experienced in a long time.

Office Anal Fun

It was a late night and when Laura called Dylan to come over for a romp, she wanted something else. When he opened the door, he saw Laura there, clad in nothing but stockings, a garter belt, and her suit jacket and shirt. But, Laura was already planning for something more, and as she shook her ass in the most tantalizing manner, he looked at her, his cock hard as a rock.

"You want in on this?" she said, wiggling her hips and smirking at the other.

Dylan immediately reached over, spreading her ass cheeks and diving his tongue into her, lapping at her pucker and her pussy. When he did this, Laura immediately gasped, feeling both the stimulation from her pussy, and from her needy ass.

She already did the prepping earlier, and when he pushed his tongue into her hole, she immediately shivered, crying out loud and immediately gasping in complete and utter pleasure. She felt like it was heaven on earth as he did this, the small touches driving her completely insane. As he continued to push his tongue in deeper, she pushed her ass closer to his face, smothering him with it.

This was amazing, but then, Dylan pushed two fingers in, letting his tongue play with her folds from over near her clit. She gasped, feeling everything start to change, and soon, she began to feel the buildup from her orgasm. He continued his motions, getting her close, but then, he moved back, causing Laura to groan.

"Don't worry babe, I'm about to give you everything that you want," he told her with a smile.

She smiled back at him, and that's when he pushed his cock against her cheeks, freeing it from the confines first and then pressing the tip against her hole. He pushed in, causing her to let out a sudden gasp in pleasure at the sensation of him filling her up. When he got all the way in, he looked at her, giving her a passionate, needy kiss before he started to move his cock.

At first, the motions were slow, but with the way her ass was positioned on the desk, and the way his cock was angled, it felt amazing. She was so full, so stuffed, that every single motion drove her completely mad. He continued to thrust in deep, enjoying the tightness of her ass.

Dylan loved her ass. It was something that he truly did enjoy on Laura. Sure, they were partners, but they did sometimes have personal romps in the office after hours. Laura usually was the top dog, but when it came to the bedroom, Dylan knew immediately what to do to turn her on, and everything that she enjoyed.

"You like that you dirty little slut," he said, slapping her ass cheek hard and causing a moan to emit from her lips.

"Ahh yes! I love it," she told him.

"Good. You're going to keep taking my cock however I want to give it to you," he said.

Of course, Laura didn't want him to stop. In fact, she scooted her body over towards the middle, causing him to move onto the desk.

"Fuck me on this desk," she said with a demanding tone of voice.

He didn't need to be told twice. Suddenly, he moved up, holding her hips as he thrust in deep, penetrating her harder than ever before. He began to watch as she sat there, desire and need growing in her body as she continued to feel him penetrate her harder and harder. Everything was so perfect, so nice, and as she felt him continue this, she could feel his hands move up, penetrating her pussy with the deepest of touches while he fucked her ass.

He tweaked her nipples too as he continued to thrust, feeling her gasp and tighten up as a result of that. She then felt everything immediately go white, and when he pushed against that bundle of nerves, she immediately gasped, feeling everything stop.

When she came, she started to moan out loud, feeling everything grow more and more intense. It was then when she came hard, feeling like she just hit the jackpot. As she finally finished, he pulled back, grasping her hips hard once again and pushing as deep as he could with all his force.

It felt like heaven when he felt his cock begin to twitch, and when he came with a groan he immediately filled her ass up. He wanted to make sure that he got it in as deep as he could, and when he finished the last of his thrusts, he pulled back, smiling in excitement.

"You good?" he asked her.

Laura was down with her ass planted up in the air, feeling the sudden shock of everything as it came to her.

"Yeah. That was...truly amazing," she said.

"Good. I'm glad that you liked that," he said, giving her ass one last smack before pulling back, eying her body one last time. If he wasn't so tired, he'd consider fucking her once again, but he was definitely not able to keep his eyes open.

"Do you need to be walked home?" Dylan asked.
"Nah, I should be good. Besides, if people know about us, I think it may cause a bit of drama, so I'd rather not have that," she admitted.
Laura wished they could be a couple, but she knew the risks. They were both highly-trained business people, and they both knew what would happen if they continued on this route. It would end up being a problem, that's for sure.
"That's true. I'm glad that I have this though. Even if it's just temporary, I'm glad I still have your cute ass that is fun to fuck," he said.
She smiled, and the two of them shared one last kiss before they pulled away, going to their own lives once again, until the next time they needed one another for a release.

Anal Fun when the Store is Closed

It was 10 pm, which meant that the only two people that were here were Lisa, and of course her coworker Carl. The two of them were close, closer than most would ever imagine, but of course neither of them would ever let anyone, let alone corporate, know about that. If someone found out about them, it could mean trouble, especially when it came to what they liked to do here.
What they liked to do was make out against the counter, both of them feeling the pleasure of one another's lips and their tongues as they continued to kiss one another in a passionate manner. Lisa was enthralled by all of this, her body aching for him, and she knew that Carl wanted this too. As they continued to make out, he pushed his hands to the edge of her pants, undoing them and pulling them off. They were right near one of the shelves that was sturdy enough for them to hold themselves up, but also not one that was uncomfortable.
As Carl started to press his fingers against the obvious wet spot in her pants, he heard Lisa let out a moan of desire. He smiled, looking at her and kissing her once again.
"You like this?"
"Fuck yes I do. I want this," she said.
The other smiled, and soon, he started to press his hands towards the edge of the waistband of her pussy, pushing the garment down along with her jeans. He started to press two fingers into her, like how he always did, and with small, succulent ouches, he began to lightly finger her, enough that it drove her completely mad with pleasure as she felt her body cling to his own.
"Fuck," she said with a moan.
"You like that babe?"
"Yeah, but I want it in the ass tonight," she said.
He looked at her surprised by this, and then she pointed to the obvious bottle of lube that was sitting there on the shelf. He smiled as he grabbed the contents and poured it on his hands, looking at her with desire in his eyes.
"Well, I guess somebody wants this then."
As if on cue, he started to push a finger against the edge of her ass, penetrating her pucker in a ready manner. She immediately

groaned, realizing and feeling the penetrative actions that came from this. She immediately felt the heavenly actions that came from this, and as he continued to push his hands deeper and deeper into both her holes, she felt as if she was losing her mind.

She continued to move her hips up to the edge of his fingers, practically begging for him to continue these actions, and then, after a few more thrusts, he added in two fingers to each hole, feeling her relax to the touch. He continued the actions, noticing the desire in her eyes.

"I want it now," she said.

"Alright princess," he teased. But then, he pushed his hands up and grasped her backside, touching the round orbs. They felt perfect in his hands, and as he felt her squirm to his touch, he immediately watched as she soon relaxed, feeling as if everything was driving her mad. He then moved his cock slowly into her, bracing her hip as he penetrated her deeply.

The sensation of this was almost too much to bear, and when he finally got all the way in, he immediately watched as she tensed up, feeling the effects of everything as he began to move his cock in and out slowly. The fact that he was bracing her like this as he continued to move himself in and out of her ass, feeling the tenseness of her body as he continued to penetrate deep into her. The feeling of this was far too much, and soon, as he began to feel more and more of this, he soon tensed up, and that's when he started to move his cock as fast as he could into her.

He could hear her squirm and moan in response as he continued his onslaught against her tight ass. The feeling of the tightness, the action that he took, the sheen of sweat that was against her body, and the feeling of her fluffy butt cheeks as he continued to fuck her mercilessly drove him completely insane. It was like heaven to him, and then after a few more thrusts he could feel his body getting close.

It was then when he moved his hand that wasn't holding her up to her clit, teasing it slightly, and then after a few more thrusts, he watched as she screamed out, tensing up and then relaxing as the feeling of her orgasm completely destroyed her. He watched with a smile on his face as he continued to push his cock in and out of her, and then, after a few more thrusts, he soon tensed up, groaning as he spilled himself all the way into her.

He could feel his cock emptying out, and she gasped as he felt his seed push all the way into her. It was magical, and she definitely didn't mind the fact that he was enjoying this just as much as she

was. After he pulled away and let her down easy, she gasped, feeling the sudden shock of being on the ground wash over her.
"Wow, that was something," she admitted.
"Sure was," he said, smiling at her.
"That was just...wow. Amazing," she admitted.
"Yeah, I enjoyed that. Plus, we've been due for a romp like that, right?" he told her.
"You're telling me," she replied.
They smiled at one another, kissing once again. It was the beginning of another long night of cleaning between them, but the fact that they had each other was enough for her. She certainly wouldn't complain, and she knew that he enjoyed this as well.

Barn Anal Adventures

Doing it in the barn was something that Abby wanted to try, but getting her boyfriend Tyler to agree to something like this was another trial within itself. She watched as he looked at her with abject confusion as she pulled him inside. They did mess around a little bit in the barn, a place that she liked to spend time with her boyfriend, but rarely did they get past third base with this.

But then, as they made out, and clothes came off, Abby had an idea. She looked at Tyler, smiling as she fished out the bottle of lube.

"Hey Tyler, have you ever thought about putting it in my butt?" she asked.

Tyler looked at her as if she had three heads for a second.

"N-no! I never have!"

"Really now? Even though you totally could?" she said with a simpering smile.

Tyler blushed, but then he took a deep breath, steeling himself before he spoke.

"I haven't. I mean, I think it might be nice, but I'm not totally sure," he said.

"Well, why don't we try it? I've done a little bit of anal play, but I haven't done much besides that," she said.

Tyler blushed. He always wanted to try it in a sense, but he didn't want to ask Abby about it.

"I mean...sure. I'lll do it," he said.

Abby smiled, feeling his hands move up towards her backside, and as he uncapped the bottle of lube, he pushed the contents onto his fingers. As he did that, Abby pulled his fly and zipper open, and when he looked at her with confusion, she simply smiled.

"I want to fuck you while you prepare me," she said.

Tyler was too shocked for words, but when she moved down onto his cock, pressing herself onto there, he immediately groaned. He started to rock in and out of her, moaning at the sensation that he felt. He didn't expect this to feel so good, but here he was, penetrating one hole while preparing another, and when he pushed the second finger into there, he immediately watched as she started to tense up, moaning out loud at the feeling of both her holes being stimulated.

Tyler was amazed at all that she could take. When he inserted a third finger, he watched as she immediately gasped, holding him as she continued to ride his cock. For Tyler, the penetration was practically too much to bear, and then, after another thrust, he pulled out, gasping.

"Okay please, I really need to be in you right now, because if we don't do it now, I'm going to cum in the wrong hole," Tyler admitted. His voice was hesitant, his mind racing and his head spinning at the sensations that he was failing.

Abby simply smiled, pushing her butt against the head of his cock, looking at him with a dark smile.

"Well don't worry, I'lll make sure you're definitely taken care of," she said.

Tyler didn't know what he was getting into, but when he felt Abby press down onto his member, filling her up with his cock, he immediately gasped. It was so much tighter than he thought it would be, and when he felt her take him all the way in, he thought he was going to lose his fucking mind.

He then watched as she, with a devilish smile, began to rock her hips up and down on him. The smallest of sensations was enough to drive him insane, and she soon moved her body up and down, faster and faster, the desire for more growing within both of them. Tyler could feel his entire body losing control, he could feel everything start to become completely out of his element. He watched as she started to thrust in and out, and then, after a few more thrusts, he then watched as she tensed up, and he began to feel his whole cock just practically burst with need.

"Fuck. I think I'm going to cum," she said.

That was all that he needed to know. He watched as she, after a few more thrusts, began to cry out, touching her clit with a few motions but then feeling the throes of her orgasm as she soon came hard. The tightness that he felt was practically overwhelming. For Tyler, he knew that his girlfriend was tight, which was one of the marvels of her, but her ass was a whole new world. He gripped her cheeks, pushing down against there one last time before he soon cried out. He then relaxed, and as he came hard inside of her, she shivered at the sensation of the cum hitting every part of her inside. She shivered, and when he finished up, he pulled out, looking at her with a smile on his face.

"Like that princess?" he asked.

"Yeah. I did," she said, her breathing heavy and her body aching.

He pulled her off, cuddling her in his arms. The hay was starting to feel a little bit scratchy, and Abby immediately placed her clothes back on. Tyler tucked himself away in his pants once again, and then, after a few moments, looked at her and smiled.
"You enjoy that?”
"Yeah. That was amazing,” she said.
"Good. I mean, I didn't expect your ass to be that tight, that’s for sure,” he said.
Abby blushed, but then, after a brief second, she spoke.
"So you want to try it again?” she asked.
"Perhaps. Maybe we should try it in the barn once more. People don’t come out here, and I think it’s pretty nice,” he said.
"Yeah, it’s definitely something that I don't mind,” she said.
The two of them smiled to one another, the excitement that grew within them driving them both mad. Abby loved the way everything transpired, but at the same time, she wondered how much more fun she could have with her ass. What was next? What would she do now? She certainly wanted to explore more of this, and with the boyfriend she adored as well.

Anal as Payment

"Shit, I broke it!" Camie cried out as she looked at the contents.

It was then when she heard the footsteps of the mysterious man, the guy whose house she was cleaning. She gulped, realizing that this wasn't going to be good, it wasn't going to be good at all.

Camie realized just what was going to happen. She probably would get sent home, but when her boss Leo came in, inspecting the area, he noticed the vase.

"You broke it!" he said.

"I'm sorry, I was just trying to clean and--"

"You know that's a precious vase, right? You can't do that," he said.

Camie blushed, but she didn't know what her punishment should be.

"What can I do? I mean, will you dock my pay, take more money out of my paycheck, make me work extra--"

"Your ass," Leo simply said.

She looked at him as if he had three heads.

"Excuse me?"

"I want your ass," he said.

She immediately realized what was going on. She soon turned around, looking at him with a flushed face as she showed her backside. His hands moved towards her skirt, pushing it up to reveal her plump ass cheeks. After a couple of smacks, causing her to let out a shudder of pleasure, he then pulled away, caressing the flesh there.

"I want to fuck this," he said.

Camie never did anal before. Would it hurt? She looked at Leo, the dashing brunette making her do stupid shit. But then, he moved his hands to his pockets, grabbing some silicone-based lube that he had around.

"I always keep this around for safekeeping," he explained.

She couldn't believe he was that prepared, but then, as he uncapped the bottle, pushing the contents onto his fingers and looked at her, he smiled a smirk that made her body hot.

"Don't worry princess, I'lll take good care of you," he said.

What did he plan on doing? It was then when he pushed his hands against the tip of her pucker, and while she expected this at first to hurt, she didn't expect it to feel so...nice. She looked at him, and he soon smiled, letting his hands move towards her entrance and penetrating her deep.

The sensation of her ass being fucked immediately drove her insane. It felt so different, and even though it was just her fingers, it was a sensation that felt better than she expected it to. She soon felt him add a second finger, stretching her out, and the first thing that she noticed about all of this, was the fact that he was actually very soft with his touches, in a way that was almost surreal in a sense.

"Fuck," she said with a moan, immediately letting her ass move against his fingers. As he did this, he smirked, watching the sensation.

"You like this, don't you?"

"Yes," she breathed out, feeling like everything was driving her mad. He continued to penetrate her, first with two, and then with three, and then, as if on cue he pulled them out, teasing the very edge of her entrance before he soon unzipped his pants. She didn't know what she was going to feel, but then, when she felt the big, meaty organ penetrate her deeply, she felt as if she was losing her mind. It was super tight, and she felt like she was practically being split open. She watched as he looked at her, sliding each inch in with small movements. She felt like her entire body was being filled up, and it was a different sensation that she was not used to. She then started to feel him push all the way in, getting straight into her completely, and when he was finally in, he waited a minute before moving.

Instead of it hurting though, it felt good. It was a strange kind of pleasure, and as he continued to fuck her tight little hole, Camie felt the need for more. More was something that she never thought she'd want to feel, but he was so good, and the tightness was enough to drive her insane.

He moved his cock faster and faster, in and out of her with movements that surprised her. He was so good, and everything was making her feel like her entire body was losing control. She watched as he continued to grab her ass, smacking it as the sounds of smacking that came from his cock filled the room.

She cried out, gasping in pleasure as he did this, and then, after a few more thrusts, he soon tensed up, and that's when he did it.

He spilled his contents into her, the heat from his cock and cum immediately making her shiver. He penetrated her a couple more times, enjoying the way that she felt, before he pulled out with a pop. He simply zipped his pants up once again before he spoke to her.

"That is your punishment for breaking the vase. I hope you never do that again," he said.

The fact that it was all that he said before walking off surprised Camie, but then she felt that it wasn't necessarily the worst punishment that she was dealt. In truth, it was a punishment she wouldn't mind trying once again, one that involved her experiencing that same feeling that he gave to her before.

Maybe it wasn't a punishment, but in fact something good that she would love to experience again and again. Maybe next time she could make the punishment even heavier, and she could get fucked even harder than she had ever been fucked in the past.

The idea made her almost want to knock something off again, that's for sure.

The Maid's Request

When Ellie went into Ben's office, she expected him to give her the cleaning duties for the day. Working for a rich businessman occasionally had the perks that she enjoyed such as lots of money, but he was a bit of a loose cannon when it came to what he wanted. Sometimes he liked to make strange requests, and when she got to the office, she heard the first request that surprised her in a long time.

"I heard that you haven't been cleaning as fast as usual," he said.

"I mean...I've been trying," she admitted.

"Trying isn't good enough Ellie. I'm going to have to punish you for this," he snapped.

How was he going to punish her? She looked at him, unsure of what he meant by that, but then he gestured to her backside.

"Turn, lay on that chaise lounge with your ass up in the air," he demanded.

Ellie followed instructions, slightly worried about what this might entail, but instead of something bad, she felt warm hangs rub her thighs, getting towards the lower part of her cheeks, and soon, she immediately tensed up, feeling a strange comfort in this touch. He then smacked it, causing a small moan to escape her mouth.

"Good girl. You like it when I spank your ass?"

"Yes sir," she said, slightly shaky from the shock of the motion.

"Good. If you want, I can make you feel good. Plus, it would be a fitting reward for you, and a good punishment too," he said.

Ellie hesithated, unsure of what to say in response, but then she nodded.

"Yes. Please fuck my ass," she said.

She knew Ben for a long time, and the fact that he was willing to do something such as this surprised her. But, with a grin he moved his hands to a bottle of lube that was on the counter, undoing the contents and pouring them onto his fingers. He slipped her panties to the side, pushing a digit into her, and when he penetrated her initially, it felt a bit strange but at the same time, a bit pleasurable. She never expected to get fucked like this, but here she was, being penetrated by her boss, the man that she did have a small crush on, so it made everything even better.

After a brief moment or so, he then started to push his fingers deeper and deeper, adding in a second finger and rubbing her clit. Her panties were already soaked, and as he continued the motions, he smiled.

"You're already so fucking wet. Does me fingering your ass turn you on that much?" he asked.

"Yes," she cried out, feeling her body shake with pleasure.

"Oh then, I'm glad that you enjoy it," he told her.

He began to thrust the two fingers in deeper and deeper, and it was then when he finally pushed a third in, causing her to let out a small moan of pleasure and desire. After a brief moment, he then pulled his fingers out, and she heard the sound of a zipper being undone, and then the sound of a groan of relief.

He was going to fuck her ass. Ellie did dream of this moment, for she wanted him to do this to her. But, she never expected him to go this far. He soon spread her apart, and that's when she felt his cock right near her pucker.

She shivered, and when he pushed in she let out a small groan of both shock and pleasure as he began to move himself deep within her. He watched as she gasped, feeling her entire body become enraptured in the pleasure. He was soon all the way in, and when he got inside, he looked at her, and she soon shivered.

"You want more princess?"

"Yes please," she said.

He then started to move his cock in and out of her, starting with slow thrusts to get her used to it, but then the thrusts became longer, and much deeper than she expected. She soon began to shiver, tensing up and moaning in desire as she felt him push his dick all the way in, groaning before he started to work at a more forceful pace. After a brief moment, she could tell that he was getting desperate, the thrusts becoming almost too fast for her to keep up, and as she felt him hit that spot each time, that strange spot that made her cry out, she wanted more.

He slipped his hands to her front, fingering her as he continued this, and it was then that, after a brief moment, she soon cried out, feeling every single fiber in her body start to go insane at the sensations. She then started to cry out, and she soon shivered, moaning in pleasure as she came hard against him. She could feel her ass squeezing his cock, the moan of approval that he uttered immediately turning her on.

"Fuck," he said to her.

It was then after a couple more final thrusts, he let out a moan, and he soon came hard, penetrating himself deep into her. He watched as she shivered throughout her body as he released deep within her. When he was done, pulled out, tucking himself back in.
"That should be enough of a reward and punishment right?" he said.
"Yes master," she said.
"Good. Well, I guess that means I'lll get to have fun with that cute little ass again in the future if you decide to disobey me," he said.
When she heard those words, she immediately realized that he did want to do this again, that he was desperate for her ass. She wanted his cock inside of her once again, and as she left his office, she smiled, remembering that she could always disobey orders once again and get that same punishment that she knew she wanted, and the one that she craved more than she had ever before.

The Boss's Need

When Vicky heard that her boss George needed some relief, she thought that as her secretary, she would just be moving to him and taking over a few of the functions of the business. But no, when he told her that he wanted her to wear this ultra-short secretarial garb after hours, she was definitely not expecting what would happen next.
But here she was, dressed in a skirt that was short, and a jacket with only a mere bra underneath. When she got in there, George smiled, and he soon spoke.
"Seems like you took my offer," he said.
"Well you said you were offering me a promotion, and I really want it," she said.
"How much do you want it?"
She hesithated, unsure of what to even think what it came to that.
"I don't know what you mean?"
"What I mean is, are you willing to do anything that I request?" he inquired.
She didn't imagine it would be anything weird, so she nodded.
"Good. Get on the desk with your ass hanging out in the air," he uttered.
She looked at him with complete surprise, unsure of what to make of any of this, but then, after a brief moment, she did as she was told. The skirt was already riding up, exposing the thong that she had on.
"Good girl. You know, you have the best as of all of my employees, and I'm very happy that you took my offer," he said.
He gave her ass a hard smack, causing her to let out a gasp of both pain, and slight pleasure.
"Really now?"
"Yes. I really like your butt, and I've wanted to get some relief for a bit. So, what do you say, I take care of that ass, we both get off, and you get the promotion," he sthated.
Vicky realized just what he wanted. He wanted to fuck her ass. Sure, she would prefer that over her pussy, but even she was surprised by the request he uttered.
"Umm, sure," she said.

"Good. I'm glad you're as interested as I am," he said with a purr. He smacked her ass a couple more times, earning small gasps from her, and soon, he moved to a drawer within his desk, fiddling with some lube that he had on hand.

"Never know when this might come in handy," he said.

He also had something else in his hands. A bullet vibrator. He settled the vibrator into her pussy, pressing in deep, and then, after a brief moment, he then pushed his first finger in.

The stimulation from the toy was enough to drown out the sudden shock that came from the fingers within her ass. She definitely didn't know what would happen next, or even what to do, but then, he pushed another finger deep into her, causing her to let out another cry of pleasure. He continued to push the digits in and out of her, making her whimper with pleasure.

He then started to push the fingers in and out, causing her to let out a series of small moans and groans of pleasure, her entire body experiencing a strange feeling a pleasure that she was definitely not used to. sure, she had sex in the past, but this was different. It never felt like this, but then, as he continued to penetrate her deeper and deeper, with the toy being teased as well, Vicky realized something. She wanted more.

Her body ached for more. She hadn'thad dick in a long time, and the fact that he was giving her this made her shiver with delight. He began to push his fingers inside, adding a third for good measure, and that's when she looked at him, the need obvious in her eyes.

"Give me your cock. Please," she said.

"My, ever so needy kitten," he said.

"I just...really want to feel good," she said.

"Well, I'lll make sure that you feel utterly amazing," he said to her. It was then when she felt him move his hands towards the edge of the toy, pushing it right up against her clit and the other hole before he unzipped his pants, lubing up his cock and getting ready to spread her cheeks. When he inserted himself into her, he did it with a slow motion, but it was enough to drive her utterly mad with pleasure.

"Fuck! Yes," she told him.

He smiled at her, pushing his cock in deeper and then letting it stay there for a moment. She did admit that it hurt a little bit, but then, after a moment, he began to thrust inside of her, causing her to let out a series of whimpers of both pleasure, and slight shock. It was tighter than she managed to feel before, and it did have a tightness she wasn't used to, but she also really enjoyed it.

George was going to town on her ass, moving as fast as he possibly could into her tight ass, enjoying the sounds that she made as he did this. He continued to smirk, the pleasure from all of this driving both of them mad. It was then that, after a few more thrusts, he soon started to increase the pace, and when he finally did, he pushed in deep, pressing the toy up, and they both came together. The feeling of the cum in her ass felt nice, and she felt like she was experiencing something that was better than anything she had ever felt before. When he finished, he pulled his cock out, and when he looked at her, he noticed that she was grinning.

"You like that?"

"Yeah. Did I get the promotion?"

There was a smirk on his face, and after he kissed her, he nodded.

"Of course. You've managed to get the top promotion this month," he said.

Vicky was happy about that, and she wondered if he would do this again. She definitely wouldn't mind making her boss happy once more.

The Roommate's Dilemma

When Regina came in and saw her roommate Ricky masturbating, at first she was a little bit embarrassed. She didn't mean to walk in on him in the living room, masturbating to some chick taking a dick in her ass.
"Oh sorry!" he said.
"No it's my fault!" Regina said, immediately flushing and trying to shuffle away.
The awkward tensions that were there seemed to linger, and for Regina, she felt a strange urge. After everything was all said and done, Ricky looked at her.
"I didn't mean to do that," he said.
"No it's okay. Besides, there was something about it that kind of...interested me," she admitted.
He looked at her, and then, she took a deep breath, blushing as she spoke.
"The truth is...I kind of want to try anal with you. Since you like it so much. And I mean, we kind of do have the friends with benefits thing going on and--"
"Are you sure Regina," Ricky asked, and she soon nodded.
"Yeah. I'm sure," she admitted.
He then looked at her, smiling as he gave her a passionate kiss.
"Then I guess we can say it's worth a try," he told her with a smile on his face.
Regina wondered what was going to happen, but then, she was brought to the bedroom. They began to kiss with a fervency, and soon, their clothes came off. Ricky played with her breasts, teasing the large orbs, and she stroked his cock to hardness, feeling him moan in pleasure. They did play around, and Regina felt wetter than ever. It was then when Ricky looked at her, and then he spoke.
"So you cool with me doing this still?"
"I really want to try this," she admitted, blushing madly at the words that she uttered. It wasn't a lie, that's for sure.
Ricky smiled, and then, he started to grab the lube that he was using earlier to masturbate. He then spread her legs apart, teasing her pucker with his fingers. His tongue went towards her clit, teasing it there, and as he continued the motions, Regina began to moan.

"This is..pretty good," she said.
"Yeah, it's nice," he said, letting his fingers dance within her. She moaned, feeling the sudden urge for more begin to flood over her. She watched as he inserted another finger, his tongue and free hand teasing her body so that she was relaxed, and Regina was definitely that and so much more.
She loved every sensation that he was giving to her, and then, after a few more moments, he inserted a third finger, causing her to let out a sudden gasp of pleasure.
"You good?" he asked.
"Yeah. More than good. I'm definitely enjoying this," she admitted.
"Good. I'm glad then," he said with a smile.
He started to move his fingers in and out, stretching her once more before he slipped them away. She heard the sound of the lube bottle being uncapped again, and then, he pulled her into his arms, holding her there as he lightly thrust down.
The sudden breach made Regina scream, but she trusted Ricky, or she knew that he wasn't doing this just for himself, but also for her. He then pushed all the way in, and when she heard that needy, wanton groan, she knew that he was enjoying this just as much as she was.
He began to thrust in and out with the smallest of motions, each and every single movement generating pleasure on all fronts from both of them. It was almost mind-blowing how good it was, and as she felt him penetrate her deeper, she could feel herself wanting more. She met his thrusts with her own ass, feeling how tight and arousing it was, and it was then when she started to meet his own thrusts, her butt hitting his cock with a force that was unlike anything he imagined. He immediately groaned, each and every single motion driving him completely crazy, and then, after a few moments, she grasped her hips, pushing down on them and penetrating the area as deep as he could go.
The force of this drove her insane, and it was then after a moment or so she tensed up, screaming out loud as she felt her body ride out the orgasm. She felt like she was experiencing little taste of heaven, and as she felt him push himself deep into her once again, he then, after a few more thrusts, grabbed her ass, plunging as deep as he could before he came in her ass.
The sudden feeling of this shocked her more than anything. She didn't expect it to feel so...good in a sense. She thought it was going to be gross, but the feeling of this was a maddening one, one that

drove her slowly to the brink of insanity, to enjoy the moment that she shared with her roommate.

The two of them stayed like this for a moment, basking in the feeling of pleasure before he pulled out. She laid down on the bed, cum trickling out of her ass, and when she looked at him, she smirked.

"Was that everything you imagined it to be?" she asked.

"Yes, that's for sure," he said to her.

She smiled, the excitement and the pleasure that she felt immediately exciting her more than anything else. She then watched as he looked at her, and for a moment, she considered asking him what was next. She wondered what now, but then, he leaned in, holding her close and stroking her hair.

"You know, I've thought about...doing things with you before, and the fact that we were able to this time...well it felt nice," he said.

"That's true," she admitted.

"I would love to do this again. doesn't have to be just anal either," he replied.

She smiled back, the excitement driving her body forward and hugging him. She wanted this too, and as they stayed there, she wondered indeed what was next for both of them.

Butt Fun at the Campsite

Hannah didn't expect her boyfriend Robert to want to go camping, but here they were, out in the middle of nowhere at a campsite, and they were in the tent cuddling. The night sounds were relaxing to Hannah, and when she looked at Robert, she felt a strange sense of happiness.

Robert was the man she'd fallen for, the one that she was madly in love with, but when he looked at her, she noticed that he had another look in his eyes, a look of something more.

The need for her.

The two of them started to kiss with a fervency that she was used to, one that she definitely enjoyed. But it was then, after a moment or so, that he pulled away, flushing as he looked at her.

"By the way babe, I've wanted to try something," he said to her.

"What is it?" she inquired, a bit surprised by this.

"Do you...want to try it in the butt?" he asked.

Hannah didn't know what to say. She did want to, but she wasn't prepared, and she didn't know if he was either.

"I'm not sure, I mean, I'm not prepared for that," she said.

"Well, I did bring a few things," he replied.

He brought forth a butt plug and some lube, and when she saw that, her eyes widened.

"Are you sure?" she asked.

"Damn sure. I really want to try this babe, that is if you're down," he said to her.

She listened to him, and as she looked at him, she immediately nodded.

"I'lll do it," she said.

She then moved her body so that it was down on the sleeping mattress they blew up. They made out, and slowly but surely clothes were being ripped off. Robert was gentle with his touches, caressing her inner folds before diving into her pussy with his tongue and fingers. Each and every single motion was enough to drive her mad, and with every single touch, she knew that she was definitely loving this more and more than she thought she would. She certainly felt some excitement, and it was then when she felt him move a finger towards her ass, touching the pucker with a massaging motion

before he slipped it into her. She gasped, feeling it completely fill her up, and it was then when, she felt him push his fingers in deeper and deeper, making her practically scream out loud and in pleasure.
"Fuck," she told him.
He nodded, moving his fingers in a skillful manner. He wanted to make sure that hewasn'thurting her, and with every single motion, every single passing second, she felt as if there was something bigger coming.
Each finger felt like a heavenly stretch that she enjoyed far more than she cared to admit, and it was after she had three fingers inside that she soon tensed up, and that's when she told him she was ready.
"Let's...do this," she said.
Robert looked at her, feeling how wet she was down there, and how she was experiencing everything that was going on, but then, after a brief moment, he then pulled back, looking at her.
"Do you want to ride or..."
"I wouldn't mind doggy-style," she admitted with a flush.
He blushed back, surprised she wanted that, but then, he started to pull back, lubing himself up as she got on her hands and knees, her ass hanging out there in front of him like a fruit that was begging to be picked.
When he pushed inside, at first it was tight. It felt almost too tight for her to have it in there, but then after he finished up and stopped, it became almost comfortable, and when she felt him sink into there, she couldn't believe how nice it was.
She felt like everything was driving her mad, and then, after a few more thrusts, she soon started to tense up, and that's when she began to feel him move in and out of her slowly. He took it easy, letting his hands move towards her breasts, fondling them as he began to penetrate her slowly. Each touch sent shivers down her spine, made her lose control, and everything began to go white.
She loved the strange feeling of need that came from this, the feeling of him completely penetrating her every fiber of her body. As he began to fuck her harder, she began to cry out with each thrust, and she was very happy that they were in the middle of the forest, or this would be hella awkward.
He started to thrust deeper and deeper, each one completely decimating her and making her want more. It was then when, with one last final thrust, she soon screamed out, everything going blank as she came hard, feeling the throes of her orgasm as it happened.

She felt like a million dollars, and it was then when, after a few more thrusts, Robert cried out as well, a manly groan filling the tent, and he came inside of her. It was a relieving feeling that coursed through her, and when she felt the way his cum filled her up, it made her want to have more.
He finished up with a couple final thrusts before he pulled away, looking at her with expectant eyes.
"You good?" he asked.
"Really good. Holy fuck," she said.
"I take it that's exactly what you needed," he admitted.
"Yeah. It honestly was. That was...wow," she said.
The two of them embraced one another in the tent under the stars, both of them enjoying the presence of one another, and both of them ready to do this again sometime in the future. It was a first time that she enjoyed, and she knew that Robert loved it too.
She definitely wouldn't mind going camping more often if it meant something like this.

The Sugar Daddy's Request

"What do you mean?" Veronica asked, looking at her sugar daddy Kain. She had been in the business of being sugared for a long time, about a year and a half now, and while the money was amazing, she never got asked this request before. Sure, sex was part and parcel of the job, but this...was different.

"I want your ass baby girl," Kain her sugar daddy said with a purr. Veronica flushed, but she certainly wasn't against the idea of it. In fact, she was morbidly curious about it, and when she looked at him, she soon spoke.

"You mean like...you want to fuck my ass?"

"That's what I want. Plus, if you do it well, I'll give you something a little extra, if that's what you want that is," he said.

She blushed, but then she nodded.

"I wouldn't mind that. In all honesty," she said.

"Good. Well get on your hands and knees baby girl, and I'lll take care of you tonight," he said.

Veronica was used to sexual favors, but this was new to her. Though, it was strange because she wanted to learn more about this. It struck a sense of morbid curiosity within her, and as she laid there with her ass up in the air, she watched as he smiled at her, a devilish grin that said everything.

"You have such a nice ass babygirl," he said.

"Thank you," she said, flushing as he touched her body with the subtlest of touches. He began with the little touches that went from her thighs, and then up to her ass, cupping it for a second before he delivered three soft spanks to her. She let out a soft moan of approval, her entire body moaning in response to the man's actions. She loved this, and as he continued to slap her, she wondered if this was what he meant by this.

But then, he moved his hands to her panties, rubbing her there, and as he did that, she let out a slight gasp of shock, her entire body immediately responding to this. She wanted more, and as she felt him press his fingers there a couple of explorative ones went to her pucker, touching it there.

What Veronica didn't expect, was for it to feel this good. She soon felt him press his fingers into her pussy, her entire body reacting to

this as he pushed one singular finger into her ass. She gasped, feeling the slight approval of the touch ghost through her body. He continued to press his fingers with soft touches against her ass, watching as she squealed and moved around with delight.
"I didn’t even know you were into that. Little slut,” he said, giving her a smack on the butt.
She gasped, feeling like everything was about to get better and better. He was using one hand to smack, and the other was teasing her pussy and ass with fingers and rubbing. All of this felt lovely, and as he continued this, Veronica wanted more.
She never experienced this need before. It felt so good, and when he pushed three fingers into there, she loved the familiar sensation of tightness that seemed to come over her. He began to move his hands over towards her ass, teasing it slightly once more before he pulled away. It was then when she heard the belt come undone and his fly unzip, and that’s when she realized that he was indeed going to fuck her ass.
Would this hurt? She honestly didn’t know, and it was then when she started to feel him move his hands towards her ass cheeks, cupping her orbs as he pushed his cock into there.
The sensation of it inside of her immediately drove her mad. She gasped, feeling everything immediately go blank as he started to fuck her ass with small motions, enjoying the tightness. But, she wanted him to go faster, and with a small voice, she voiced that very need.
"Give me more,” she said.
"You sure babygirl?”
"Yes. I want more,” she said.
He smiled, moving his hips slowly, but then thrusting faster and faster, enjoying the actions that he was feeling. Everything was maddening, and it was then when, after a few more thrusts, he then started to hold her there as he practically jackhammered his cock into her tight asshole.
For Veronica, this was a pleasure that she never thought she would get to experience, but then, after a few more thrusts, she could feel his hands rubbing her clit, in the way that she loved it, and as she felt this, her body keened to the touch, moaning out loud at the sensations that were bestowed to her.
"Yes! Fuck yes!” she cried out.
It was only a moment later that she came hard, her entire body losing control, and everything becoming almost surreal in a sense. It

was then when, after a few more thrusts, she felt him groan out loud, and he soon came inside her ass.

She shuddered at the warm feeling of his cock deep within her, but then, after a few more thrusts, he then pulled out, looking at her with a loving glance.

"You good?" he asked.

"Very good," she said. It was so much better than she anticipated, that's for sure.

"Would you do that again babygirl?" he asked.

In truth, Veronica wanted to. She wanted to feel her sugar daddy's cock deep within her, and it was then when she nodded, smiling at him.

"But of course," she replied.

"Well, I can certainly cater to that need, if that's what you want," he said to her.

She smiled at him, and she knew for a fact that she was enjoying this far more than she thought that she would. Everything about this was heavenly, that's for sure, and it was after a moment that she laid there on the bed with her sugar daddy there. He did give her money, but she was just happy serving someone that she cared about a lot.

A Rock Star's Need

Nick didn't expect his groupie Sandra to stick around after the show, but she was there, hanging out with him for a while. Nick thought Sandra was fucking gorgeous, and he loved fucking her whenever she wanted. But tonight, she seemed a bit off, and Nick felt the urge to have her.

"Something the matter?" he asked.

"Yeah. it's just...I've wanted to request something for a long time, but I didn't know how to ask," she said.

A request? What the hell could she possibly want? He looked at her, and then she blushed.

"Well, what I want is to have you fuck my ass," she said, a flush present on her face.

He looked at her, and in a sense he wondered if she read his mind or something.

"Funny, I really want this too," he said with a purr.

"I mean you don't have to if you don't want to! it's just something I've considered trying," she admitted.

He leaned in, giving her a kiss, and it was then when he smiled back.

"Trust me my dear, I definitely want this as much as you do. I mean, we can make this work," he told her.

She began to blush crimson again, but not before she laid down on the tour bus bed and blushed.

"Well, if you want to, my ass is ready," she said.

He loved the way her butt looked, and the fact that she was so ready to explore made nick hard as a rock. He reached forward, stroking Sandra's ass and giving it a small smack. She blushed once again, and then, it made him want to do more, so much more.

He pressed a digit against her entrance, testing to see if she liked it. When he heard the purr of approval, he realized that she indeed did want this, and that this was definitely something that he could get used to. It was a tight heat that practically sucked him in, and that's when he started to move his hands slightly, pressing in deep against her with soft motions.

She responded by letting out the cutest moans possible. He didn't expect her to enjoy this, but as he prepared her ass, he could feel her

practically whimpering for more. When he pulled back, he spread her open, causing her to gasp.
"I'm sorry, this is just something I've wanted," she said.
"This is something I think I've wanted deep down as well," he admitted.
He touched the little pucker, watching her squirm, but then, he pressed his tongue there, rimming her with small strokes. As he did that, she let out a sudden gasp, immediately enraptured by what he was doing.
The truth was, Nick wanted to do this for a long time, and the fact that he was so enraptured by the way her ass looked in front of him, the way that the pucker was just begging for him, made him shiver with delight. He wanted this, and he knew that she did too.
With a couple more strokes, he pulled back, his cock achingly hard in his pants.
"Are you sure about this?" he asked.
"Yes. I want this. Give it to me," she told him, desperation obvious in her eyes.
He could tell that was the green light to go. After a brief moment, he pushed her legs apart, pressing his cock into her ass, and as he sank into there, he started to moan.
It felt so nice, so perfect, and whenever he pushed himself all the way in and started to move, he enjoyed every single aspect of it. He started to thrust in and out of her with small, exact motions, causing her to let out a series of cries as he began to fuck her softly, but then his need to go harder began to take over, and it was then when he started to push his cock in deeper, plunging himself all the way into her. When he finally got there, he looked at her once again, and she looked completely enraptured by the way that he was fucking her.
He began to thrust in and out, taking each thrust as deep as possible until he felt like his cock couldn't take it anymore. He went in a rhythm, desperate to fuck her, and his whole body aching for more.
After a few more thrusts, Nick moved up, playing with her pussy, and he remembered that she was sensitive. That was enough to get her to cry out, moaning out loud as she came hard against him. The tightness of her ass at that point immediately made him groan in pleasure, and it was then when, after a couple more thrusts, he came hard, his body tingling as he filled her with his seed.
Everything about this felt perfect, and when he finished up, he pulled out, looking at her with expectant eyes.
"You good?" he inquired.
"Better than good," she told him.

"I'm glad. Because I want to make sure that you're taken care of as well," he said.
"You've done that and so much more. I...I love it," she admitted.
He reached in, touching her hair and looking into her eyes. She was a mere groupie, but she was someone that he could enjoy, and it made the rockstar life less insane.
"You know, I'm happy to have you, and I'm definitely happy to know that you're here with me. I think it's safe to say that you certainly do make life way more fun," he told her with a smile.
"I'm glad. I know how ti can be, the rockstar life taking a lot out of you and all," she admitted.
"Yeah, I feel that. But, I'm here and I'm happy," he said.
They stayed together for a bit, and while he knew that they couldn't be together forever due to the fact that he was a rockstar, he was definitely a happier guy.

Her New Boss

When Karen heard that her new boss was a younger guy, she immediately was on the prowl. At first, it was little touches and gestures, but then it evolved into subtle touches and little tingles that made her squirm. She loved everything about this, and she knew that he did as well.

Of course, Karen and her new boss Cody started talking, and Karen, being the hot cougar that she was, knew for a fact that she was going to certainly have a lot of fun with this. When she looked at him, she noticed his eyes always gazing at her ass. She did have a good butt, but she was surprised that he was so forthright about it.

A couple months passed, and Karen decided to test these waters. She would let his hand move towards her butt, barely touching there, and when he looked at her, instead of anger, there was something else.

Lust.

He wanted this, and she did as well. He soon moved his hands downwards, letting his hands move towards the two orbs, caressing them there. As she looked at him, he then moved over towards her hole, touching it through the confines of her thong.

'Someone seems interested,"Karen said.

She knew that she was playing a dangerous game, but it was a game that she was willing to play. He slyly smiled, and then, after a moment or so, he pulled back.

"I mean, if you want..."

She quickly pushed him over to his office, closing the door and furiously making out with him. She started to watch as he groaned, the excitement immediately hitting his pants. After getting off of him and moving towards his cock, she lightly lapped at it, and then took it halfway down her throat. She hummed, watching as he suddenly tensed up, moaning out loud and in pleasure.

"That's right, you like that don't you?" she purred.

He then pulled her head up, and then, he stopped, looking at her with a serious glance.

"It's not me I'm interested in, it's you. I want your ass," he said.

She flushed, realizing what he was saying, and soon, before she knew it, he had his hand near her pucker, teasing it with the smallest of strokes. He then moved his hand towards there, and then, after he fetched the lube that was in his drawer and pouring the contents on here, he looked at her, smiling.

"You good?" he asked her.

"Yeah. I want this," she told him with a smile on her face.

He put the first digit in there, and although the hole was tighter than he expected, she keened into the touch, moaning out loud at the sensations that this brought her. He started to finger her ass as he kissed her, adding in a second digit to the fray. She sighed, feeling everything change within her, and soon, before she knew it, he pushed a third into there. Each of these digits greeted her hungry ass, all of them sinking in, and it was then when she looked at him, and she noticed it.

He was enjoying this just as much as she was.

She couldn't believe what was happening, but here she was, horny and desperate, with three fingers in her ass, and soon, he pulled them out.

"You want to ride it cowgirl?" he asked.

"Don't mind if I do," she purred.

She moved her body so that she was right over the very tip of his cock, her ass teasing the very tip of it with tantalizing motions. After he groaned in need, she slipped her body down, watching as he threw his head back and moaned.

"What's the matter? Enjoying this?" she asked.

"Y-yes," he finally managed to reply.

She smiled at him, pressing her ass down completely, and then, he moaned once again. She started to ride him, watching with satisfaction as the man sat back, taking in the sights. She was so happy she got a chance to do this. She knew that this man was the type who wouldn't be able to resist her. She began to move her body up and down, watching as her ass began to hit the very base of his cock. She groaned, feeling everything start to get deeper over time. She watched as he started to moan as well, each and every single motion making him drool with desire. For her, she knew that it was the beginning of more fun, and then she started to pick up the pace. Karen knew that she was doing him in. he moaned, each and every single groan that emitted from his mouth making her want to ride him harder, so that's what she did. With each one, she saw the desperation in his eyes, the need for her to continue with this, and the desire for so much more. It was the beginning of a new relationship, she knew this for sure.

She did acknowledge it was taboo, but as she continued to thrust down on his cock, he moaned out loud, and when he came, she moaned, touching herself and getting herself off as well. He watched as she pressed two fingers inside, snaking them up and touching her insides with each and every single succulent touch. She gasped, cumming hard, and he got to watch the spectacle right in front of her.

When it was all said and done, Karen pulled off of him, smiling at him with a smirk.

"You good sweetie?" she said.

"Yeah. That was just...wow," he said.

"I know, it was something. But I'm glad that you enjoyed it. Perhaps we can have some more fun too," she said.

Karen gave him a kiss, and she knew that the younger man wasn't going to say no. she clicked her heels away, smiling at her antics. Of course, her thoughts were confirmed when she got a text about ten minutes later saying the following:

I would love to do that again.

Ditching the Party

"This is lame," Lance said as he looked at Sherri.
"I have to stay here. My dad is definitely not going to be happy if I leave. This is his gala, and I'm his daughter," she said.
"Yeah and I'm just some errand boy. But don't you feel like you could do so much more? Like you could easily ditch this shitty place," he said.
Sherri sighed. She wished that she could leave. But then, Lance jumped the fence, smiling.
"You know we are going to get in trouble," she admonished.
"Come on Sherri, let's ditch this place," he said.
She looked at him, thinking he was utterly insane for doing any of this, but she followed him, and soon, they were at his house. When they got inside, she laid down on the bed, sighing.
"This is the life," she said.
"You're telling me. Better than a party, isn't it?" he asked.
She blushed, but then nodded. "You're right. It is.
"Anyways, I was thinking we do something a bit different tonight," he offered.
She tensed, looking at him with worry. "Like what.
"Like, I want to try fucking your ass," he said.
She blushed, but then she spoke.
"I mean, I've never done it before," she admitted.
"Yeah but, don't you think it's better to try something new rather than sit at that dumb party," he told her.
He did have a point. She nodded, sighing.
"Yeah, you're right," she admitted.
"Anyways, let's try this," he said.
She looked at him, and soon, he started to kiss her. She kissed him back, and the two of them let their tongues mingle with a pleasurable sensation for a little while, both of them enjoying the feeling of this. As they continued to make out, he pushed his hand to her plush ass, and as he did so, Sherri threw her blonde hair back, moaning in pleasure at the way he touched her. He moved his hand up, stroking her pucker as he teased her through her panties.
"You good with this?"

For Sherri, she didn't expect this to feel so...good. She expected it to be something wrong, that she would hate, but in truth, she liked the way this felt, and when she moaned, he took that as a good sign.
"Good girl," he said, playing with her once again. Sherri moaned, feeling excited about all of this. He continued to smile at her, playing with her ass as he continued to make out with her. He pressed a finger in once again, but then pulled out, grasping a bottle of lube he kept for this moment.
"I've been preparing," he admitted.
"Oh really now," Sherri said with a smirk.
Lance looked at her with a mischievous glance, but then he pushed another finger in. both of these fingers sank into her, and when she felt these, she tensed up, moaning out loud at the sensation. He pressed them in and out, letting each of them move deep within her. She then started to feel her body become even more stuffed than she thought he would make her feel. Everything was amazing, and then, as if on cue, he pulled his fingers out.
"How do you want to do it?" he asked.
Sherri paused, thinking about how she should do this. It was then when she spoke.
"I mean, missionary works. it's my first time," she said.
Lance nodded, spreading her apart and lining his cock up against her hole.
"Tell me if it hurts," he said.
She nodded, and soon he pushed the tip in, watching as she threw her head back, crying out loud at the sensation of being spread apart. He then moved in deeper, letting his cock sink into her, and at first, she thought about telling him no, she couldn't do this. But, she didn't want to disappoint him, and then, as soon as she thought that, the pain went away.
"What the heck?" she said.
"What's wrong?"
"It feels...good," she admitted.
"Well good, that's how I want it to feel,"he teased.
He started to move his hips against her, thrusting his cock as deep as he could. For Sherri, at first it was a bit painful, but then, it hit a spot that made her tense up, and when it did, she cried out in pleasure at the sensation that she felt.
"Fuck!" she cried out.
She definitely was enjoying this. He smiled, continuously fucking her tight ass with his cock. She held onto him for dear life, and as he

continued to fuck her relentlessly, she soon felt as if everything was driving her to the point of madness.
She was so close already. She knew that it was something that she couldn't hold back, and when he reached forward, massaging her clit as he fucked her, she knew that this was the beginning of it. When he pushed against it, she screamed out loud, letting her hips move up and her pussy throb. She came, and the tightness was too much for Lance. He tried very hard to keep himself together, trying to make sure that he didn't cum too fast, but it was too late. He shivered, cumming hard inside of her, causing her to let out a sudden gasp in pleasure at the sensation of this.
"Holy fuck," she said.
"You good?" he inquired.
"Better than good," she told him.
He reached forward, pulling her close and kissing her. She kissed him back, and soon he pulled away, smiling at her.
"Better than sticking around at some boring party, don't you think," he teased.
Sherri nodded, lightly elbowing him.
"Okay fine, maybe you were right and it was better than a party," she teased.
"I know I'm right, because I see it on your face," he replied back.
She smiled, feeling a strange feeling wash over her.e she wanted to do this again, wanted to feel him fuck her ass again, and she knew that it was better than a party, that's for fucking sure.

Work Breaks Made Fun

It was another boring work day, but at least Izzy and Andrew got to work together. As the cafe's newest and hottest couple, people would congratulate them, but of course Izzy and Andrew hadn't had much time together.

Which was why, during their break in the break room Andrew locked the door, pushing Izzy against the wall and making out with her with a fervency that even she was supersized about. She kissed him back, feeling the need grow within her as time started to pass on by. Soon, Andrew had her up against the wall, his hands right near her round ass, touching the cheeks.

"You look so good," he said to her.

"Thank you," she moaned, feeling his hands massage the area. It felt so nice, so perfect, but then, he started to slide her pants off. She knew what was coming.

Andrew had recently tried anal with Izzy, and to say that it woke up some monster within him was an understhatement. He loved it, and for some reason, he grew almost addicted to it, and as he started to tease the puckered flesh, she began to moan, feeling excited about everything that was happening. She started to move towards the touch, feeling everything begin to change within her. It was heavenly, and then, as if on cue, he pushed his finger into her.

She didn't know he even lubed it up but when it was inside, she let out a moan that was a bit of a surprise, but also a relaxed one. He began to push his fingers in and out of her, starting with the smallest of touches and then moving towards the inner thigh. When he pushed his fingers in, she tensed up, gasping I surprise at the sensation of being filled up. He then started to press his fingers in and out of her, watching as she moaned, feeling everything as he continued to do this. Each and every single touch was enough to drive her mad, and then, after a few more thrusts, he added in a second finger.

Izzy learned that she really liked anal as well. At first, she thought that it was wrong, but then she r3slized that it gave her intense pleasure, and she soon pushed her butt against the two fingers inside of her, causing him to groan as the ring of muscle sucked his fingers in. watching as she got off to this was something that she enjoyed, and then, she noticed that he was already hard as a rock. When she pulled back, she smiled at him, a coy little grin that said it all.

"You want to stick it in," she said.

Andrew knew that the only had about fifteen more minutes. Nobody figured out that this was what they did on their breaks, but he soon pushed his hands to the side, spreading her cheeks and then, with awkward hands, he covered his fingers in lube and then rubbed his cock, looking at the two wonderful moons that were there.

"Fuck," he said to himself.

He watched as she gasped at the feeling of his hands as he began to spread her cheeks apart, and then the feeling of his lubed up cock as he started to penetrate her hard.

She gasped, tensing up at the sensations that were happening within her. She loved this, and she knew that with him, this was the type of feeling that she wanted to have. He began to fuck her with a fervency that she loved, and he soon started to press his cock as deep as he could into her. She immediately moaned, tensing up and pushing her body against his own. The sensation of his cock inside of her tight ass made her want more, and it was then that, after a few more thrusts, she knew that they needed to finish up soon.

It was obvious that they only had a limited amount of time, and it was then when he started to thrust into her hard, and she met his own. He pressed his fingers towards her clit, rubbing it so that she could get off, and then, after inserting a finger into her pussy with everything else, they both stopped, the sudden feeling of cumming immediately overwhelming their senses.

The first to cum was Andrew, and he filled her ass up with his seed. He groaned at the sensation of the feeling that he shared, and as he looked at her, he noticed that she was enjoying this just as much. After a few more moments, she let out a sudden gasp, feeling everything become blank as she rode his cock, cumming hard as a result of his actions.

She watched as he pulled away, a little bit of cum moving out of her hole. She reached over, grabbing a couple of paper towels to clean up the excess. Quickly, they both got their clothes on, looking at one another with lustful glances.

"God your ass is so much fun to get into," he said.

"Look who's talking, your cock feels amazing in there," she said with a flush on her face.

He looked at her, smiling warmly, and soon, both of them started to kiss one another hard. The sensation of this was almost too much,

and they knew that if they continued in this line, they'd end up fucking once again. But then, he pulled away, smiling.
"Let's do this later," he said.
"You think tonight after our shift?" she asked with a purr.
Andrew smiled, knowing this. "Yeah, I'm cool with that," he told her.
She gave him one last kiss before she pulled away, winking.
"Good. We should probably get back to work though. Don't want anyone to think we're doing some naughty now, would we?" she teased.
Andrew blushed, but he followed her, and soon, they were back to the tedium of life, their jobs, but they still had one another.

What to Do Instead of Hitting the Books

The last thing Sally and Brendan wanted to do was study. Fuck finals, and fuck the element of studying. Plus, it didn't help that Brendan was very attractive, and Sally was having trouble focusing.

"You okay there Sally?" he inquired.

"Oh! Yeah I'm okay," she said.

"You sure? You look a bit distracted, you know," he said.

"No it's just...I have something on my mind," she said.

"Like what?"

Sally blushed, wondering what her friend might say. She then took a deep breath, looking at him with a red face.

"Have you ever...thought about anal?" she asked.

"What brought that up?" he asked with a laugh.

"Don't make fun of me, but I was watching some porn the other night, and I saw it and like...I wanted to try it," she told Brendan with a blush.

Brendan looked at Sally with surprise.

"Are you sure? It tends to hurt."

"I'm sure. I mean, it's something I've been curious about, you know," she admitted with a flush on her face. As Brendan heard this, he blushed as well, surprised by how forthright she was with this.

"Well, I guess we can try it," he told her.

"Okay. I want to," she said.

He then looked at her, tossing the textbook to the side and kissing her.

"Fuck studying. Not worth it," he said.

She then kissed him back, moaning in surprise and shock at the sensations that he gave to her. He soon started to kiss her harder and harder, each and every single touch driving her mad. He then pushed her down, pulling her skirt up and letting his tongue lick the edge of her pussy. Brendan knew that he wanted to get her off first before he tried anything like this.

Sure enough, it did them both good. Sally immediately whimpered, crying out loud at the sensations that were bestowed to her. She knew that he was enjoying this as much as she was, and soon, they both were making sounds of satisfaction, and of desire.

For Sally, she loved being eaten out, but she was curious about butt stuff. She did buy lube, and she did get a toy at one point, and she knew for a fact that this was the sensation that she wanted to feel. She soon looked at him, and soon he grabbed the contents pressing a singular finger into her.

"You good?" he asked.

The sensation of her ass being filled with something like this was...strange that's for sure. She didn't expect it to feel so foreign, so different from what she was used to, but she soon moaned, bucking her hips in happiness and pleasure as he started to push the digit in deeper and deeper. The sensation was almost too much for her, and as he pushed in deep, she tensed up.

He continued slowly, feeling her relax to his touch, but then he started to insert a second, and she felt filled up once again. She began to moan as he started to push his fingers in and out of her, loving the feeling of her tight ass against his fingers. He continued with the third digit, waiting until she was ready for the real thing, and then, when he pulled back he patted the bed.

"I'm going to sit down. I want you to ride me," he said.

She blushed. Sally had a feeling that the reason for this was because she didn't want him to hurt her, and he was hesitant about taking control the first time. Sure enough, she soon pushed herself against the tip, feeling it fill her up, and then, Sally wondered if she made the right decision.

It was tight. Almost too tight, and when she felt him get all the way in, she shuddered. She didn't know if this was it, but then, when he was finally inside, it soon got easier. She then relaxed, liking the tightness, and when she started to move, she noticed it hit a part of her body that she was definitely not used to.

She started to cry out loud, feeling the pleasure sink through her body. After a couple more thrusts, she noticed that Brendan was sitting there, ogling her body.

"You're beautiful," he told her.

"Thank you," she replied, feeling everything become almost magical as she continued to ride his cock. The sensations were overwhelming, that's for sure, but she loved the feeling of this, and then after a few more thrusts, she soon tensed up, crying out loud in pleasure.

She came hard, feeling her entire body lose control at the sensations that were there. He soon pushed himself all the way down, and when he groaned, he felt his cock empty out, filling her up completely with his seed. She shuddered, for it was a different sensation than how it felt when he came inside of her pussy, but she wasn't complaining, that's for sure.

When he finished, she pulled back, blushing red.

"That was just...wow," she said.

"Good for you?"

"Yeah. Amazing, really," she admitted.

"Well, I'm glad I could help then," he said to her.

The two of them looked at one another, kissing once again. Sure enough, their study session took a very different turn, but neither of them were complaining. Rather, they were both happy and satisfied with the feelings that they shared.

"I wouldn't mind doing that kind of studying again," Brendan said.

"Same here. But next time, we should make sure that we have our work finished before we consider doing that," she admitted.

"I think that's a smart move," he admitted to her.

She laughed, planting a kiss on his lips.

"You know, I never thought that it would feel this good. I'm happy," she admitted.

"I'm happy as well," he told her.

Both of them smiled, their eyes glistening with happiness, the desire growing within them. For Sally she felt that this was the beginning of something more, but she didn't want to push it. But it was better than studying, that's for sure.

Paying Her Debt

Jackie felt the familiar tightness in her ass as Dan began to press the toy into her, turning it on.
"You have to keep it in my dear, or else that's another 500 added to your debt. But, if you manage to make me cum with your ass I'lll take away 2000," he said to her.
She blushed, and as she felt him push the toy in deeper, turning on the vibrations, she began to shudder, the excitement filling her body as he began to penetrate her deeper. She began to tense up, feeling everything change, and as she began to feel him push the toy right up against that spot that drove her crazy, she felt her entire body start to sweat.
"Fuck," she muttered, feeling everything go blank.
"You handle it?" he asked, his voice almost mocking.
"I can," she spat back with confidence. Course, even she didn't know for sure what might happen. He clicked it up higher, and she soon cried out.
The one thing about Jackie was that she came from anal play, and when she bit her lip getting close, she realized over time that she may not be able to hold her ground. She then tensed up, gasping out loud as she felt her entire body shake at the sensation of her orgasm.
Dan loved seeing her come undone whenever she came too hard. She was a total mess right now, moaning and gasping in pleasure at the sensations that were happening, and he smiled, knowing that he was the one to create those. After he turned off the toy, he pulled it out, looking at her with a smile.
"You did so well my dear. I think it's safe to say that you're ready for me. And, you still were able to reduce your debt by 500," he said.
"Thank you sir,"Jackie said.
Jackie had this debt for as long as she could remember, but she was just now taking her life back. Dan was a rich businessman who found her on the street, offering her a chance to take care of it. What she didn't know, was that she was going to use her body for this.
But, his large, thick cock was right there, a familiar sight to her, and as she looked at him, she realized that he looked bigger than usual.
"Did you get thicker?" she asked.

"I've been trying these enhancement pills. I didn't think so, but that's really up to you," he said.
She shivered, realizing the truth of all of this. She was at the mercy of his actions. She watched as he stroked himself completely, looking at her body.
"God you're so pretty," he said.
"Thank you," Jackie replied.
He positioned himself so that his cock was right near her entrance, and then with a groan, he pushed himself into her.
She tensed up, feeling his thick cock completely breach her walls. She screamed out loud, shocked by the sudden feeling of this, and as he started to push himself deep inside, she began to shiver, feeling as if she was about to get broken by this man.
Would he break her? Would he actually completely destroy her? She didn't even know, but when he thrusted his fat cock into her completely, she let out a sudden scream, her entire body losing control at the feelings she was feeling.
"Fuck," she cried out loud. She was whimpering by this point, and that's when she felt Dan give her a hard smack on the backside.
"Come on, take it," he said to her.
He started to press himself deeper and deeper, fucking her faster than she was used to. She had to endure this. She had to make him cum.
She knew that if she did that, she would at least get closer to her debt being paid, which was something that she didn't mind.
She started to feel him push himself into her at a faster pace, and she felt as if she was being split in half. But, when he managed to make it so that he was hitting the bundle of nerves there, she screamed out loud, shuddering in pleasure at the sensation that she was feeling.
"Holy fuck," she said, feeling as if everything was driving her insane.
He continued his onslaught against her body, watching as she shivered, loving every single moment of this, and then, as soon as she felt him press all the way in, he tensed up, and she lightly gasped as he touched her clit with the smallest touch.
He came hard into her, and the sensation of cumming inside of her sent something through her body, a shiver of sorts, and she soon lost her mind.
"Holy shit," she said to him.
She then started to gasp, feeling as if everything was on fire. She then started to tense up, feeling her body soon reach the brink of

orgasm. As quick as it happened, she then relaxed, riding out her orgasm.
"Holy crap," she finally managed to say after it was all said and done.
"You like it, kitten?" he asked.
"Yeah. That was something all right," she admitted.
"Well, you managed to get another two grand off your debt. You still have a long ways to go, but with that ass of yours, I'm sure you'll manage to get this paid off in no time.
He left Jackie on the floor there, a shivering mess with cum trailing down her leg. She then realized that her ass did have the power to get her out of this mess, and although she was doing this to pay off her debt, she wasn't going to complain, because it also felt amazing as well, and she also felt that it was something she did enjoy, even if she did have ulterior motives for doing everything that she did with this man at the moment.

Book 2:

Fantastic Beast Sex

8 Stories of Fantasy Creature Erotica

Victoria Gray

What's in the Box?

"I'm telling you, you must go," said Vera with a smirk as she stirred her tea. Little wisps of vapor escaped the porcelain cup in the chilly autumn morning.

"You want me to leave?" said Vivien who wasn't really paying attention to what her friend was saying. She had become easily distracted lately. There was something about the cold autumn air and lack of daylight that made her feel sluggish like she was living underwater.

"No, silly! You have to go to the new gift shop in town. It's quite a wonder. There are trinkets and gadgets there that I couldn't even name!"

That wouldn't take much, Vivien thought to herself as she watched the slice of lemon bob in her steaming tea cup. She had grown up with Vera and appreciated her invitations to the estate, but as Vivien got older, it seemed as if her friends were being pared away like petals from an artichoke. Vera was kind enough, funny at times, but could be downright frivolous about the things in her life.

"The antiquities there must be worth a small fortune. I would like to plan a visit there this afternoon and would like for you to attend me." Vera set her tea down and placed her hands in her lap as if Vivien would hand her her answer.

"I don't know...I'm kind of busy." Vivien knew she wouldn't be busy. She was a writer and a dedicated one at that, but even on a good day she could manage five hours of work maximum. Vera didn't care enough to ask her about her work, so for all she knew Vivien labored for days on end in her tiny cramped office.

"Oh, please, Viv! I don't want to go alone. And you really should get out of the house more. When's the last time you met a nice fella'?"

Vivien narrowed her eyes at her. If Vera didn't care about her work, she absolutely cared about who Vivien was seeing. The truth was it had been over a year since any man had drawn water from her well. It didn't bother her as much as it seemed to bother Vera. She had learned to keep herself company even though the life of a writer gave her an excuse to stay in and read. Her salacious novels and hand provided her anything a man could provide and with none of the headache of pleasing a guy.

"Fine...but we should go now, I want to get some writing done today."

"Perfect! I'll let Winston know we'll need some spending money. Just wait here and go easy on the cookies." Vera stood and scooted across the parlor on heels, each click echoing through her massive home. After marrying into money, she had taken on many bizarre airs. She was always nice but always had a way of saying something mean that almost sounded considerate. Now she walked different, talked different, and seemed to be a completely different person. They had gone to university together, working together in the laundry room to pay their tuitions. Vera had dropped out and married the first man she met there. Vivien had earned her literary certificate and squeezed out a living writing adventure novels that critics bemoaned and her followers devoured.

In the den, which was somehow different from a parlor when you were rich, Vera spoke with her husband Winston who was counting his money or whatever rich people did to make a living. Vera often spoke of the erotic favors she did for Winston that had earned her her wedding band as if it were a trophy to claim. Winston was quite a bit older than Vera with shiny, combed back, silver hair and a prominent mustache that dominated lip. It was difficult to imagine such a proper and stoic man having such a large sexual appetite. Vivien held her face and blushed every time Vera brought up her sex life, but at night would often fantasize about her friend and her friend's husband inviting her into the bedroom for the type of debauchery rich people participated in. Vivien had a profound and unyielding imagination that made her a darling writer among her fans but could also generate sexual scenarios so intense she embarrassed herself.

"You ready, dear?" Vera stepped into the parlor with a small bulging sack of silk that was surely stuffed with gold coins. Vera was superfluous and obsessed with the appearance of wealth, but she was always generous when she had money to spend. Her husband owned several merchant ships so she was almost always generous.

As Vivien stood, Vera took her arm and the two friends stepped outside to await their carriage. Vera was beaming in the morning light, much like anyone would beam if they had been handed a sack of gold. Vera and Winston were almost a perfect match. Vera loved spending money and according to her, Winston loved taking her to the docks and showing her the eels, as the merchant captains were fond of saying. Their black carriage circled in the carriageway and stopped in front of them. It was an absolutely gorgeous vehicle with golden trim and black paint so shiny it looked fresh. Vera guided her in by the hand and followed before closing the door. The inside smelled like flowers and smoke. The seat cushions were down stuffed, covered in silk, and the carriage probably cost more than Vivien's house and all the books in it. Even the walls were upholstered inside the vehicle.

The ride was smooth as they left the countryside and entered the seaside town of Watervale. Winston had once regaled them with the history of Watervale which had been originally called Salt End. The harbor built the city up boat by boat and eventually the rich people decided they didn't want to live in a city called Salt End and renamed it Watervale. The town was gorgeous on the rich side, though Vivien lived on the fringe of the poorer, eastern side of town known as Salt Pit. Their carriage clicked down the cobble stone row to match the trot of the horses and Vivien found herself nodding off. Vera had sent for her early in the morning even though she liked to stay up all night reading and writing then sleep in during the day. The peacefulness and isolation of deep night allowed her to enjoy her books to the fullest and accomplish several hours of unbroken work at a time. The season wasn't helping her energy levels or her mood. Meeting a guy, even just to scrape the barnacle off her bow, wouldn't be the worst idea. She didn't hate sex, liked it in fact, she just doesn't like having to deal with the guy after he spent his load. She barely had enough energy to care for herself and get all her work done, she certainly couldn't manage the emotional needs of another person. Maybe Winston could take her on as a paramour? There would probably be a lot of gold involved...

"We're here!" exclaimed Vera who snapped Vivien out of her daze. She blinked her tiredness away and stared out the carriage window. Judging by the state of the surrounding buildings and the cleanliness of the road, they were in a nicer neighborhood. A few pedestrians walked by the carriage, but it was still mid-morning, hours before the road would be filled with rich spouses who had too much money to work. Vera practically sprang out of the carriage door and Vivien nearly tumbled out after her, holding onto the rail to stay upright. The carriage rolled away and Vivien stretched out her arms and twisted her back to a series of pops. She let out a yawn and looked to Vera who had her face pressed against the window of a building. She might have been mistaken for a child devouring the inside of a candy shop with just her eyes. The building itself was made of black bricks with sanguine trim around the doors and windows. It looked thoroughly strange surrounded by buildings of a more common architecture. Crimson curtains guarded darkened windows that must have made it nearly impossible to see the contents of the shop. Above the door was a large sign painted in red and gold that simply said "Curiosities" in a stylized script nearly impossible to decipher. With her face still pressed to the glass of the shop window, Vera let out a childish squeal then ran up to Vivien.

"Oh, I can't wait for you to see it. This is going to change your life," Vera squealed and held her arms to her chest.

"I don't know...maybe I should just head home," said Vivien just to tease her. Vera looked as if she had just been stabbed. Her jaw dropped and her face went white.

"Viv!"

"I'm kidding, let's go outside. I'm sure at the least this will be great material for a book."

Vera snatched her arm and dragged her through the front door. Inside was a dim antiques shop crowded with all makes of rare and valuable items. Many of the pieces could be recognized as urns or vases, bowls and cups, while the uses of other contraptions were a mystery. The building had a strange smell like burning herbs and flowers. Vivien almost felt insulted that this was what Vera had dragged her here for until they passed two aisles and came upon a vast collection of ancient sex toys. Vivien's face flushed and her pussy pulled tight to see all these erotic contraptions out in the open. Vera released her hand to fuss and coo over all the strange and tantalizing items. There were hundreds of dildos made from polished stone and wood lining the shelves. Many looked to be modeled after human cocks, but others must have been modeled after orcs, goblins, leonese, zera, and more base animals such as dogs, lions and horses. Vivien's heart raced as her creative mind imagined the artisan who had sculpted their own horse cock from marble and had surely presented it to a royal or aristocrat for use. The room suddenly felt insanely hot.

On some racks off to her right were gorgeous lingerie made of fine fabrics and frills. She had never worn anything more elaborate than chest bindings and a breechcloth and couldn't imagine donning such elaborate underwear. Though she could imagine Vera dressing up to please her husband. Near the dildos on an adjacent shelf were a collection of gorgeous eggs made from stone and inlaid with delightful gold and silver designs. Surely one would make an excellent paperweight.

"Those are for your bum," Vera whispered in her ear and made her flinch. It was a lot to take in, both figuratively and literally. Some of the eggs were the size of cuckoo eggs, while others could have been dragon eggs. *How could anyone fit such a thing in their butt comfortably, let alone at all?* On other racks and shelves were clamps, chains, and crops which looked more like they were used for aggressive interrogation than pleasure. Off the wall was a glass case which contained several small bottles. The labels on many of the potions had faded, but others promised the virility of a bull or the fertility of a dryad. Vivien dreaded to think Vera would risk her health on such questionable tinctures. In an adjacent glass case were several wooden boxes, polished and stained, with no obvious purpose.

"Finding everything alright?" said an elderly woman who was suddenly standing in front of her. Vivien flinched back from the apparition but Vera caught her around the shoulders.

"Mrs. Belsworth!" declared Vera who bent over the counter to give the old woman a huge.

"So good to see you again, dear. I take it you and your husband enjoyed the ointment I prepared?" the old woman said with a pleasant smile. Her gray hair was up in a bun and she wrapped herself in a plush violet robe. Her face was almost pretty and the plumpness of her frame resisted wrinkles.

"And then some! We went all night and didn't stop until lunch! It was a wonder! He nearly broke me in half," said Vera who finished with a loud hard laugh that made Mrs. Belsworth chuckle. While Vera put on the airs of a highborn daughter, when it came to sex, she couldn't conceal her lowborn roots. Modesty was not in her nature and she loved to discuss sex with anyone who would listen.

"I'm glad," said Mrs. Belsworth, "and who is this lovely creature you brought with you? A paramour perhaps?"

Vivien blushed at the implication that she was Vera's sex servant.

"I wish, she's just my good friend Vivien. Viv, this is Mrs. Belsworth."

"Nice to meet you," said Vivien who held out her hand. Mrs. Belsworth smiled and shook it. Her hands were remarkably soft.

"Seems it's been awhile since a man visited you," said Mrs. Belsworth.

"Vera!" Vivien snapped.

"I didn't tell her."

"I can tell from your countenance, dear. A woman needs a good dusting once in awhile or her house starts to creak. I can tell from your eyes that it's been quite some time since a man dusted your parlor?"

Vivien dragged her hand down her face and sighed. It felt like her mom was lecturing her about men to have such an old woman discuss her sex life.

"Two years...maybe I should just buy one of those dildos over there to keep me company."

"Perhaps...though I think I have something more appropriate for you." Mrs. Belsworth knelt by the glass case and slid the back door open. She removed one of the plain, polished wooden boxes and set it on top of the case. Vivien moved her hand to open it, but Mrs. Belsworth slapped it away.

“Ow! What’d you do that for?” Vivien yelped and shook the sensation back into her hand.

“This is a very special gift. You must take it home and open it after midnight.”

“Uhhh, what is it, and why?”

“You’ll understand. Only open it in the quiet of your home, when you feel that longing for a man’s touch.”

“Why are you selling it to her when you wouldn’t sell it to me?” said Vera who moved to reach for the box but hesitated when Mrs. Belsworth moved her hand to slap it away.

“I can tell from her eyes she is alone at home and longs to feel a man’s touch. This gift will help her. You have a man at home, my dear. This gift is not for you.”

“You still didn’t tell me what this is,” said Vivien.

“You’ll see,” said Mrs. Belsworth with another warm smile.

“Well, how much is it?” said Vivien.

“Two gold.”

“Gahhh, I don’t have that kind of money to waste on trinkets. I--”

“You said this will help her get laid to bed?” Vera hip checked her out of the way and counted two coins from her coin purse.

“In a sense. I promise if she follows my instructions she will be immensely sexually satisfied.”

Vivien blushed and covered her cheeks as the two women discussed her sexual satisfaction. Their conversation made it feel like they were undressing her with their words. She just wasn’t capable of that kind of talk. She knew Vera loved her for her frankness and honesty, but when it came to sex, she couldn’t be open the way Vera was. They spent a little more time in the shop as Vera browsed and Mrs. Belsworth wrapped up the strange box in tissue and giftwrap. Vera ended up purchasing a handsome marble dildo for herself and a strange animalistic dildo for Vivien.

“Goodbye, dears,” Mrs. Belsworth called to them as they stepped outside into the daylight. Vivien looked down with apprehension at the small gift-wrapped package in her hands as if it might explode. She had no idea what might be inside, probably one of those suspect aphrodisiacs, though judging by Vera’s response, they might be legitimate.

“Guess you want to go home now, huh?” said Vera with a bit of misgiving in her voice.

“We could grab lunch first I guess. I really do need to go home and get some writing done, but I have some time.”

The two friends boarded their carriage and were taken to a fine dining establishment up in the bluffs near the harbor. The restaurant was up in a crosswind that blew away the otherwise unpleasant smells of the harbor. The view was spectacular and the two friends ate their meals out on the patio. After placing an order for food and drinks, Vera immediately began sharing stories of her sexual escapades with her husband. Winston gave off the impression of being a stuffy aristocrat, but apparently he was an absolute beast in the bed sheets. Vera explained how she had slathered his manhood with a special balm Mrs. Belsworth had sold her and how they had made love through the night and into the middle of the day when they were both overcome with exhaustion. The balm had invigorated Winston and sent him into a bout of heat, just like an ungelded stallion. Vera had been completely overwhelmed by his tenacity. Fortunately the balm had had an effect on her own inner workings and her sexual appetite grew to match her husband's that night. They did everything including bum stuff, as Vera put it. Vivien was eternally grateful that the patio was mostly empty in the opening hours of luncheon.

Vera and Vivien ate their meals without much fanfare and returned to their carriage. They rode across town to Vivien's home where she was dropped off outside. Her home was a small brick house with a slate roof that seemed to lean off to the side. Like her home, all the surrounding building looked like they were slowly sliding into disrepair. She thanked Vera for the outlandish gifts and hugged her friend goodbye.

"Let me know how it goes," said Vera with a wink and a smile. Whatever magical balm was contained in the box, she wasn't sure she wanted to share the effects with her friend. She unlocked her front door, making sure to lock it again when she stepped inside. Her small home was cramped with small stacks of books everywhere as if they were part of the furniture. She absolutely loved books and couldn't bring herself to throw them away or afford a carpenter to build her an adequately sized case. She went directly to her office and set the gifts down on an end table also covered with novels. Her office was cramped with books as well. The entire left wall was a bookshelf packed so tight that removing one book threatened to bring the whole collection down. She had brought in multiple end tables to stack her books on and what was left for work was only her desk with just enough space for some parchment and an inkwell. She grabbed the book she was reading off her desk chair and primed the pump as it were before she started writing. It was an old text she had spent far too much money on. The tome told the firsthand story of warrior who had descended into the unholy hells, written as if it had happened firsthand. The style, like many old texts, was dry and sometimes difficult to comprehend at times, but the novelty of such a creative story from so long ago sparked a special interest in her. She leaned back in her swivel chair and devoured the story, only looking up hours later when the light made it difficult to read by.

Vivien sparked a candle with a black-mold spark stick and stood up to stretch her legs. On the end table were the gifts Vera had bought her, just where she had left them. She was so engrossed with her book she had become a bit too addled to write effectively. A good hand session with herself would be the perfect thing to clear her mind. She picked up the package that was clearly the dildo and unwrapped it on her desk. Her nipples hardened as the toy emerged from the tissue paper. It was an elegant thing if you didn't mind the subject matter. The dildo was carved of a beautiful, blood-red stone with small striations of gold-black that resembled veins. The shape was hardly human with a huge bulb at the base and the shaft coming to an accusatory pointed tip. Vivien felt flustered just looking at it, knowing it must have been modeled after some animal. She picked up the dildo which had a good weight to it and felt herself go slick. Despite the chilliness of the night and the season, the dildo was a comfortable, neutral temperature. She stroked her toy imagining that she was masturbating some monster or a dragon. Taking a deep breath, she slid the dildo in her mouth and fellated it, imagining she was pleasuring one of the strange creatures she had read about in her books. Despite the cold she yanked off her bottoms and plain breechcloth to have at herself. She moved her hand through her untamed bush to find her hard little nub and massaged it delicately. With one hand she pushed the dildo down her throat and masturbated with the other.

As she masturbated, she imagined Vera watching her be taken by some great beast that was overpowering her. Knowing Vera, she would thoroughly enjoy such a display. The though of Vera enjoying her sexual submission made her loins roil. She released the wet dildo and slid it up inside her where it stretched her to a satisfying and comfortable degree. As she slid the toy in and out of her warm, needy pussy, she pulled her blouse up and pulled her chestbindings down which caused her chubby breasts to bounce free. She pinched and pulled her nipple with one hand as she dildoed herself with the other. In her mind, the faces of Vera and Winston flashed. She imagined them watching her, finding it mildly amusing how quickly she had taken to the dildo and how good it felt to be stretched open again. For a moment she desperately wanted Vera to watch her masturbate and wished to the gods that Vera was here with her. She had never felt any such tendencies towards women, but there was a special intimacy she shared with Vera and her outgoing sexual nature.

Vivien worked herself into a frenzy until her orgasm broke across her body as she imagined Winston mounting her as Vera watched. The ecstasy was incredible as it washed over her like a warm wave of water.

The dildo was truly something special. After composing herself, she redressed and wandered into the kitchen to find a snack. She found some butter and a good sized chunk of black bread which she quickly devoured after such an intense session with herself. She almost felt cleansed after her orgasm. Surely Vera would want to hear about this the next time they met for tea. After devouring her snack, Vivien returned to her office and began writing. She whipped up a frenzied storm of dialogue and character development, and not for the first time in her career did she consider interjecting a sex scene into the story. Her publisher would hate it as erotic fiction was only traded discreetly and never in fine reading establishments, but this night she was feeling especially randy. Despite having masturbated less than two hours ago, she felt like she could go another round. Instead of pleasuring herself with the magical animal dildo, she poured her energy into her stories and got a considerable amount of work done. She wrote deep into the night and only stopped when the moon was high in the night sky. Hours must have passed since she started as her candle had burned down to a pathetic nub on her desk.

Satisfied with what she had accomplished, Vivien grabbed her candle and dildo and made for her bedroom for one, last, personal massage before she turned in for the night. As she stepped out of her office, there was a rattling noise behind her. She whirled around as her heart jumped, but there was nothing in her office besides books and paper.

Vivien slowly moved down the hallway to check the kitchen and her living area, but the house was truly empty. Then the noise came again, almost like a quick set of knocks. She stopped and listened for it, brandishing the dildo like a cudgel. Another rattling noise, this time distinctly coming from her office. She hurried down the hall and raised the stone dildo above her head, ready to bludgeon whoever dared to steal her precious books. But again, her office was devoid of life. She checked under her desk just to be sure, but no one was there. The rattling happened again and this time she saw movement out of the corner of her eye. She whirled around, dildo brandished, to find the second gift of Vera's on the table. Her eyes focused for some sign of movement when the wrapped packaged wiggled on the table and made that rattle noise she heard.

"Gods help me," whispered Vivien as she neared the package. What on earth had the old woman sold them? She set her candle on the floor and piled several of her heaviest books on top of the gift. Too frightened to pick up the box and toss it outside, she would weigh the gift down and bar her office door until morning. Just as she lifted her heaviest tome onto the gift, the stack of books shot across the room which caused a small avalanche. Vivien backed away until her plump butt bumped the side of the desk. Emerging from the small box and torn wrapping, what Vivien initially perceived as a snake was actually a dark tentacle that moved on its own accord. She held her breath and tried to remain perfectly still. The candle on the floor shined off the slimy skin of the appendage and cast a stark shadow against the office wall. Vivien crept towards the door, never taking her eye off the thing. She would have swore it could have heard her heart raging in her chest, but it didn't seem to have anyway to perceive her.

Just as she stepped inside the hallway, something grabbed her leg and lifted her off the ground upside down. The tentacle was somehow holding her up in the air. Vivien screamed for help, but doubted anyone in her scrappy neighborhood would hear her or much less help. Reasoning had gone out the window in this moment. She screamed again when another tentacle emerged from the box. It shot at her screaming mouth and began plunging her throat. She grabbed the thing with both hands and clawed into it, but it continued to move back and forth in her throat. She gagged and fought with the entity, kicking and thrashing in the air, but whatever it was, was extremely powerful. Vivien felt dizzy as she gagged on the tentacle and thought she would faint when it pulled out of her mouth and sprayed her face with tendrils of dark goo. The other tentacle dropped her unceremoniously on the stone floor, leaving her disoriented. Despite the horror of it all, Vivien felt a strange desire move through her hips. Whatever that thing had done to her, it was humiliating, and something deep in her mind had loved it. Still, it could be dangerous.

Vivien stumbled from the room and to her front door when once again her leg was seized and she was dragged across the floor back to the office. Sprouting from the box were three more tentacles this time. The appendages lurched at her and ripped her outfit to pieces, leaving her naked and embarrassed. She covered her breasts and furry pussy but didn't know why she was trying to hide her modesty from this thing. Like several precise fingers, the tentacles turned her over facedown. One slipped inside her already wet pussy and began to fuck her. There was no other word for it. It slipped back and forth inside her and felt absolutely divine. It had been years since a man had touched her, and even longer since one had given her a orgasm. The tentacle throbbed and pulsated inside her, filling every inch but not hurting her. Despite her fear and apprehension over the situation, her sexual needs won over her rational thought, and Vivien allowed the thing to fuck her brainless. In moments her orgasm erupted out of her and moments after that, the tentacle sprayed her insides with warm thick goo.

She thought the ordeal was over, but the creature had other designs. Even more tentacles emerged from the box, too many to count in the dying light. She was lifted into the air by her wrists and ankles, and one of the tentacles slipped inside her needy pussy. Then another slipped in her mouth. A final one, smaller than the rest, slipped into her asshole where no man had dared to tread. The creature fucked her into mindlessness. Not only was her mind going somewhere else while her libido stayed home, but she felt absolutely used to be fucked by this thing without permission. The combination of the two brought her multiple orgasms that splashed across her hips and chest like warm liquor. Every conceivable, fuckable hole was being satisfied, and Vivien could barely function. Some tentacles left, filling her holes with a load of goo, but others reclaimed purchase and continued to pleasure her. This continued all throughout the night, hours after her mind had stopped thinking and her body gave in.

When the sunlight peeked in through her office window, the tentacles quietly slithered back into their box. On the floor Vivien lay naked on the verge of unconsciousness. Her pussy and asshole gaped and leaked strange dark ooze. She felt like an absolute whore and loved it. Vera would absolutely need to hear about her wild night.

The Expedition

An expedition had been sent to the Foracee Jungle by a lord thousands of miles away after his court historian had uncovered tablets that might have indicated the final resting place of a powerful and forgotten artifact known as the Lich Crown. According to the fractured texts, the wearer of the crown would be bestowed with the power to raise the dead. What that meant for a lord was an unstoppable army which would allow him to seize any territory he desired, even those held by rival lords.

Billie didn't give two piles of horse shit for the geo-political struggles of lands she had never even visited. In the deserts of her homeland she was known as a prodigious thief who could snatch any prize if she was properly motivated. The guards and paladins of her native lorddom called her "The Mist" for trying to prevent her from entering was like trying to stop the mist itself. She was also deathly quietly and had the uncanny ability to hide in plain sight.

A milk-faced man who was clearly visiting the region had approached her in the tavern and proceeded to ramble on about an expedition they were making into the Foracee Jungle. No one with half a mind would enter the jungle unless they had a death wish. Despite being hundreds of miles away from the quiet desert village where Billie hid from authorities, tales of the legendary jungle made their way into the inn. The jungle cats and vegetable bats were enough to keep even the dumbest adventurers out. A jungle cat was covered with pleated green fur to blend in with the surrounding vegetation and would only make its presence known when it ripped out your guts, letting you live long enough to watch yourself be eaten. Vegetable bats were cute enough with their pink fur and giant shiny eyes, the few bravest explorers said, but one bite and you'd fall over stiff like a tuber until your last breath slowly drifted out of your paralyzed lungs. Then there were the swarms of insects who carried diseases with no names because anyone who had been there to observe their symptoms were also dead. And finally, some adventurers claimed that the flora itself fought back against those who would dare enter the jungle. Tripping travelers to break their necks, poisoning them, or strangling them in their sleep.

Billie had a mind that these were often tall tales the men told to impress the serving girls, but she had no inclination to find out for herself.

But still, the small pale man from another land was insistent that The Mist accompany his expedition. He had reason to believe that the temple they were seeking would be riddled with traps and safeguards to prevent anyone from purloining its treasures. He didn't believe that all the deterrents would be operational, but wanted someone with an expertise in such matters.

She had the pasty man buy her several drinks as he explained their expedition and its purpose. At first he was unwilling to divulge the exact purpose of their quest, but on threat of withdrawal, the man confessed they were seeking an ancient crown rumored to possess magical powers. Still she refused to join the expedition until the stranger offered her a mind-boggling eight hundred gold for her services. With an agreement to be paid more money than she'd earn in eight lifetimes, Billie joined their expedition.

The journey was uneventful trek across grasslands and desert, almost always along roads that had seen countless travelers and were well known. That was until they crested a desert bluff and first laid eyes on the Foracee Jungle. From the desert bluff, a colossal wall of vegetation rose up from the sandy loam. Trees far larger than any Billie had seen in her lifetime towered over the jungle floor, draping curtains of moss as long and as wide as crop fields. Everyone in the eighty man expedition was in awe of the natural wonder as they stepped into the jungle. After so much mindless topography and a constant, flat horizon in the distance, stepping into the Foracee Jungle was like stepping into another world, one where you couldn't see five feet in front of you but were constantly dazzled by the natural wonders that blocked your path. Fern bushes as large as houses and in every color of the sun blocked their passage into the jungle. Their expedition leader Randall stepped forward and cut a path through the vegetation with his two swordsmen by his side. Randall was a tall, weathered man with dark skin and fine toned muscles. He had no sense of humor or appreciation for the challenges of their long voyage that the less experienced bemoaned. He was the opposite of Johnson, her doughy white handler, in every conceivable way and she had immediately taken a fancy to him during their journey.

Billie was a proud, sexually self-possessed woman who enjoyed a wank session after a good heist. She also appreciated a man who could put her in her place in the bedroom. Outside the bedroom she had no patience for men who thought too highly of themselves or too lowly of women, but between the sheets she needed a man who could take charge. At night during their expedition she often thought of their leader as she touched herself in her bedroll. She would imagine his taut brown muscles pinning her down and having his way with her. How ruthless he would be with her tiny tan body. How he would smack her flat little butt or bite down on her small, unimpressive breasts. Billie was a supremely confident woman after a career of successful heists, but every time Randall caught a glimpse of her she felt like a little girl again, and she liked that feeling.

It was only the second day after entering the jungle when their troubles began. The second morning after the second night saw one of their journeymen asphyxiated in his sleep. They all gathered around the man in his bedroll whose head looked like a giant blueberry. There were no marks on his neck, and no blood on his hands from defensive wounds. All the explorers whispered among themselves about who or what might have done it. Randall didn't expect foul play, so the man was wrapped in tarpaulin and dragged behind their caravan.

The next night, the camp awoke to screaming. One of the explorers claimed he had been completely wrapped in vines as he fell asleep and had begun choking. Billie expected the pragmatic Randall to dismiss the man's outrageous claim, but instead he examined a nearby hanging vine. The camp watched and waited for a decision. The air was menacing and strangely quiet that night as if the jungle was holding its breath. Randall removed a small knife from his hip and sliced into the vine. The thing, for surely it was no ordinary vine, screeched and recoiled into the canopy. Randall cast his eyes all around.

"New sleeping arrangements. Half of you sleep while the other half watches each individual person. keep an eye out for anything even mildly suspicious and report to me or Johnson with any unusual discoveries."

Randall counted off the expedition into one's and two's and ordered everyone to bed. Each night the camp alternated who slept first and who watched first. Despite their reserved and arguably secure sleeping arrangements, three more people died in the next two days. The expedition discovered a beautiful blue flower that bloomed at night and released a deadly toxin which probably caused the first two deaths, but the third was a complete mystery. Over the course of the ensuing week, a quarter of the men abandoned the expedition in the night. Johnson promised their wages split evenly among the men who stayed in an effort to keep the quest from completely falling apart. Randall looked visibly distraught each morning to find more men had abandoned them. The next morning, Billie took it upon herself to relief his tension.

Drinking plenty of water, Billie woke herself early with the powerful need to make. Not braving the dangers of their dense jungle hells, she squatted and pissed just two strides outside of camp. It had become a common sight in the past week as no one was foolish enough to leave camp just to make. After wiping herself with the back of her glove, she pulled up her trousers and stepped across her sleeping comrades until she stood outside Randall's tent. She quietly slipped inside and was shocked to see him sitting up, halfway into dress. Their eyes met for a moment as Randall reached for his knife on his crumpled trousers beside him.

"Tell me you're not the one responsible," he said in a raspy whisper, implying she had been the cause of the unknown deaths so far.

"No! No, listen," she whispered loudly, "I just thought. You look tense, and I want to help out."

Billie placed a hand on his bare thigh that might as well have been carved of wood. His cock immediately rose to attention inside his breechcloth.

"I, I..." It was strange to see him stammer after seeing so much confidence from him. Billie pressed a finger to her lips and moved towards him. She lay across his lap and freed his beautiful thick cock that sprung to attention. His shaft was brown like the rest of his skin, but his cockhead was more pink than brown and delightfully plump like the head of a mushroom. Without a word she slipped his cock in her eager mouth and sucked it lovingly. He gasped and placed his heavy hand on the back of her head. She bobbed her head up and down and slobbered on his warm, smooth cock. Her hand found his balls and fondled them as she loved his cock with her mouth. He pet her head as she fellated him and she loved feeling like his little pet. Shockingly he was quick to cum and blew a massive thick load into her mouth that she had trouble swallowing. His cum was thick and bitter and stuck to the back of her throat after being swallowed. She sat up and smiled at him, wiping the stray cum from her mouth.

"Th-thank you," he managed to stammer out.

"Anytime," she said with a grin and slipped out of his tent. Something about stealing a guy's cum felt amazing to her. She knew the kinds of guys who frequented the tavern thought a girl was a whore if they were willing to suck on a cock, let alone eager to do so. But sucking cock made her feel beautiful and sexy, and if a guy could keep his stupid opinions to himself, she absolutely relished the chance to suck him. It was a treat for her and she doubted a guy could understand the emotional satisfaction of sucking a guy off.

Despite the splendid morning in Randall's tent, the expedition continued with increasing peril. Randall seemed much more sure of himself as he led, but people continued to disappear. One night a jungle cat snuck into their camp at night and ripped the guts out of three men before Billie put it down with a knife to its throat. She had been sleeping when the screaming started and the watch swore they never saw the cat enter.

Randall took it upon himself to be her personal watch after that and the men seemed to understand her importance to their survival. This gave her and Randall many opportunities to exchange oral favors. She contemplated performing her oral love for all the men left in the expedition to keep morale up. Randall said it was a beautiful and generous idea but the men would quickly move to hurt feelings after becoming infatuated with her. It made sense but didn't stop Billie from fantasizing about blowing every guy in the camp in a single night.

After forty days of travel, fifteen at a tortoise's crawl through the Foracee Jungle, their expedition finally came upon the temple, just where Johnson said it would be. All the men smiled and hugged each other as if their journey was finally over. Eighty had set out from the lorddom, and only forty-three lived to see the temple. The shares would be massive for whoever lived to step outside the Foracee Jungle. The first night camped outside the temple almost felt like the first night without any deadly incidences. Just when Billie and Randall thought it safe to exchange oral favors, Johnson approached them with charcoal etchings of the tablet he had discovered for his lord. They were written in a script Billie didn't recognize, though she never bothered to learn to read. Johnson explained that the temple held great religious significance in a time out of time and that many traps and safeguards had been put in place to protect its treasures. He didn't suspect that many of the traps would be functional, but some might be of such a simple design that they were failsafe. Despite these helpful warnings, he had no information on the traps themselves.

The first group into the temple consisted of eight people including Billie and Randall. Johnson had no information on the exact location of the crown within the temple, only that it once existed inside and was in fact the last known location. The jungle had done its part to invade the temple grounds as vines snaked through every crumbled hole and bare patch of dirt in the floor. Trees sprouted up through the structure and must have shattered the roof hundreds of years ago. The Foracee Jungle was dark even during midday because of the dense canopy, but light was even more limited inside the temple. Most of the expedition resorted to black fungus torches lit with spark kits, but Billie had a pair of fae goggles she used for night time heists. An alchemist had sold them to her for a hefty sum promising perfect night vision, and she had delivered. The goggles were a simple band with two lenses housed in copper frames that left green rings on her face after prolonged use, but the magic was in the lenses themselves. The alchemist had taken two identical lenses and pressed a film of fae blood between them inside the frame. Not only could you see a little further with the inflection of the lenses, but the entire world was lit up from the glowing fae blood. Tiny sparks danced in the glass itself, but their light allowed incredible vision in the dark.

Still, the goggles didn't help Billie see the first trap. While creeping down a dark hallway totally overtaken by thick corded vines and hanging moss, a large section of the sealing crashed down and crushed three of the men. The block was near head height, over eight feet long, and must have weighed thousands of pounds. Billie pissed herself in fear as the obvious trap crashed down inches from her face. The remaining members tried to move the massive block but were unable to. Randall called for a retreat and the expedition left the temple to regroup at camp and discuss what had happened. The high spirits of the expedition quickly fell when they learned of the fate of their fellow explorers. Johnson nodded stoically as Randall relayed what had happened. The pale man gave their plans some thought before he spoke.

"I believe to ensure that we succeed at all in this endeavor, that Ms. Billie remain in camp while we send a new team in to discover the location of the crown."

An agitated murmur spread the survivors.

"Once we find the location of the crown, the team shall return and bring Ms. Billie with them to overcome what are surely the most devious traps in the temple."

More angry whispers.

"It doesn't have to be this way," Billie spoke up, "I'll go back in. I'm getting paid to risk my neck, not sit on my ass."

"I deeply appreciate your willingness to re-enter the temple, but I believe it is critical you survive long enough to find the crown. It will only increase our odds for you to wait here," Johnson countered.

"But I have experience with traps. I can protect them and scope out any more traps."

"Yet you failed to perceive the first one."

It felt like the air had been pressed out of her chest. Maybe it was her fault those men died. *Shouldn't she have been able to see such a massive deadly trap before it was sprung?* She had no response.

"Alright then. Who wants to volunteer?"

Not a single person except Randall stepped forward. His bravery moved none of the men to action.

"We already went in there. We shouldn't have to go back," said a man Billie believed to be named Damian. It had become too painful to get close to anyone or learn their names. The other two survivors of the first expedition nodded their agreement.

"Come on now, don't make me pick names," said Johnson, looking around for anyone to volunteer. "Alright then."

Johnson dug through his rucksack, removed a parchment, and unrolled it on a nearby table.

"First pick is D--"

"Wait!" Billie cut him off. Johnson pulled his head back as if her interruption had physically affronted him.

"I know it seems like you guys are risking yourselves for me, so I want to do my part. I'll suck off anyone who volunteers...before you go." Billie felt her face flush red hot as she offered such a whorish promise. It worked though, and several men pushed past each other to offer themselves up to the temple. Randall choose the seven he deemed the most competent. Those seven men gathered around Billie expectantly.

"You don't have to do this, Billie," said Randall with a hint of sorrow in his voice.

"No, I want to. We might never make it out of here alive. These guys deserve this and I'd rather leave this world with a treasure in my arm and a dick in my mouth."

The seven men all smiled at her declaration. Billie lifted her tunic off to reveal her tan chest and small breasts. The men reached out and began to paw at her. She felt so whorish showing these men her teets and letting them touch her, but that whorishness felt amazing, especially against the looming specter of the temple. Their rough hands squeezed her tiny pale breasts and pulled at her hard brown nipples. She gave them several moments to paw at her before she knelt down to receive them. The men began to furiously undo their trousers and press their cocks to her face, jostling to be the first past her lips. She grasped the first one carefully and took him in her mouth. She made sure to make eye contact so he could maybe accept risking his life for her. She had sucked plenty of cocks in her short life and had enjoyed most of them. But being surrounded by seven eager cocks and seven pairs of eyes was dizzying. She could feel her pussy drip into her breechcloth as the men watched her perform oral. Her first man was quick and blew a considerable load across her face and into her short dark hair.

To speed things up she grabbed two cocks and took turns sucking and kissing them. Despite sharing her attention, the two men seemed happy to have their cocks loved. She had to resort to stroking them towards the end as her mouth became dry, but they were more than happy to blow two separate loads in her face and on her chest. Randall pushed his way through and offered her a canteen of water. She drank happily and returned to her promise. The next two men had impressive cocks, one a long powerful thing like a claymore and the other dark and thick like a cudgel. She kissed and sucked them happily though was unable to swallow them. The two men appreciate her willingness to engage with such massive cocks by painting her face with warm sticky cum. Her blood ran hot and her mind spun and danced like she was drunk. The sixth man stepped up and received an eager blowjob as her mind seemed to lift out of her body. She could imagine what those men thought of her for sucking all their cocks. She hoped at the least they were appreciative for what could be their final blowjob ever. The sixth man came quick and filled her mouth with bitter cum. The seventh stranger, for they certainly felt like strangers, grabbed her head and fucked it. Normally she didn't like to be facefucked, but a new special whorishness had overtaken her that evening, and she relished feeling like a whore. The man huffed and grunted until he whined out and blew a load directly down her throat. She collapsed to the jungle floor, covered in the cum from seven different men.

Moments later, Randall scooped her up and placed her on his lap. His rough calloused finger spread her bushy mound open and found her aching clit. With some dexterity he massaged her clit while the men watched fascinated. She didn't need to fantasize about anything; what she had just done was far and away the most whorish act in her life. In seconds she screamed out and ejaculated all over the jungle floor. Ecstasy spasmed through her small frame and made her limbs tremble. Randall wiped the cum from her face and chest and wrapped her in a blanket.

"Thank you, Billie," said one of the men, followed by a chorus of the others that she had serviced.

The Gorger

Despite the beautiful and amazing night Billie had shared with her camp, their situation in the Foracee Jungle did not improve. Blowjobs were no ward against the traps that awaited in the temple. Eighty men had braved the Foracee Jungle, but only forty-three had arrived at the long forgotten temple. Many had fallen to the deadly fauna and flora of the jungle, and just as many had abandoned the expedition to never be seen again. In the first day of their survey of the temple, three of the men had been crushed by a trap. The lord who had financed the expedition had sent his steward who hid behind the name Johnson to manage the endeavor along with the expedition leader Randall. Billie was a master thief and was brought along to overcome the traps and safeguards that would protect the Lich Crown: an ancient and magical artifact believed to have the power to raise the dead. After the very first survey of the temple, the rest of the expedition refused to enter, and Johnson refused to allow Billie to risk her life until the location of the crown was discovered, claiming he needed her expertise with traps if they should have any chance of reclaiming the crown. To encourage the men, Billie promised to blow any man who volunteered and she did in fact suck off the seven men who volunteered to enter the temple, becoming beloved by the camp.

Despite their optimism, more men fell in the second survey to poison darts. Morale fell even lower when the third survey returned two short and reported that they had fallen into a spiked pit. Blow jobs could motivate men to do great things, but even well given head could not motivate the men for a fourth survey. The survivors insisted on returning home, believing none would survive this expedition. Even their leader Randall had misgivings about entering the temple again. Only Johnson seemed insistent on continuing in their folly.

"It is not up to me!" he yelled as the men insisted on turning back for good.

"What does that mean?" Randall spoke up.

"You will not be paid unless you return with the crown."

At such an outlandish statement, several of the men brandished their swords and knives and moved towards Johnson with murderous intent.

"If you kill me, you'll never be paid!" Johnson wailed as they closed in.

"Guys!" Billie spoke up. Though gentle of voice and cantor, Billie carried great love and respect in the camp. The entire trip had been a living nightmare, but her loving mouth kept the morale from crumbling. The men lowered their weapons and remained silent for her.

"Thanks. Look, I don't like this anymore than you do, but we came here for a reason. We can't just turn back and say all those men that died, died in vain. I'm going in there, alone. I'll bring the crown back, and then we can all retire together in a reverse harem."

Some of the men smiled at her attempt at humor.

"We love you Billie," Randall spoke up, a single tear sliding down his cheek. The men chorused his words.

"We should go with you to protect you," said Randall.

"No, too many men have died. I have more experience with traps and burglary than any of you. I'll go. I'll bring back the crown. You guys have made this nightmare somewhat bearable."

The men gathered around and embraced the camp's de facto comfort woman. They rubbed her head and wished her luck as she stepped into the temple alone. It was midday but might as well have been twilight inside the temple halls. The structure was huge, as massive as an entire city, though its size was concealed from the outside by the dense foliage of the jungle. The reports of the previous surveys indicated they had not gotten far inside the temple. Every area seemed to be riddled with deadly traps. Each area had new hazards that made it impossible for infiltrators to recognize and adapt to the hazards. Whatever was in this temple, the architects did not want it taken out.

Billie sidestepped a tripwire down one hallway, then hopped over a suspicious pile of dead vegetation that probably concealed a trap. Turning around one corner she found a small room with an elaborately carved door on the far side. She took a handful of pebbles from her pouch and tossed them in. A slab of stone crashed down to seal the doorway and on the other side she could hear the grating of stone on stone until it finally stopped with a dull crash. This place was quite literally a death trap, but that gave her hope something extremely valuable could be plundered. Rich people didn't build these kinds of deterrents to protect people, only things. She had learned that after two decades of separating the richest lords from their most prized possessions. There was a certain satisfaction into throwing all their efforts into futility as she overcame expensively built deterrents only to rid lords and aristocrats of their most prized possessions.

After two more pressure plates and a pendulum gore ram, Billie found a massive main hall. The room was larger than many of the towns she had lived in and stolen from with several fractures in the ceiling to let obstructed light in. With her magic goggles she could see several ruined statues in the grand hall, probably of long forgotten deities that these ancient people once worshiped. She moved carefully through the hall, half in wonder of deities and kings never seen by any living soul, and half in tentativeness for the traps that most certainly lurked. Despite her apprehension, the room seemed to be free of traps. Halfway across the colossal hall, she had not seen or triggered a single trap. That was until she stepped into a beam of light and the room shook. Billie looked down, but whatever she was standing on surely was not a pressure plate. She quickly scanned her surrounding and ceiling to look for falling or swinging traps, but nothing was coming. Then the room rumbled again. Across the ways, on the north side of the room, a massive creature stepped out from behind a crumbled ziggurat.

The creature was a gorger. Half man, half beast, about twenty feet tall on its hind legs with more muscles than an entire army combined. It looked right at her. She kept her eyes on the deadly beast, holding perfectly still. From its head grew one, massive, jagged horn taller than she was. Around that horn was a golden crown. *What were the chances they would find a crown in the exact building they were searching and have it not be the Lich Crown?* It had to be it. This heist wasn't impossible, she would just have to be smart.

The gorger inched closer. Each step it took shook the ground slightly. She couldn't kill it with just her daggers, but she could snatch the crown and flee back to camp, maybe even trap the beast in the temple hazards. She wasn't sure it could see her but it was certainly moving towards her position. Not wasting a good distance, Billie sprinted for one of the massive eroded statues against the far wall to her left. The beast thundered after her, shaking the floor in its rumbling gait. The statues were huge, at least fifty feet high, and if she got the thing to smash into one, the collapse could crush the beast, allowing her to snatch the crown. Billie was fast for a human, but the gorger displayed insane speeds as it lumbered after her. She circled around the statue's platform, slightly relieved to have an obstacle between her and the beast.

The gorger smashed through the legs of the statue in an explosion of debris, and the entire structure came crashing down on it. Billie ran into an alcove carved in the wall and prayed to the gods she didn't believe in that she'd survive the impossibly loud avalanche of stone. The beast wailed and roared as it was crushed by several tons of rock and mortar.

Once things were finally silent, Billie uncovered her head and opened her eyes to see a pile of stone where the mighty statue once stood. And simple enough, the upper half of the gorger's torso stuck out of the rubble. It's horn was snapped in half but it still wore the crown. Billie's heart jumped as she realized how close she was to bringing this long deadly quest to an end. She ran up to the hill of stone and began scaling the pile. The gorger didn't move or breath at all. Just steps from its mouth, she stopped and stared to make sure it was dead. It didn't seem to move at all, so she carefully climbed the last few feet and lifted the crown off its horn.

As Billie turned to climb back down, the gorger broke throw the stone and threw her against the wall. She clutched the crown against her chest as she was slammed into the stone wall, stunned and disoriented by her impact. Slumped and curled on the floor, the gorger shoved its snout up her crotch and sniffed. The blast of hot air and the unceremonious rub of her vulva made her wet against her will. She turned over to see the face of the beast inches from her body, sniffing at her. It was an ugly thing, its face halfway between a hound and a dragon. She stumbled to her feet and was pushed against the wall as the gorger sniffed her pussy again.

"Fuck, it's horny," Billie thought as she clutched the crown. Under the creature's chest she could see its large, animalistic cock dripping pre-cum on the floor. The tip was flared like a stallion's and seemed to almost stare at her. She slid across the wall to escape slowly when the gorger knocked her down with its massive claw. She felt it press its snout into her butt then rip her trousers away. The gorger licked her once then stepped over her.

"Oh, fuck no," she whispered right before its animal cock impaled her cunt. She cried out in surprise as she was penetrated by the terrifying creature but still kept the crown clutched against her. Whatever happened, she needed to leave with the crown. The gorger seemed to hesitate with it's position until suddenly it pistoned into Billie. The force of penetration was like being fucked by a god as the gorger fucked her senseless. It's powerful hips rotated as it pumped her full of cock. She was stretched to her limit and felt like a little toy as she was fucked brainless. Her mind totally vanished as she became an object for this thing. Orgasm after orgasm spread through her body as she was fucked harder and faster than ever before by the fattest cock she had ever taken. The beast was relentless. At one point she pissed all over the floor but didn't even notice. The force of it's cock pushed her along the floor until the gorger pinned her body with its massive claw and fucked her with full force. Her head lulled side to side as her body became one continuous orgasm.

Finally the gorger bit into her shoulder and pumped her full of cum. The cum exploded with pressure and pushed her off his cock like a geyser. Heavy tendrils of cum slammed into her and coated her entire body. By the end she lay motionless in a large pond of musky cum. Once it was finished breeding, the gorger walked off several steps then fell on its side and went to sleep, completely uninterested in the crown she carried.

Billie spat out a mouthful of dense cum and lay in the puddle, awaiting for her mind to return to her. It was as if the monster had fucked her identity away. Her hands instinctively held the cum covered crown. Somewhere in the back of her mind, she knew she had completed her quest.

When the Wolves Howl, Run!

"Something must be done!" Mayor Abbott roared. The townsfolk roared and murmured a similar affirmation. Something indeed needed to be done.

"These bandits have looted our town eight times in the past year and the town watch does nothing. NOTHING!" Mayor Abbott's face seemed fit to explode as it turned a terrifying shade of crimson. His wretched finger pointed at the head of the watch, Master Townsend. Townsend was an older man, but more fit and powerful than any of the young bucks in town. He stared back at the mayor solemnly. He was a quiet man, never prone to violence. He carried his office with all seriousness and was a beloved figure among the townsfolk.

"And what is it you would have us do?" said Townsend, his eyes scanning his men before locking a stare on the portly mayor. Half of them were fresh faces that had been trained up in only the past month.

"Stop the bandits! What do we pay you for if you do not protect the town!"

The rowdy townsfolk echoed his sentiment and tossed a few, choice, rotted vegetables at Townsend that fell short on the platform, almost as if they were frustrated, just not frusrtated enough to antagonize The Master of the Guard who made no move to react.

"We have sent thirteen men into the foothills to find the bandit camp. None have found the bandit camp or even returned at all. Thirteen good men. The bandits move with a massive pack of feral hounds. We cut down thirty of the beasts and it seems sixty return the next month. We are too few in number," said Townsend. The room settled down. Everyone knew the scourge of the bandits and their feral hound pack. They were big powerful men covered in furs who ran with a massive wolf pack. Even with all the guards at arms, the town's numbers were too few, and the hounds too many.

"The bandits pillage our stores and capture our women. If this should continue, there will be nothing left of Waterbridge," said the Mayor.

"I have done everything I can, Mayor. It may be time to consider mo--"

"Excuse me," a woman spoke up. She wore the elaborate gown and boots of a mage and was clearly not from Waterbridge. Her crimson gown and boots were like a bloody mote in the crowd of plainclothed townsfolk. Beside her stood a powerful dark woman in heavy, platemail armor, and a third sandy skinned woman in leather armor and green cloth.

"Who speaks?" said the mayor.

"My name is Dorthea and these are my companions Maggie and Fastul. We are a traveling guild and it seems your town is in danger. We would like to lend you our aid," the mage spoke loudly and with confidence.

"You are sellswords, beholden to the highest bidder. Waterbridge has no place for the likes of you," declared the mayor as foam spittle formed at the corner of his jowls.

"It seems to me that you don't have many other options," said Dorthea, crossing her arms with a grin.

"How dare you!" raged the mayor, "We will not be coerced into hiring a pack of mercenaries. Leave this town at once and never return!"

"I'll contribute ten gold," Townsend spoke up. The stoic master of the guard stood, reached in his pocket, and counted out ten gold coins on the table near the podium, the entire contents of his wallet.

"It's going to be a hundred gold, sweetheart," said Dorthea with a "lay-me" smile.

"One hundred GOLD! That's outrageous, prosperous, I, I, I, never!" The mayor worked himself into a frenzy and gripped the podium for dear life as if he were the helmsman in a terrible storm.

"I have a gold," said Pickett, one of the local merchants. The handsome merchant approached the dais and placed a single coin on the small stack Townsend had started.

"I can give two," said the local boywer who contributed his share. Each person in the assembly hall eventually formed a line and contributed what they could to the trust. Rafton, the local carpenter, presented a sensible chest for the fund to be stored in. After all the silver, coppers, and gold were counted, they had amassed seventy-eight gold in total. Dorthea counted it all to be certain.

"Close enough," she said with a smile which caused a collective sigh of relief to sweep through the hall.

"Hey, I didn't see the mayor contribute anything," someone in the back shouted. The townsfolk surged at the mayor, knocking him over and grabbing his ankles. Four men hung him upside down and shook him vigorously. Trinkets and coins tumbled out of him like a sliced purse. Two women gathered the treasures and placed them on top of the chest.

"Alright folks, leave it to the Red Hens! We have never failed a quest and don't plan on starting now!" Dorthea declared. The townsfolk, infected by her confidence and bravado, cheered her on as she left the assembly hall with her companions Maggie and Fastul. Already packed and ready in anticipation of receiving the quest, the three women made their way into the foothills outside Waterbridge. Afternoon quickly turned to evening at they made their way deeper into the foothills in search of the bandit camp.

"Why did we take this quest again?" Maggie grumbled as they crested a shallow rise into another timberline. Wearing heavy armor and carrying a claymore made the walk far more difficult for her than for Dorthea or Fastul.

"Because they were desperate and seemed to have a decent amount of money. You saw that gold, right? Hundred gold? I almost couldn't believe it myself when they agreed," Dorthea said with a smirk.

"I didn't think they'd really agree to it. Frankly, I was kind of mad that you started with a hundred gold," said Fastul with her bow out and an arrow nocked. Her dark braided her was tied back out of her face to better scan their surroundings.

"Fortune favors the bold. And we have certainly found our fortune," said Dorthea.

"And how are we supposed to kill a pack of one hundred hounds?" said Maggie.

"We kill the bitch whelping them and eventually they'll die off. Pack will splinter after the alpha is killed," said Maggie.

"We should focus on the men involved. No doubt they are directly responsible for the size of the pack," said Fastul.

"Oh, no doubt. You see where they're coming from?" asked Maggie. The forest grew darker as the sun set behind the distant mountains. The sound of insects sprang to life in the twilight like nature's chorus.

"Tracks go this way. There's at least four dozen in the pack, maybe more. Hard to tell when there's that many. Tracks go deeper into the forest. See here, tufts of fur caught in the low broken branches. They definitely come through here. Towns that way, that means their den is this way."

A single wolf howl broke the soft silence of the twilight and was answered by what seemed to be hundreds of other howls all throughout the dark forest. The three women stopped.

"Do they know we're here?" asked Dorthea.

"They do now," said Fastul as she scaled a nearby oak.

"Tell us what you see," Dorthea called up to her.

"Nothing. Light's too dark, forest is too dense. There's a clearing up ahead, let's move towards it." Fastul hopped from tree to tree with ease and led her companions to a wide clearing in the woods where they would have a broader field of vision for the upcoming battle. In the brush outside the clearing, bushes and saplings twitched and shivered as the wolves approached, but none were visible. Maggie had her powerful claymore drawn in front of her and Dorthea's wand trembled in her hand.

"Sit rep!" Dorthea called up to Fastul.

"At least two dozen, use your flames. Try not to burn the whole forest down!"

Dorthea sparked a fireball on the tip of her wand that roared to life and lit up their surroundings. Only the glint in the wolves' eyes could be seen in the brush.

"Come on!" Maggie roared at them. Fastul drew her bow and fired, killing a wolf with a single yelp. The other wolves barked and ran into the clearing. Fastul caught the first two to break the timberline with well placed arrows behind their necks. Dorthea followed up with a torrent of flame that set one of the wolves aflame and fleeing into the woods. More wolves stepped in to surround them. Fastul let two more arrows fly, ending one and wounding another. Unwilling to be completely surrounded by the bloodthirsty beasts, Maggie let loose a battle roar and charged a trio. Her massive claymore swung in sideways, slicing the first two in half and becoming embedded in the third. More wolves moved to attack but Fastul and Dorthea were on them with their arrows and fire respectively. Twelve wolves fell in under two minutes before the rest of the pack fled into the forest.

"Well that was easy." Dorthea wiped the sweat from her brow with the back of her hand and turned to Maggie who was wiping the wolf blood from her sword.

"That was too easy," Fastul called down to them, "we should keep tailing them. That was probably just a scouting party. We need to find the den."

"Wolves have scouting parties?" asked Dorthea. Maggie held up her hands and shrugged. The three friends continued deeper into the woods, carrying torches that Dorthea lit with her magic. Fastul hopped from tree to tree, scanning for the drops of blood that glistened in the torchlight. They trekked for hours and the evening turned over to a moonlit night. Miles deep into the woods, the treeline ended and the hinterlands began. Sheer cliffs rose up out of the foothills and descended into canyons. Hundreds of paw prints were visible in the barren dirt outside the forest. Dorthea made to speak when a wolf crested the ridgeline, howled, then ran off into the canyon. Fastul leapt from her perch and joined her companions at the entrance to the canyon.

"We have to be ready for this. They won't have any cover in that canyon, but I bet there will be a lot more of them," said Fastul who already had an arrow nocked. The three women entered the canyon by moonlight. Their torches cast long creepy shadows on the canyon walls and their boots clicked against the bedrock. As they moved deeper into the canyon, the only sign of wolves were the innumerable paw prints in the dust and the occasional droppings.

"Where are they? This is starting to wear on my nerves," said Dorthea.

"Stay focused. We find them when we find them," grumbled Maggie.

A howl echoed through the canyon into a hundred echos and was joined by others until the night air was filled with the sound of a thousands wolves. This first howl was different somehow, deeper, angrier. It did not altogether sound like a wolf's but something much bigger.

"What the fuck was that?" Dorthea whispered loudly.

"Sounded like a warg. Nothing we can't handle. Do what Maggie said. Stay focused."

The click of claws on stone echoed through the canyon, but no wolves or wargs could be seen. As they moved into the lowest depths of the canyon, a line of wolves appeared in the torchlight. None of them moved or even growled, they simply stood there and stared at the women.

"That's freaking me out!" hissed Dorthea who already had a fireball conjured on her wand. The eyes on every wolf glared in the torchlight like copper coins.

"Wait!" Fastul grabbed her wrist. "Look."

The center of the line parted and six massive wargs stepped through. Their fur was midnight black and took on an almost bluish hue. Their eyes were all red and contained no pupils or irises. They were truly massive beasts, the size of horses.

"Can we do something now!" Dorthea hissed as her hand trembled. The three women stared at the six wargs and the beasts stared back.

"There's no way we can defeat all of them." said Fastul.

"What now?" Dorthea cried. One of the wargs approached her. Its muscles rippled under its stretched fur with every step it took. Its jaws dripped slobber and its eyes stared hatred. The beast moved closer and sniffed at her. Her two companions watched. The warg stood on its hind legs and began to hump the air. It's massive red cock slipped out of its sheath and glistening in the torchlight, spraying watery tendrils of cum high in the air. It performed this strange act for several seconds then returned to all fours and bellowed at Dorthea.

"What the fuck!" cried Dorthea.

"It wants to mate with you," said Fastul.

"I don't want to fuck that thing. I don't even have a sheepskin!"

"It's not going to get you pregnant, stupid. You're going to have to give up the goods if you want to survive," said Fastul. "We probably all are..."

The warg bellowed and stood on its hind legs to hump the air again. Dorthea spun in a circle and finally realized they had no chance of escape. They would have to fuck their way out.

"This is so humiliating," she said as she slipped her panties off under the hem of her gown and presented for the warg. The mighty beast hobbled over to her and covered her with watery cum as it searched for her opening. Fastul and Maggie could only watch in erotic fascination as their friend was about to be mounted by a warg. Its huge animal cock poked her ass several times until it found her opening. As soon as it found purchase, the warg thrusted its hips up and fucked Dorthea violently. Her entire body trembled and her cries of pleasure vibrated in her throat as the warg mated her. Its hips moved violently fast and pounded Dorthea's with a rapid series of slaps as its balls bounced off her vulva. The mage crumpled to the ground from pleasure as the warg mated her viciously.

Fastul was fascinated by the display. As a ranger she had mated with more than one magical beast. Spending years out in the wilderness could make a girl mighty lonely and monsters were always willing to mate a tiny tan human with a warm wet pussy. She slipped off her breeches and breechcloth then presented herself for one of the other wargs. A new suitor wasted no time in sniffing her cunt and lining up behind her. It stood on its hind legs and drove its hot, powerful cock inside of her. Her mind was a white flash as the beast's cock overrode her senses with unadulterated pleasure. No man had ever fucked her a quarter as good as the warg did. There was nothing she could say or do to stop the beast. Her only option was to ride out the pleasure and accept she was the bitch being mated. Orgasm after orgasm seemed to line up as her pussy was destroyed by this sexual monster. She felt the warg's knot swell up inside her, trapping her on his cock for breeding. She was vaguely aware of Maggie who had finally given up her pussy to the wargs. Her powerful warrior friend was on her hands and knees, completely helpless as the beast conquered her with just its cock. She had never seen Maggie show an ounce of weakness, and it was intensely fascinating watching her get fucked and succumb to forced orgasms. Her two friends lolled in ecstasy as the wargs thoroughly punished their mounds. She could feel her beast pumping her full of monster cum that she was thankfully protected against as a human. Having mated with multiple monsters, she knew there was no chance of birthing one.

The warg finally stopped, leaving its knot painfully swollen inside of Fastul as it pumped her full of cum. She had experienced so much pleasure that she was numb and couldn't focus on any rational thought. Just as the warg finished trying to breed her, several men covered in furs appeared in the moonlight, Still addled by the mind-dissolving sex, Fastul could only stare at their peculiar presence. Then her warg stood up and started to pull its swollen knot out of her. She whined in pain as the beast stretched her to her limit, finally passing out as the knot popped free. The last thing she remembered was being lifted up in a man's arms.

Den Mothers

Fastul awoke in a luxuriously appointed cavern on a large bed of furs with her two friends. It took her several moments to recover her mind as her body and thoughts adjusted from the absolute hardest fucking she had ever received in her entire life. Slowly, fragments of the previous day came back to her. The people of Waterbridge had commissioned her and her friends to rid the town of a local bandit camp that traveled with a massive pack of wolves. They had battled a pack of wolves in the hills and forests before they tracked the wolves into the hinterlands but were forced to give up their pussies to the warg pack leaders in order to survive. Now she and her companions were completely naked in a well appointed cavern except for the furs covering them. Inside the cavern was beautiful furniture and candelabras as well as a vanity mirror. On the table, a selection of food had been laid out. Seeing the food, her stomach immediately grumbled and she climbed out of bed to eat. Because they hadn't had a chance to camp for the night, the last time she had eaten was midday of the previous day. On the table was a bowl of fruit, several wedges of cheese, loaves of bread, and three separate roasts, one lamb leg, one cow shoulder, and a chicken, crispy black but bleeding on the platters. She hesitated to grab a bite to eat as something seemed off about the delicious spread. That's when she realized that almost all the food had deep puncture wounds in it like bite marks from a wolf. Had the wolves set the table!?

Hunger overcame any misgiving and she quickly ripped apart the chicken and began devouring it. The roasted meat was delicious though a bit underdone as if the cook didn't have any experience. The sounds of her feasting awoke her friends on the bed who staggered over and joined her in the small feast. They must have been as hungry as she was, and assuming the food was safe, they joined her in her binge. After thoroughly stuffing herself, Fastul stumbled to the bed and fell backwards into the furs before letting out a loud burp. Once she was nice and full, the strange reality of their situation finally set in. They had been surrounded by wolves last night, and then wargs appeared. And they mated with them...and then...

"Does anyone know what we're doing here?" Dorthea sat on the edge of the bed and pulled a fur around her naked pale body. Maggie stood at the table proudly as if showing off her powerful brown body.

"Some men brought us here. They must be the bandits," said Maggie as she searched the room for clues. Fastul turned her head and watched Maggie's plump brown butt as she searched the drawers of a dresser.

"All this furniture and no clothing or weapons. I don't think they intend for us to escape this place," said Maggie as she planted her hands on her hips. She was a powerful woman with a powerful body from a decade of combat training. Her skin was dark and her hips broad. Dorthea was nearly the complete opposite. She was a narrow pale woman with some impressive teets but nothing else of note. Fastul had seen them both naked before on their travels, but never for so long and in such a brightly lit area.

"Guess we'll have to sneak out of here," said Dorthea.

"Can't." Fastul sat up next to her.

"Why can't we?"

"Even if we escape, the wolves will be able to track us down. No weapons, not even any armor, we won't have a chance," said Fastul.

"So the wolves are keeping us prisoner?"

"The bandits are," said Maggie solemnly, "we kill them and we can escape. They're commanding the wolves. They've trained them or something. We all saw how organized they were in the canyon."

"I think to survive this, we need to get close to them. Let them think we're defeated. Then when we have the opportunity, we kill them," said Fastul.

"I like that plan," said Dorthea. Maggie nodded her agreement.

"Let's go see what's up," said Fastul as she moved to an opening in the cavern wall. Her two friends followed her lead. Outside the bedroom was a long cavern lit with kerosene lamps mounted to the walls. Fastul slowly led them down the hall and popped into the first doorway. Inside was a bedroom very similar to theirs only less beautifully appointed. On the bed space, two young women slept. Both of them were naked.

"More women?" whispered Dorthea.

"Bet they're from the village. That angry mayor said the bandits made off with the women. They keep them here, but why?" said Fastul.

"Who doesn't want women around?" said Maggie. The three companions left the room and found another bedroom down the hall. In this room, three naked women sat around a table and happily enjoyed a large spread similar to the ones the sellswords had enjoyed in their room. Upon seeing Fastul and her friends, one of the women waved her over. She was a tall blonde woman with bountiful breasts and a pleasant smile.

"Hey there!" said the smiling stranger as she loaded a tin plate with food. Her eating companions greeted them.

"Hi..." said Fastul, "what is this place?"

The blonde woman giggled.

"What do they call this place, Jenny, do you know?"

Jenny was a small redheaded woman with a petite frame who wore her hair in two large braids.

"Awoo?" she said and the other two dinner guests giggled.

"Why are you here? What's going on?" said Fastul who began to wonder if these women were simple or just addled.

"Why, we live here, silly. Do you want to join us for breakfast?" said the blonde woman.

"Why are you here? Why are you naked? Are you from Waterbridge?"

"Why, yes, I was from Waterbridge, but now I live here. We were all taken here and this is our home. No one in Awoo wears clothing in case you haven't noticed." the blonde woman cut a slice of cheese with her knife and fork and ate it. As she chewed she smiled at Fastul knowingly.

"The bandits took you here right? Why did they bring you here?"

"I guess they did, but we chose to stay here. We're the queens, they said so themselves."

"What do you do here as queens?" For every answer the blonde woman gave, Fastul only seemed to have more questions.

"We replenish the pack with our bountiful womb. Isn't that how you found your place in Awoo?"

Fastul touched her tight, sand-colored belly. *Was that really why they were here?*

"The wargs..."

"Uh-huh!" The blonde woman nodded.

"And you?"

"Mmm-hmm!"

"My queens," a man in the doorway spoke. He was covered in furs but his cock hung freely.

"What now?" said Fastul.

"If you would come with me. I am sure you have many questions." The man gestured for them to follow. The three companions left the bedroom and followed him down the entire length of the hallway. At the end was a massive cavern at least five stories high and decorated with chandeliers, candelabras, and even more furniture. The man led them to a collection of sofas where they sat around a low table. On the table the man poured water into mugs for each of them.

"What's going on here? Who are you?" said Fastul.

"It must all seem very confusing. My name is Wolf. I--"

"Really?"

“Yes...we are not very creative here. This is our home of Awoo. We seek out fertile women to carry on our pack. We bestow upon them the spoils of our raids in exchange for the service of their womb.”

“Wait, so we’re prisoners here?”

“No, you may leave whenever you want. Though none of our queens have chosen to do that since I’ve been alive.”

“And you breed with us?”

“Only if you want and only after you are with pup.”

“Wargs can’t breed with humans. I’ve been with a dozen different monsters. It’s just not possible.”

“Tully!” exclaimed Dorthea who must have been utterly shocked at Fastul’s sexual revelation.

“I do not mean to contradict a queen, especially one as beautiful and as powerful as yourself, but I have witnessed countless conceptions, it is indeed possible,” said Wolf. A small pack of wolves moved through the cavern and stopped to howl at them. Wolf stood up and returned a convincing howl.

“What did he say?” said Fastul who felt herself disassociate at such an outlandish situation.

“She said you are all very beautiful and she would be happy to have you in the pack.”

“So now that the wargs have mounted us, we’re going to give birth to wolves?”

“Or weirs. I am a weir myself. If you choose to stay in Awoo you will have many litters and many pups, some weir and some wolf. We will do anything you ask of us, so long as you stay and mate with our kings.”

“What do you girls think?” said Fastul. Maggie and Dorthea looked at each other.

“I mean, I’m not going to lie, that was the best sex of my life by far,” said Dorthea. Maggie nodded her agreement.

“Does seem like an incredible arrangement. And we can leave anytime we want?”

Wolf nodded.

“Alright then. Guess we’ll be staying in Awoo for awhile. At least until we get bored.”

“We only ask one thing of you,” Wolf spoke up.

“What’s that?”

“You must mate with all of our kings so none of your pups is given any favoritism among the pack. This arrangement leaves us peaceful and content.”

“Alright...”

Wolf stood and unleashed a stupendous howl that echoed down the cavern. Heavy claws clicked the stone floor and echoed down the chamber until six massive wargs appeared.

"If you would present for your kings."

Fastul, Dorthea, and Maggie all got down on their hands and knees, facing each other. The wargs circled them, stuffing their cold wet snouts up their crotches and sniffing their pussies. With no warning they were mounted in turn. The warg on top of Fastul pummeled her mercilessly, fucking her into a line of endless orgasms. She let loose a stream of urine as the sensations overrode her bodily functions. She looked up to see her two friends receive a similar vicious fucking. Fastul placed her hand over Dorthea's as they were both bred brainless by the wargs. Her male's knot slipped inside her and stretched her to her limit. She gasp and whined as it expanded and filled her up. Hot warg cum sprayed against her womb as she was fucked mercilessly. Finally, its hips stopped moving and she could feel her entire insides fill with cum. The warg pulled out with an audible plop and a new beast took his place. Nothing could stop the wagon train pulled on the three companions as they were bred mercilessly by the warg pack. After the third rotation, the floor of the cave became a large puddle of cum they were forced to lay face down in. Their entire bodies were coated in a sheet of semen as they were ridden into the heavens. Their thighs were scratched heavily, but the endless forced orgasms erased any pain. After six kings had each taken turns inside their delicate human pussies, the three friends held each other, collapsed in a puddle of warg cum. Intermittently their legs would twitch as their brains caught up to what their bodies had just gone through.

"You are now officially our new queens," said Wolf.

The Boy Who Loved The Sea

The ocean tossed the St. Maurice as if the gods themselves were affronted by the humans who dared to conquer the waters. Walls of water higher than any chapel rose and crashed all around the ship. It was the worst storm any of the crew had ever seen, including Captain Wilhelm who had lived to see three other ships founder in his long and arduous career. He was an old salt but extremely knowledgeable about rigging, navigation, and managing a rowdy crew. His confidence and decisiveness was a rocky promontory in dark times. But when the captain yelped in fear as he was tossed from the ship, Conner knew that the end had come. Once everything that could be done about the rigging was set, including striking the topmast, the crew battened down in their quarters and waited to see if they would survive.

A low roar emerged from the depth of all time over the drizzle of the rain and crashing of the ocean waves. It sounded as if the ocean had come alive as some great beast. The storm seemed to subside for just a moment, and the entire crew held its breath as the roar steadily grew louder, blocking out all other sound. The 350 ton St. Maurice was tossed end over end like a child's toy, sending the crew slamming back and forth through the lower deck and quarters in a bloody heap. Conner survived the first toss in a daze and would have swore to any man that he heard the voice of the gods themselves as the ship was lifted high in the air out of the ocean.

Conner awoke unknowable hours later in a shallow lagoon. His body was sprawled over a considerable section of the St. Maurice's hull as it bobbed in the semi-shallow waters. The sun was high and blazing brightly. His entire body hurt, and he had no idea where he was. Conner lifted his face off of his divine raft and looked up to see a tropical vista on the near horizon. He was floating in a wide lagoon that poked off the edge of a tropical island. His body ached something fierce and he didn't feel the energy to move, let alone swim for shore. He had survived that nightmarish storm or at the least woke up in another world.

For hours he bobbed in the lagoon, slowly moving closer to the shore. On the sands were several pieces of debris, almost certainly from the wreck of the St. Maurice, but no signs of survivors. After hours had passed, he finally drifted into a tidal pool and rolled off onto soft ground. He lay there for several seconds, contemplating what he had just survived and what his next action could possibly be. A heavy wave washed over him and nearly drowned him there after surviving such an ordeal. He shot up, coughing the salt water out of his lungs. His head spun as he sat up, and he shot his arm out in the dense mud to steady himself. Taking several minutes, he gathered his bearings and made to stand when pain shot up his left leg. Something was most certainly broken, and it caused too much agony to put any weight on the leg. Willing himself, if for no other reason than to survive the next hour, Conner dragged himself inch by inch out of the tidal pool. Pulling himself up a shallow stony ridge, he tumbled down the other side onto the hot dry sand of the beach. He realized then he had taken on a deep chill from drifting in the ocean, but the hot yellow sand warmed his body like a well seasoned skillet.

Once the sand had given up its heat, he rolled over to a new warm spot. He repeated this process every few minutes, giggling to himself like a sanitarium patient. He continued in his folly until he rolled over onto one of his crew mates. Conner yipped in fear and pulled himself up higher on the beach. It was impossible to tell who it was, but judging by the facial hair it might have been the carpenter Wilson. His body was fat and bloated, still sloshing from when Conner had rolled over onto him. The beach was littered with smashed crates and pieces of the rigging, bow, and deck, but Wilson's body was the only one he could see. He didn't know yet if the gods had blessed him or cursed him for leading him to survive.

Conner took a deep breath and tried to imagine what captain Wilhelm would do in this situation. Why, he would come up with a plan. That's what captain Wilhelm would do. But Conner was not good at coming up with plans which is why he had been so successful as a rigger. It was an easy living on a galleon when someone was always telling you what to do. He didn't have to ever think about what he was supposed to be doing. And even if he was doing it wrong, someone would find out soon enough and correct him with some stern words or a smack to the back of his head.

His leg still ached from trying to stand on it. Bracing his leg would certainly be a good place to start if any. Conner dragged himself down the beach to the tatters of a barrel that had probably held their fresh water. The planks of the barrel had been bound with rope and he tied them around his leg as tightly as possible. Once he had fixed the best brace he knew how to make, he stood to test his contraption. The pain was still there but it was manageable. *What was the next step?*

He was as thirsty as an abbot during shore leave, so his next step would have to be finding some drinkable water. Conner marched down the beach in hopes of finding an intact water barrel, but almost all the debris ashore had been smashed along with a few wooden shards of gods only knew what. He found two more bodies in his search and meant to bury them as soon as possible, but figured surviving would be a little more important.

"Is anyone else here?" he cupped his hands to his mouth and shouted. The silence was deafening and sad. *Was he the only survivor of the St. Maurice?* The notion fell heavy on his heart. He fruitlessly continued his search for water barrels until the sands of the beach ended and climbed into cliffs on the far end. If there were no water barrels, he would have to find a lake or river in order to survive. He was already thirsty from gods knew how long at sea, and figured he wouldn't have many days left without water. So Conner trekked inland in search of fresh water. Off the beach, Conner Island as he took to calling it, was dense jungle. Small trees, ferns, broad leaves, and long grasses all jostled for the scant sunlight in the dense foliage. Something must be watering these plants, he reasoned to himself as he trekked further inland. The plants were green and beautiful but there were no signs of other people on the island or even other animals save for a few small birds that sang in the brush but remained unseen.

Conner stopped to rest on a fallen tree. He was dripping with sweat, exhausted, and his leg ached from all the walking. As he caught his heavy breathing, he heard the distinct trickle of water. He stood and chased after the noise as if it were something to be caught, but his heavy steps and the swoosh of the plants he pushed past dispersed the life saving sound. He stopped again and once more he could hear the steady trickle of water. This time he moved slowly, containing his eagerness to live. He walked deeper inland until he stepped into a small stream guarded by broad leaves. He ripped the stupid plants away and discovered a tiny stream less than two inches wide hidden in the foliage. Conner threw his body to the jungle floor and slurped from the tiniest river discovered by man. The water was cool and sweet and tasted better than any liquor. He sighed happily to himself as he slurped up the clean, saltless water until he had completely quenched his thirst. He followed the stream backwards until he discovered a stony grotto bulging from the ground. It stood like a small altar of stones with an overflowing pool on top. He scooped the water into his hands and splashed it in his warm sweaty face. The relief was immense and with it, his faculties seemed to return completely.

Now that he had water, shelter would be of the utmost concern...probably. He followed the stream back to sea where it petered out several dozen feet from the source. Still, he was able to locate the beach and begin gathering driftwood for a shelter. Hours in, and as the sun made its descent for the horizon, a loud hunger overtook him, and Conner cradled his stomach. The island seemed completely uninhabited, so maybe shelter was less important than food, at least on the first night. Leaving the scrap wood he had gathered near the grotto, he continued his quest into the jungle with a firm piece of lumber to smash any animal that he could possibly feast on. Though the sounds of the birds were numerous, he never actually saw any, and figured it would take more than a trusty piece of wood to capture them.

Afternoon turned to evening, and evening to night when Conner decided that he would have to stop. He lay down where he stood and fell into a quick sleep from the unrepentant exhaustion he had experienced that day. On the second morning he traveled back to the grotto and slaked his thirst once more. The water was a godssend and brought quick but temporary relief to the ache in his stomach. He continued his search of the island for more food but only found more dense jungle. The island rose away from the beach to a high cliff on the opposite end. There were no notable features save for the beach, the tide pool that surrounded the lagoon, and the grotto he had discovered. During midday he saw his first bird. The creature's wings looked exactly like leaves which probably made it impossible to see if you weren't staring right at it. Even without the help of camouflage, the bird was too fast to smash with a board.

Convinced he had thoroughly scouted the island for food, Conner returned to his grotto to feast on water, then to the shore for the off chance some rations had washed ashore. He gave serious consideration to eating his dead crewmates, but their bodies had bloated and began to stink. Burying them would be an intense effort, one that he couldn't sustain while starved. The washed up crates on the beach yielded nothing. His eyes focused on the tide pools as he followed the length of the beach, and that's when he realized it was the one place he hadn't searched for food. There could be yummy clams or crabs or even lobsters swimming around there. Just the thought of those snacks had him running down the beach, ignoring the pain in his leg. But despite his hope, the tide pools were barren. Defeated, he slumped in one and lay on his back in the water warmed from the sun. *Was he really going to die here?*

Another day passed, and another. Conner got it in his mind to dig for food, but found nothing in the jungle, beach, or tide pools. He resorted to eating the leaves and bark off the trees but eventually threw them back up. He tried just the leaves, but threw those up as well. His energy was low, and he had decide to sleep near the grotto in his half completed shelter. The water stopped helping with the hunger pains. Everything felt so unbelievably hopeless. He tried to think of what his captain would have done, but at this point Conner had even forgotten his name. His brain wasn't working right anymore. He began to contemplate forgoing water so he could die peacefully. It was a nice plan. Still, it would be awful if he were rescued only days after he decided to die. As a compromise, he would make one more sweep of the island for food. He rested all the day before so he would have some iota of strength for his final forage.

The next morning he rose, drank plenty of water, and went on his final quest. The dark jungle interior took on a dreamlike quality as he searched for food. He scratched at the dirt with his board, hoping to find a root or an insect to eat. The shadows seemed to swirl and bend as he traveled. Dizziness was frequent and he stopped often to gather his bearings. He could have sworn he heard the sound of women conversing but never saw anyone. The birds seemed to be harbingers of madness on that day. They sang so beautifully but only promised food that could not be obtained.

As he sat and gathered himself a tenth time, one of the strange green birds landed on his log and began to sing. He moved his hand slowly with the full intention of snatching the bird and devouring it beak and all. His hand shot out but the bird flapped away, landing on a nearby branch. Conner crept after it and shot his hand out once more, but the bird saw him and flew off to a nearby bush. He continued the chase, figuring this would be his only chance at meal. The bird evaded every attempt, but never moved far, as if toying with him. Stumbling out of the jungle, he fell face first into one of the tide pools surrounding the lagoon. It was there he decided to die.

Conner fell asleep during the evening and woke up some time in the early dawn. He hadn't died yet, though he half expected to from his utter exhaustion. It took him several minutes before he could even will himself to blink his eyes open, not wanting to see the damnable island he was stranded on. When he finally did open his eyes, he saw a massive fish in the tidepool next to him, gasping its last breaths. The fish was quite large, about the size of an expensive wine bottle, and still alive, though clearly dying slowly. Pain radiated out of his jaw as he smiled. He grabbed the gift of the gods and took a big bite out of it without thinking. The flavors were mild and sweet but he gagged as he swallowed, his breathing disrupted by the scales. Frustrated, he beat the fish against a nearby rocky outcrop, sending the scales flying like woodchips from a falling ax. Satisfied with his cleaning, Conner took another bite of the gift and relished the sweet mild flavors of the raw fish. Nothing on the planet ever tasted so good as that second bite. After another chomp he ripped the fish open and pulled the guts and length of bones out and tossed them aside, maybe saving the guts for later. After devouring the entire fish including the collar, Conner lay back and stared at the cloudless sky. Whoever was watching over him, they clearly wanted him to live a little longer.

With rejuvenated strength, Conner explored the lagoon that was surrounded by the tide pools. A crescent outcrop of stone and mud surrounded a shallow portion of the ocean. Underwater, despite the burning sea water in his eyes, he saw many fish swimming through the lagoon which may have been fifteen feet deep and noticeably warmer than the deep ocean. Despite his efforts, he was unable to catch any fish. Even after spending all morning fashioning a net from some grass he had wove, the fish were too elusive for a swimmer to catch. He needed a hook and line, but such tools had not appeared in the wreckage that continued to wash ashore.

Exhausted from a day of diving, Conner rested in one of the tide pools and nodded off. When he awoke, another fish similar to the one he had devoured lay in the tide pool near him, gasping for air. Now this was just plain weird. *Were the fish offering themselves up to him? Did they think he was the god of Conner Island?*

Regardless of the situation, he took his offering and cleaned it against a rock once more before devouring it. This fish was near identical to the first, but nothing could mirror the flavor of fresh fish devoured after days of starvation, and he wasn't about to try. Still, the meat was sweet and mild and filled his belly. After a good night's sleep and a healthy slurp of water, Conner got it in his head that maybe napping in the tide pool was the key to retrieving fish. So he lay down in one of the pools and pretended to snooze. With one eye barely opened, he waited to see what would happen. Hours passed and no fish appeared, but Conner was patient. There was virtually nothing to do on the island and the anticipation of finding the solution to this mystery was very interesting all things considered. Just when he was about to give up and explore to kill the daylight, a woman's head popped out of the lagoon. She was utterly gorgeous with deep blue lips and hair that ran from ocean blue to seaweed green. Pulling herself out of the lagoon, she revealed a pair of gorgeous pale breasts and a tail! The entire lower half of her body was one massive fish tail shining like a thousand silver coins. In her arms she carried a floundering fish.

As she scooted closer to Conner as he pretended to sleep, he sat up to greet her.

"Hi, my na--"

Before he could even finish his sentence, she tossed the fish at him and flopped back into the lagoon with one elegant motion.

"Wait!" he cried after her, but she had disappeared in mere seconds. He dove into the lagoon after her, but she was already several feet away when he submerged. Knowing he could never catch her, he returned to the fish and completed his ritual of scaling and eating it raw. Not one to be deterred, and with near infinite time on his hands, Conner pretended to nap again in hopes the strange woman might return. He spent all afternoon and evening considering what he might say to her, but she did not return. He went back to his grotto and fell asleep that night. But that woman did return, just in his dream. She swam through the darkness, looking over her shoulder once at him, before swimming off forever. Conner awoke that morning with a heavy heart. He would have to try and speak with her again. He had no other options and no real plans. So he walked out of the jungle and into the tide pools and there he sat, awaiting her return. Several hours went by when suddenly the woman's head popped out of the water. Seeing Conner awake and waiting for her, she dove back down immediately.

"Wait!" he cried after her on the verge of tears. This time he would not chase her. He thought maybe he had scared her last time when he yelled and chased her. He would remain still and let her know that he was no threat. An hour seemed to past, though it was hard to tell when you were bored and alone, when the woman returned and popped her head out of the water. Seeing Conner, she tossed the fish on shore and dove back down. He repeated his ritual of cleaning and eating the fish but remained in the tide pool on the off chance she might return. She didn't that day and Conner returned to the jungle to sleep.

The next morning he was more hopeful. She had returned, so he hadn't completely scared her off. She was giving him fish, so she must have liked him or at least felt bad for him. *Maybe if he had something he could give her?* He searched the beach again as more debris drifted a shore even after weeks of being on the island. Conner was shocked and a little humored to find a chest washed ashore with several gold coins inside. There were twelve total but twelve gold could set you right for a few years. It was painful irony he now possessed more gold than ever before in his life time but had nothing to spend it on. Still...

He gathered up the gold and returned to the tide pools. He set the gold out in a small stack between him and the lagoon and waited. Hours passed and the strange woman popped her head up again. She had large eyes, a bit larger than any human's he finally noticed. They were a deep brilliant blue. This time she didn't dive immediately but instead watched him. He watched her back and smiled, trying to look as non-threatening as possible. His eyes fell on the gold and her eyes followed. They widened on seeing the shiny pieces of currency. What she would possibly use them for the gods only knew, but everyone liked shiny things, and Conner hoped she did too.

She looked at the gold, back to him, then at the gold again. He nodded to indicate it was hers but declined to speak for fear of scaring her off. He watched her and she watched him. Then her hand shot of the water, snatched a piece of gold, and she dove back into the lagoon. It was a small bit of progress, but it was indeed progress. Just when he realized she hadn't brought any food, a fish leapt out of the water and into the tide pool.

Conner repeated the same plan the following day. He could almost time her visits by the sun's position, four fingers over the horizon. That day and the following day she snatched a piece of gold and delivered him a fish. At first his hopes were high, but he soon realized he wasn't making any progress with the fish woman. On the fourth day of their peculiar trade agreement, he decided to say something. That morning he waited, and when she arrived at the same time as everyday, he decided to speak up. Her head popped out of the water and looked at him.

"Please wait, I, I'm stranded here and I don't have anywhere to go. Can you help me?"

While she was clearly a benevolent creature, her blank expression seemed to convey she didn't understand what he was saying.

"Please help me," he said, tears sliding from his eyes. She stared at him a moment longer then held out her hand. He crept slowly to the edge of the lagoon, terrified he might scare her off for good this time. He took her hand and was yanked into the lagoon. She pulled him down to the lagoon floor. Through his burning eyeballs he could see a collection of large fish eggs on the floor and a small stack of gold coins. She pointed at the eggs then at his crotch. Conner wasn't sure what she meant. Then he desperately needed to breath. He began to thrash and claw at his throat, pulling away from her to swim up. His lungs burned and his throat ached as she grabbed him under his arms and rocketed him to the surface. Once he broke the surface of the lagoon, he gasped for air with one big breath followed by several smaller ones. The woman bobbed in the water next to him, watching him, looking for an answer.

"I'll be glad to help you, but I don't understand what you want." He smiled at the absurdity of their situation. She smiled back confused then dragged him to shore. He sat on the edge of the lagoon and watched her. Despite the absurdity of the situation, he couldn't take his eyes off her gorgeous pale breasts and her pink, flesh-toned nipples. His cock pressed against his ratty trousers and didn't escape her notice. She grabbed his trousers and ripped them free, nearly pulling them into the lagoon. His cock sprung free and she started at it fascinated.

"You can touch it if you want, it's okay," he said and wagged his erection at her. She reached out with a cold clammy hand and grasped his warm cock. She stared in fascination as if she had never seen one before. *Were there men just like her in the sea? What in the hells did their cocks look like?* She stroked his shaft and watched him for a reaction. It had been months since he had known the comfort of a woman. She was gentle but curious. His warm skin must have felt strange to her.

"My name's Conner," he said, feeling slightly stupid for telling her his name only after playing with his cock. She dipped her head halfway under water and blew several bubbles as she seemed to screech.

"Might have trouble remembering that...maybe I should just call you Aria like the herald of the sea."

Aria tilted her curiously, never relinquishing his cock.

"Conner," he said, pointing to himself, "Aria," he said as he pointed at her. She mimicked his motions but struggled with his strange human words. Suddenly she flopped onto the tide pool next to him and lay flat. She was a gorgeous woman even if she was half fish.

"Can I touch you?" he asked and placed a hand on her cold bountiful breast. She watched him as he touched her but didn't seem to mind it. He bent down and placed his mouth on her cold pink nipple and suckled. She stroked his hair as he nursed.

"Ah, Aria," she forced out in a light beautiful voice. His eyes widened in surprise.

"That's right. Why did you show me those eggs, Aria. Are they important? They must be." Conner leaned over her as he spoke, his warm cock pressed against her fishy thighs. She covered her mouth and blushed a strange blue color. As she did she spread open a slit in her lower half to reveal a deep red opening that could never be mistaken for anything but a pussy. Conner's eyes opened as far as they could go as she revealed her pussy to him.

"Do you want me to fuck you? Is that it?"

She reached out for his still hard cock and pulled it towards her. He hoped to the gods that she was asking for sex, because he didn't want to do anything that would harm this beautiful and generous woman. Conner climbed over her and guided his cock into her opening. He slid in easily as she was slimy in anticipation of him. Her pussy was cold though, so very different from every woman he had ever been with before, but she felt no less amazing wrapped around his cock. He postured up over her and thrusted into her, gentle at first. He didn't know what kind of fucking she was used to and didn't want to hurt her. Her beautiful breasts sloshed with each thrust and it took some effort to keep his eyes on her eyes. Her blue eyes were easy to get lost in though. He increased his speed, fucking her the only way he knew how. She let out a little coo and pulled him closer to her. He fucked her as hard as he could and she whined in his ear. Her erect nipples grazed his chest with every thrust. Finally he let out a garbled cry and blew his load in her. Immediately she slid away and dove back into the lagoon.

Conner rolled over with his cock wet and still erect, shocked at what had just happened. Every time she left it felt like she would never come back, but she returned minutes later, hopped out of the water, and lay next to him. She smiled at him and pet his soft, tender cock with her cold hand.

"Hope I was alright," he said with an awkward smile. She climbed up on him and lay against him. He thought she meant to go another round when she sneezed and sprayed him with a strange dark liquid from her pussy. She sneezed two more times and each time it covered his body with thick, inky goo like when you harpoon an octopus. After sneezing, she flopped back into the water. Conner stared after her, unsure of what to make of what just happened.

If You Want to Catch Fish, Use the Right Bait

Conner's ship the St. Maurice had been foundered by a mighty storm. Conner survived and he washed ashore on a desert island where no other humans lived. Days passed, but no survivors of the St. Maurice appeared. Water was plentiful on Conner Island, but food was non-existent. As he lay dying in the tide pools, a strange woman who was half human and half fish presented a fish for him. Each day she'd bring him a meal and then disappear. After days had passed, a bond grew between the man and the mermaid. He named her Aria and she coaxed him into sex. Once he had spent his seed in her she covered him with thick inky goo and then vanished once more into the lagoon.

Days passed. Each morning Conner went down to the tide pools in search of Aria, but the only sign of her was the freshly caught fish she laid out for him each morning. The thick sticky ink clung to his body no matter how much water he splashed on himself or how hard he beat himself with ferns. Over the days it had formed a hard scaly carapace against his body. The scaly formation didn't hurt, nor did it restrict his movement. He would spend all day at the edge of the tide pools in hopes he might see her again, but she had begun to time her fishy offerings with his sleep cycles. Even when he arose early, he only caught sight of her tossing the fish out of the lagoon and into the tide pools but never her beautiful face.

He initially assumed he had hurt her but then reasoned she probably would have stopped feeding him if that was the case. The second time in the pre-dawn hours when he caught her leaving a fish he dove in after her, but she was far too agile a swimmer to be caught. The days continued, and the loneliness wore heavy on Conner. It was on the eighth day that Aria finally reappeared. Her beautiful face popped out of the water right at the edge of the lagoon and her dreamy blue eyes fell on him. He moved slowly to the edge and crouched, terrified that he would scare away his only friend in the world. Once he was close enough, Aria snatched his arm and dragged him underwater. She darted to the bottom of the lagoon, and in the morning light, Conner could see that her eggs had grown massive in size. They were at least three times bigger than the petrified bird egg his former captain had kept in his quarters. She held his hand and they watched as tiny arms and legs burst forth from the eggs. In moments, newborn fish people just like her tore through the iridescent membranes of the eggs and swam into the lagoon. Aria released his hand and began to dote on her newborn children. She swam around each one several times, gently pinching at them and fussing with their hair. Conner smiled to himself then surfaced.

After several moments, Aria surfaced too, along with her school of children. They all had deep blue eyes like her except the one who had brown-coppery eyes like him. Aria leapt out of the water and into the air, coming down with a heavy splash. Her school of children imitated her to varying degrees of success. Then she submerged her face and blew screeching bubbles into the lagoon, once again mimicked by her children. Conner was awe struck by what was happening. *Had he helped her breed?* It seemed very likely.

Over the next few days, Conner would sit on the edge of the tide pools and watch his family swim and leap and splash in the lagoon. The children were natural swimmers and within days could achieve speeds no human could match. When Aria submerged her face and squealed bubbles into the water, the children would immediately come to her. It was heartwarming to see Aria and her children happy and safe. Conner didn't know where he fit in with this family, but had developed a deep affection for them. The children would often urge him into the water, pulling on his arms or legs. They would become frustrated as they out swam him or when he rose to the surface for air.

Weeks went by. Then one fateful morning, a galleon passed maddeningly close to the island. The ship had drawn everyone's attention. Conner began to shout for help, but the ship was far too distant for them to take notice. He stopped himself, but not out of futility. *Was there a better life away from the island?* He did miss talking to people. He taught Aria and the children some words but they picked it up very slowly. Some nights Aria would join him in the tide pool and they would lay together again. Each time he would fill her with his seed and she would cover him with ink. They shared kisses now, and cuddled. *What life could compare to the one he shared with this woman now?* Aria looked at Conner then at the ship. She squealed into the water which caught the attention of her children playing nearby. She squealed again then swam out into the ocean with her children in tow.

"Where are you going?" Conner cried after her. He saw her breach the water as she swam like a dolphin. It was obvious she was heading for the ship. He could only watch and wait for what happened next. Hours passed as the ship skirted the island. Then it slowly began to change course, turning back for Conner Island. As the galleon approached, Conner could see Aria and her children slipping the water in front of the bow as if being chased. As the ship approached the lagoon, Aria and her children slipped under the waves and disappeared. Several men stood at the gunwales of the ship who must have spotted her in the water and gave chase.

"Ho' there!" one of the men called from the ship. The galleon might have been too large for the lagoon so a ship's boat was sent out instead. It had seemed like years since Conner had seen another human and he stared in dumb fascination as they approached. There was almost a threatening sense as the men brought the ship's boat into the tide pool.

"Whoa there fella', how long have you been on this island?" said one of the crew, a big burly man with an open shirt that exposed the dark hair on his chest.

"A...long time," Conner answered meekly. The men had a hardy chuckle at what they thought was deadpan humor.

"Would you believe we chased a mermaid to this island and found you here? I didn't believe it when Jackson started raving about a mermaid, but I swears to you I saw one in our wake."

"I believe you. She lives in the lagoon. She saved me. Aria!" Conner called out but she would not appear. He tried calling for her once more, but nothing happened.

"You alone on this island, friend? Best gather whoever is here with you. We have a schedule to keep," said the burly man.

"It's just me..."

The crew of the St. Clementine rescued Conner from Conner Island that day. As he rode with them back to the galleon, he saw Aria and her children bobbing in the lagoon. She had saved him that day. Maybe a part of her understood he needed to be with his own people.

Once Conner finally returned to a civilized harbor, he began his career as a wharf fisherman. Nothing in heavens or hells could make him set foot back on a ship after the ordeal he had been through. Still, every night he dreamed of Aria and descending the depths of the ocean with her. Her inky ejaculation still clung to his skin and gave him the appearance of disfigurement, though it in no way was detrimental to his ability to work. He made a modest living as a wharf fisherman. Each catch would only remind him of Aria though. Her blue eyes and large pale breasts haunted him.

One evening during a swell, Conner marched out onto the wharf like he always did after supper and cast his line. Most of his rival fishermen would not brave such a swell, but he knew that some of the largest fish could be caught if one were brave enough to attempt it. The waves crested well above the tallest buildings in the harbors, and every building had shuttered its windows. The waves sprayed over the wharf in dull hisses. It was all very exciting to Conner to be out in the swell. He cast his line and waited. The waves put pressure on the thin line, but experience had taught him the difference between wave pressure and the tension of a caught fish.

Without warning, the line snapped taut and Conner was pulled into the swell. He fought to return to the wharf but was tossed end over end by the waves. Water flooded his mouth and nostrils and waves tossed him, making him unable to gather his bearings. Then he was pulled down.

He awoke later in a cave. The swell continued outside, but inside, water lapped lazily against the walls. He must have been at sea level. He was on a rocky outcrop just above the water level. And next to him was Aria! But as he gathered his bearings, he realized it wasn't Aria at all, but a completely different mermaid. This one had short dark hair and smaller breasts that could fit easily in his hand. Her tail wasn't silver either, but a mossy green that blended to copper. The mermaid stared at him and pulled her head back as he reached out for her.

"Are you...a friend of Aria's?" he asked. She reached out and touched his hand then pulled her own away. He lowered his. She reached out again and touched the dark, ashy patch of dried ink Aria had covered him with.

"What is this, do you know?" he asked. Despite visiting a librarian and a physician, neither of them could say what the black crust on his skin was. This new mermaid seemed to at least recognize it, but didn't have the words to share. At least, that's what Conner thought.

"You've been inked," she said as she stroked the black crust.

"You can talk!" he exclaimed. It was like discovering a fish could talk.

"Of course I can. Why should I be silent?"

"Well, it's just, I met another mermaid like you and she didn't talk."

"I see. I learned to talk from listening to the men and women on the docks speak."

"My parents taught me..."

"My mother taught me much about swimming and catching food, but it was from the humans I learned your language."

Conner nodded.

"How did you find me in the swell? I for sure thought I was a goner. This is the second time I was saved by a mermaid."

The whole time they spoke, the mermaid stroked the black patch on Conner's stomach and chest. It seemed difficult for her to make eye contact with him.

"You have given a mermaid great pleasure and she has marked you as good. I could smell her ink not far from where I nest."

"She thought I was good?"

"Yes. There seems to be many layers of ink on you. She must have loved you deeply."

Conner's heart warmed in his chest upon hearing the revelation regarding Aria. She had loved him as much as he loved her.

"I miss her a lot..."

With no warning, the mermaid jumped on him and began humping him. Her powerful hips slammed into his cock that was guarded by his trousers.

"Stop! Wait!" he cried as she humped him.

"I need a male to fertilize my eggs. I would seek a good man, a friend of the mermaids," she said as she continued to hump him.

"At least let me get my cock out first. This isn't how it works." Conner fought with the lacing of his trousers, nearly ripping the rawhide to free his cock. His pink-pale cock sprung free and the mermaid stared in fascination. Her cold clammy hand wrapped around his shaft possessively.

"At least tell me your name," he said.

"My name is Bermuda, like my mother before me."

And with those words, Bermuda enveloped his cock and humped him vigorously. Her hips were fast and powerful, pistoning on his cock. Her pussy was cold and tight and felt like velvet heaven wrapped around his cock. Leaving no time for foreplay or cuddling, Bermuda battered his cock with her pussy until he erupted inside her moments later. He gasped and cried a little as her cunt tightened around his refracting cock.

"Be right back, love," she said and disappeared into the water. He lay in the dim cavern with his half erect cock, trying to understand completely what had just happened. Minutes later, Bermuda returned, or at least he thought it was her. There were two mermaids now. One was Bermuda, but the other cozying close to him had blood-red hair.

"You're right! He has been inked," said the redhead as she reached for his cock. He flinched from her clammy hands but his cock rose to attention in her grasp.

"Fascinating," she said as she played with his cock.

"You're supposed to put in you, ya' stinky starfish," said Bermuda as she climbed on the rocky outcrop to watch. The redheaded mermaid climbed up too and wrapped her ruby lips around his trembling cockhead. Conner gasped as her tongue tickled him.

"Not like that! Here," said Bermuda, who spread her scaly vulva with two fingers to reveal a dark pussy hidden in her fish tail.

“Ohhhh!” said the redhead as she flopped onto Conner and tried to position herself.

“At leat tell me your name!” he cried as she struggled to guide him in her.

“Hehhe! It’s Pearl. Sorry, it’s my first time.”

“Oh for the sake of the Ocean Lord,” said Bermuda who grabbed his cock and guided it into Pearl. She was painfully tight and gasped as he slid into her. She trembled from the pressure and Conner held her close to comfort her.

“It’s okay, just breath,” said Conner as he pet her hair. She took a deep breath and finally relaxed around his cock. He grabbed the shape of her ass and pushed inside her, making her coo aloud.

“I’ve never watched before. This is exquisite,” said Bermuda as she lay next to him. Conner had to admit that the sex was doubly intense as Bermuda watched them fuck. In only moments Pearl cried out and warm ink gushed past his cock and covered his hips. He hurried to finish inside her, clinging as he pumped her full of cum.

“That was it?” Pearl gasped as she rolled off.

“Now go fertilize your eggs, dear,” said Bermuda as she touched Pearl’s shoulder. Pearl jumped into the water leaving the two alone.

“Do, do you know Aria? She has dark blue hair and beautiful blue eyes like the ocean?”

“Sorry, love. Never met an Aria before. Cute name though,” said Bermuda as she stroked the ink stain on his chest. If he thought that was the end of it, Conner was gravely mistaken. Five mermaids in total found their little love grotto and bounced on Conner’s cock until he finished in each of them. Each time the girl would cum enthusiastically and leave to go fertilize her eggs. He felt a strange new sensation he never knew before as girl after girl used him and made him cum. By the fifth he could barely maintain his erection and Bermuda mouthed his cock between exchanges to keep him hard. She had clearly done this before and he nearly came in her mouth. By the time he had finished providing the mermaids with much needed seed, the swell had calmed and Bermuda took him back to shore. He sat on the beach naked in the failing light of evening as Bermuda bobbed in the surf.

“Until next year,” she called to him and then disappeared underwater.

“Next year?”

What Water Mages Want

Avida awoke to her master Aga calling her from the basement. She looked out the window of her bedroom to see that the sun had not even breached the horizon, casting the sky a pink bruise behind the mountains. She yawned and stretched then climbed out of bed before the sleepies could overtake her again. Aga got dreadfully mad whenever Avida allowed the sleepies to pull her back to bed. She pulled off her gown and shivered as she stood naked in the cold castle tower. She was a thin woman with a flat butt and small breasts, neither of which helped her to stay warm at night. She quickly dressed in some trousers, a tunic, and quilted doublet to keep out the chill.

"AVIDA, WHERE ARE YOU!" her master howled from the lower floors. Avida slipped on her slippers, lit a torch, and hurried down the stairs. The kitchen was empty, so the most logical place to search was the cellar. Her master had set up many contraptions and fixtures in the cellar to carry out her magical experiments in private. Avida cleaned the castle and ran errands for her master like retrieving mail and purchasing groceries. She was paid well and had been taught history, math, and how to read and write. She would also pay visits to her master's bedroom when she was lonely and needed Avida's body. Avida was a young eager woman who was more than pleased to pleasure her master who had given her so much. She grabbed some fruit and bread out of the pantry and hurried into the cellar just in case her master had forgotten to eat as was often the case. At the bottom of the dark staircase she paused to catch her breath and then knocked on the thick wooden door that guarded the cellar. Even when called, she knew better than to enter the cellar without announcing her presence.

"Come in, come in, what are you knocking for?" cried Aga from the other side. Avida pushed the door open with her flat butt, a torch in one hand, a loaf and apple in the other. The sight of the lab never failed to inspire awe in Avida. The walls were lined with hundreds of potions, many of which lit up the lab in beautiful neon colors. There was scant furniture, but many contraptions for which she couldn't discern their purpose. She found an empty space to set the food down and rested the torch in its catch on the wall.

"What are you doing? Come here, girl," said Aga on the far side of the room. Despite being a shut in, Aga was a beautiful woman. She was only in her late thirties but acted like a woman twice her age. She had dark hair she always wore in a sloppy bun and a loose robe that allowed Avida glimpses of her soft body. More often than not, Avida lay in bed at night and touched herself, imagining her master taking advantage of her.

Aga was dedicated to the study of the arcane and had made many discoveries on the uses of magic. At university she had mastered the use of fire and lightning, the two primary schools of offensive magic. She subsisted on grants from various colleges and had been gifted this castle for her studies. The castle was situated far up north and had a chill three seasons out of the year. Avida didn't understand the first thing about magic, but was happy to help someone who was so clearly passionate about their work. With the silver Aga gave her she was able to take care of her mother who could finally retire on the money after raising eight children.

"What can I do for you, mistress?" Avida asked. She was always polite and the nicer she acted, the more civil Aga seemed to behave. Aga wasn't evil, but she could be very severe at times, especially when she was days into a project like she was currently. Aga had told the mage's council that water could be channeled the same way as fire or lightning which had brought skepticism and even derision. Some of the elders trusted her profound insights, but others thought she had finally succumb to her eccentricities. The way Aga explained it, she was questioning if there was a third temperature besides hot or cold, or a third light besides dark and bright. When Avida had mentioned warm and dim, Aga chuckled and patted her head.

"Come here, girl," said Aga as she fussed over several glasses filled with liquid. Avida sat on a nearby stool and watched her master. Aga waved her hand over a jar of water and suddenly a tendril of liquid arose. It seemed to danced in the jar like how the druids entertained snakes at the carnival on reap day.

"You did it," Avida whispered and clasped her hands to her chest. Aga gestured in a wide swinging motion and the tendril grew longer and moved towards Avida.

"Can you imagine the applications? To be able to move water with just your mind? We could completely cleanse the cities of filth, or farm once barren soils. The expeditions that could be undertaken with a Water Mage."

Aga raised her other hand and another tendril of water sprouted forth from a new jar. She waved her hands slowly in the air and the tendrils seemed to follow her movements.

"The council is going to be so mad when you show them," said Avida.

"Furious. The damn fools. Maybe now they will learn to simply accept my authority instead of questioning it because it does not conform to their preconceived misconceptions towards the nature of reality."

"Yes, mistress," said Avida, addled by her master's words but excited that Aga was excited. She loved to see Aga excited. It almost always meant a trip to her bedroom for some rough cuddling and forced orgasms.

"Avida, I need you to do something for me," said Aga as she moved the tendrils through the air.

"Anything, mistress. I brought food if you're hungry. I--"

"Not that. I want you to disrobe for me. Quickly now."

Avida swallowed. She had been naked for her master many times, but Aga had never been so blunt. She felt her whole body flush at her request. Carefully, she disrobed in the cellar until she wore nothing but the dark bush between her legs. Her arms at her side, she allowed her master to stare at her small naked body.

"You are truly a beauty, dear," said Aga as her hungry eyes fell on her.

"I, I, if you say so, mistress," said Avida who fought the urge to hide her body from her master. Aga stepped forward, clasped her face, and planted a tender kiss on her lips.

"You've been such a good girl, Avida. You have enabled me to do great things."

"You're the great one! I'm, I'm just a dumb girl who cleans up messes..."

"No, you're my student. And now I want to take care of you the way you've taken care of me." Aga gestured her hand forward and one of the water tendrils moved towards Avida. She manipulated her fingers as if casting a spell, and the tendril slid closer to Avida's hairy pussy. She stared dumbfounded as the living water slipped under her legs. Aga cast her palm up by the wrist and the tendril moved up inside Avida. She gasped and clung to her master. As Aga moved her palm up and down, the tendril slid in and out of her, stretching her tight pussy that had never known the touch of a man. She clung to her master, whimpering as she was fucked by the water magic. The tendril was comfortably warm and stretched her just enough to feel pleasure. Aga hung onto her but continued to fuck her.

"Your whimpering is so cute," said Aga as she continued to fuck her student. Avida whined as the tendril stretched her and fucked her. She felt dirty getting fucked in front of her master, even though it was her master causing it. A high pitched whine escaped her mouth as the tendril fucked her rapidly and surge over her clit. The sensation was more intense than any she ever felt and she screamed her orgasm as she sprayed the cellar floor. Gasping, she gripped her master's robe for balance. Aga led her to a bench in the cellar and loosened her robe. Her pale breasts spilled out and Aga guided Avida's mouth to her nipple where she sucked lovingly. Her master pet her furry pussy as she suckled on her teet.

"Such a good girl, my Avida. You're such a good girl. Now I want you to eat me."

Avida obediently kneeled and Aga spread her plump pale thighs open to receive her mouth. Avida kissed her master's bushy pussy then spread her lips open. A drop of her juices dripped out in a long tendril and hit the floor. Avida exhaled on her master's wet cunt and began to suckle her engorged clit. As she sucked her master, a warm tendril of water found her pussy and began to fuck her again. Avida gasped as she was stretched open but performed her oral services dutifully. Aga gripped her hair as she served, and urged the tendril to fuck her student faster. She sprayed her orgasm in Avida's face then another tendril found Avida's asshole. She cried out as she was fucked in both holes. Aga held her face down in her mound and made her student breath in her musk and juices. She continued to kiss and suck her master's swollen clit, whining as she was fucked out of control. Aga brought her hips up to fuck her face as Avida cried out in orgasm. The tendril of water played back and forth over Avida's clit as she was forced to eat out her master. Together the two women cried out in riotous orgasms before both crumpling to the floor. They cuddled together as they caught their breath, Aga planting little kisses all over her student's body. They lay together for several minutes until the rush of eroticism had calmed.

"This is going to change the world," said Aga as she kissed Avida's plump bottom lip.

"You're so amazing," said Avida, still recovering from the orgasms that were forced from her body.

"Ready to go again?" said Aga with a smirk.

"What? Wait--"

Before she could protest, the tendril found her pussy and fucked her viciously. Her hips moved up and down from the pressure of the water cock inside her. She latched onto her master who kissed her lovingly. Her lips bobbed up and down and Avida looked down to see her master was also fucking herself. They were being fucked together, in each others' embrace, lips together. Aga climbed on top of her and cried out as the water cocks ripped orgasms out of them. They trembled like strangers lost in the cold, but the water cocks continued. Whines joined cries followed by futile coos, but the water cocks would not stop. Orgasm after orgasm was stolen from them. Avida's mind went numb. All she could remember was her master's lips on her and the sensation of being stretched and fucked endlessly. The cocks never got soft, never relented. They pumped over and over, firm, and amazing as they punished. Avida was in tears by the end as an orgasm sent her into tremors. The two women had their thumbs in each others' mouths and suckled as more orgasms were forced out. She almost felt herself regressing, becoming an animal as her hips became pleasantly numb. She thought about men and being bred as she suckled Aga's thumb. Aga's eyes were closed by the cute little coos that escaped her mouth after each orgasm let Avida know she was still conscious. Eventually Avida blacked out from the pleasure. She awoke later with Aga snoring gently near her. The tendrils were gone for now, at least while Aga was asleep.

"We're going to change the world," Aga whispered in her sleep.

Book 3:

Lusting for MILFs

11 Hot and Sizzling Milf Stories to Satisfy Your Desires

Victoria Gray

Preface

MILFs are always something enjoyable to read, and they're something I love writing. They are fun to bring alive, and it's a very popular topic for my readers. Whether they are older cougars, or young moms looking for a hot fuck, I definitely love bringing their stories to life for readers to check out.

Thank you for picking this up, and I hope you enjoy my hot and sizzling MILF stories guaranteed to turn you on and arouse you.

The Milf He Delivered to

Brandon took the package out of the delivery van, sighing as he walked over to the gate. He hated delivering all the way to the Anderson's. It was always a bit awkward, mostly because they were at the end of his route, and he seemed to come here a lot. They were rich for one, and two, he hated trekking all the way over there just to deliver items. But, he sometimes did get the benefit of seeing Katie, the hot woman who resided there. He never really uttered more than a few words to the woman, but he enjoyed looking at the beautiful lady. The only downside, was that he could never have her, for she was probably married to some guy, no doubt some rich fuck who was nothing more than an asshole that married her for convenience.

Still, it was a huge home, one that dwarfed the small place he currently lived in. He went to the gate, pressing the button, and then moments later, a familiar voice echoed.

"Yes?"

"This is the postal service. Here to deliver a package," Brandon explained.

There was a click, and then the gate unlocked. Brandon walked up to the doorway, knocking and waiting a moment before he heard the sound of the door open. In front of him was a super hot brunette with giant tits, shapely legs, and a plump ass. Brandon tried his best to contain his arousal, but his eyes kept wavering around.

"Oh, it's you again. That delivery boy," she said.

"Name's Brandon. And if you could, you can sign here and I'll be on my way," Brandon said.

He gave her the sheet, expecting her to sign it and be done, but then, after she signed it she handed it back to Brandon.

"You can have it back, but you don't have to leave yet. This is your last stop, right? If not, I'll let you go," she said.

He stiffened. It sure was his last stop. He didn't have to go to any other house, and he'd be able to head back home after he clocked out.

"Yeah, it is," he said.

"You wanna come in? Bring your truck in, my son is having a sleepover, and lord knows my idiot ex already moved out," she said.

Ex? So she wasn't married? Brandon nodded, smiling at her.
"I'd love to," he replied.
He went to the car, pulling it in and killing the engine. He was super early anyway, so he'd make it back in time. Even if not, nobody cared as long as you gave them the hours at the end of the week. Brandon stepped into the living room, and as he looked at the woman, she smiled.
"Never seen a place this big before, huh?" she said.
"I'm surprised it's yours," he said.
"Trust me, I made sure during my divorce I walked out with so much more. Plus, I make money writing novels anyway, so I'm doing something with my life. What about you? what's your story?" she asked. She grabbed a cigar, lighting it and puffing out smoke. Brandon was mesmerized by the smoke as it created a ring in the air.
"Delivery driver. I'm nineteen. Just trying to do something with my life, since I don't have much going on," he said.
"That's a damn shame. So, do you have a girlfriend?" Katie asked, pushing her large breasts together.
"N-no," Brandon said, trying to keep his eyes off of her.
"Aww, don't be shy sweetie. Unless it's your first time. Or, do you not want to have a little fun? You're a handsome man," Katie purred, moving closer.
Brandon couldn't believe this. She was right there, up against him, and he could feel her ample cleave there. He was struggling to keep himself together, and then, he spoke.
"I-I mean as long as you wouldn't mind," he said.
"You should know my son is gone, and I'm free as a bird, so why don't you give me a little...celebration," she offered.
Brandon felt like he was under her spell. She moved her body so that her breasts were against his chest. She hiked a leg into his lap, and Brandon felt completely mesmerized.
Katie loved seeing a man like this. In truth, she was turned on by his young, spry body. And she knew that, despite the youthful looks, he was definitely going to be fun to play with. She ground her hips against him, and she watched with delight as he groaned. What Katie also noticed, was that he was packing.
He was bigger than her ex-husband's. Being alone in this house was lonely, and she knew that this young man would be fun to mess around with. She moved in closer, pressing her lips to his own, immediately taking control of the conversation.

She smiled with delight as he tried to fight for dominance with her, failing miserably as Katie snickered against his lips.
"Seeing you try to fight me like this is such a fucking turn on. You're making me wetter than I've been in the past," she said.
That was the phrase that made him gasp, and she immediately took the opportunity to push her tongue into his mouth, mingling it with her own. He tried to fight for dominance, but he was younger, not as experienced, and she could tell it was his first time with a woman.
With a smile, she pulled away, their lips still connected by a trail of saliva, and she soon tugged at her shirt, pulling it off over her head. His eyes widened like saucers as her large breasts appeared, barely able to be contained by a bra.
"These got so big after I had little Georgie, though I can't complain because the guys love them," Katie said with a purr. Katie then groaned as Brandon pressed his face against her luscious mounds, pressing his face between them and inhaling her luscious scent.
Brandon was already hard as a rock, and he could see that Katie was smirking as she looked at his aching member there. He blushed, but then, she moved towards his pants, pulling the fly off along with the button. He groaned as he was released from the confines, and soon, she placed her luscious tits in between there.
"I heard guys like this," she teased, letting her hands move towards her breasts, squishing them as she started to move up and down against the shaft. She looked over at Brandon, who had his eye closed and his lip was being bit. He couldn't believe she was doing this, and Katie was surprised at how he seemed so compliant to her actions.
In truth, Katie hadn't gotten some in a long time. She was a lonely woman, who had all of this but she felt like her life was missing something. Now that she got a taste of Brandon here though, she wanted more. She started to flick her tongue against the tip as she moved her soft breasts against there.
She could see that Brandon was losing all control. He grasped her head, pushing it down slightly as he groaned, releasing into her mouth. She was surprised at the sudden action but lapped it up, and when he finished, she looked at him with a smile.
"Seems like you enjoyed that," she told him.
"I did. I've...never done this before," he said.
"Oh, so you're a virgin? That's adorable. I haven't had a virgin in a very long time, and I'll make your first time memorable," she replied with a purr.

She then moved over towards his cock, which was still rock hard, and she teased the very edge of her pussy against there, shivering as she felt the hard member dance against the tip. She groaned, feeling her body ache for this. In truth, she hadn't gotten any in forever, and she struggled to satisfy herself, but as she looked at Brandon's large cock, she licked her lips, moaning as she moved down on it, feeling the hard member fill her up.

She shivered at the sensation, shocked at how good this felt. She couldn't believe her insides were practically begging for more. She looked over at Brandon, whose eyes were dilated. She groaned as well as her pussy took him all the way in, and then, he shivered.

"Fuck I'm so sensitive," he said.

"I know dear. But don't worry, I'll make it feel amazing," she said.

She could tell this was his first time. He was writhing in pleasure at the feeling of her pussy. For Brandon, she wasn't too tight that it suffocated her, but not loose either. It felt so perfect, that he didn't know what to do with himself, and soon, he started to relax, completely amazed by how amazing this felt.

Katie started bouncing up and down on his cock, and he started to groan. He felt like every fiber of his body was on fire, and as she started to move slightly faster, he could barely contain himself. He moaned, aching for more from the lustful Milf, and soon, he started to push his tongue against one of the nipples, sucking on it, letting his other hand move towards the free nipple. Katie continued her bouncing, feeling completely free and excited about everything. She couldn't believe how amazing this man felt, how she was enthralled by it all, and how she wanted more.

He then started to push up against her, and despite her riding, the way he pushed in completely astounded her. He got in deep, and soon, he grasped her hips, pushing her up and down while he thrust himself into her as well.

"Fuck," she moaned out loud, feeling at the mercy of all of these touches. He began to move faster and faster, but then, he picked her up. He was glad to have the strength training from work, which allowed him to push her down on the couch and plow into her.

"Yes! Just like that!" she screamed out loud. For Katie, this was what she dreamed of. Being a lonely mother who was recently divorced did make things hard, and she couldn't believe how nice this man treated her. He angled his cock so it kept brushing against those nerves, something she discovered herself but not even her ex-husband could do.

"Fuck!" she screamed out, feeling at the mercy of everything that was transpiring. After a few more thrusts, he grasped her hips, thrusting in as deep as possible, and it was then when she cried out loud, feeling at the mercy of every single motion that was there, and it was then when she felt her orgasm pile up forward, making her shake with delight as she felt her pussy clench around him, hugging that cock against her walls.

Katie wanted all of him, and she wasn't going to let him go. She did already have a hysterectomy a while back, which allowed for anyone to cum in her, and when she achieved orgasm, she could see that Brandon was super close too. He groaned, tensing up for a second before he spilled his entire load into her, thrusting in deep so he could get everything that was in him out.

Katie missed this warmth. She wanted it again and again. She loved every single moment of this, and she could tell that he did as well.

When he finished up, he pulled away, collapsing on the couch there. Katie sat there as well, basking in the afterglow of her orgasm, and she couldn't believe that it happened like this. In truth, she wanted to be fucked like this for a long time, but she didn't really know how to approach this. She was older, so she feared what might happen if she did go out into the dating world and tried to find someone. But, this guy satisfied her in a small romp than her ex-husband did in a long time. The two didn't say much, but then, she noticed Brandon look at his watch, shock plastered on his face.

"Fuck, the guys are totally going to ask about what happened!" he said.

"Oh relax. I'll put in a good word for you. Just say that you had some extra business," Katie said with a purr.

Brandon nodded. "True. I can lie."

"And don't worry, if you want to come here after your delivery routes anytime in the future, you're more than welcome to. I'll always have my door open. The kid is usually off with friends, and he's always ready to leave, so if you want to come back again sometime in the future I'd love that," she said with a smirk.

Brandon couldn't believe she wanted this, but Katie was lonely, and with the way her life had been going, this was one of the best things to have as of late.

"Thank you, Katie. I enjoyed this a lot. I'm happy we got to share this," he said.

"Oh, same here. I'm very happy as well," she replied.

The two of them shared a kiss, and Katie helped walk Brandon to the door. She then pulled out her phone, smiling at him with a subtle smile.

"If you ever want to, you can always text me too," she said with a purr.

He blushed, but he agreed to that, giving her his number. Brandon seemed to be on the spot, but Katie loved how awkward he was. She certainly wouldn't mind this, and she definitely would love to take him up on the offer once again. It would be a ton of fun, and by the time he got up and was ready to leave, she could see in his eyes that he wouldn't mind doing it again as well.

Katie knew that the delivery boy would be back, and she would make sure to request him when it came to packages that she wanted to get. That way, she could still have a lot of fun and definitely get exactly what she wanted, that's for sure.

Tutoring and Lusty Desires

Holly sat there with her son, who was struggling with math. Holly didn't really have the time, nor did she desire, to sit with her son and figure out math problems. Math was definitely not her forte either, but when she saw how bad her son was doing in school, she knew that something needed to give.

"I need to hire a tutor," she said.

Holly scoped out for one, seeing a few that had potential but wasn't really what she wanted. However, when she read the profile of Jonathan Brooks, she immediately was interested. He was a very attractive young man, 25 years old, and was a professional tutor. Holly did have the money, so she decided to hire him.

The first day he came in, Holly's eyes widened. She knew that he was attractive as all hell, but she wasn't expecting this. With long, dark hair, beautiful hazelnut-colored eyes, and a cute smile, she felt that urge to fuck him grow and grow. He looked at her youthful frame, and, being only 37 years old, she was much younger than most mothers he probably had to deal with.

What Holly didn't expect, was how good of a tutor he was. Steven loved working with Jonathan, who was docile and gentle with him. It was the first time Holly saw him truly happy, and there was something about the young man that not just made her pussy ache, but also warmed her heart.

She wanted more of this man, craved more, and she would stop at nothing to have this man all for herself.

The next couple of weeks involved little flirty touches between both parties. Holly's hand would brush against his own, and he would let his hand touch her shoulder. They would steal little glances at each other, small, smoldering looks that made Holly want to jump his bones and fuck him senseless. It had been a long time since she got some, so she could feel the craving grow within her.

After one of the study sessions, Steven immediately ran off to his room to play games.

"Get ready for bed in an hour," she said.

"Alright mom," he said.

Holly wanted to make a move on Jonathan, but every single time had been inopportune. After all, she had the child hanging about, so it wasn't like she really got an opening. But, that night Jonathan kept averting his eyes, and she smiled at him, a small, seductive grin.
"Something the matter?" she said.
"Oh no, it just seems like you wanted to talk to me," he said.
"Oh, I do. Come with me," she said.
She motioned for him to follow her, and soon, they were in her office. She closed the curtains and made sure to lock the door. Course, Steven knew that when those doors closed, it was mommy's work time, so he usually let her be.
The two sat in the office, and Jonathan kept staring her up and down.
"So, it seems like Steven is doing much better. Are you sure you want me to stay here?" he asked.
"Of course. I like having a cute, attractive man over here. And plus, you're doing so well. But, I can tell that you're a bit worried about something. You're confused on how to feel. Care to tell me what's wrong?" she said.
She crossed her legs multiple times, showcasing a hint of panties. He gulped, trying to keep his eyes on her.
"I'm sorry, usually most of the women I work with are quite old, but you don't look a day over 30, so it's a bit distracting. I'm sorry, I know I shouldn't be doing this and--"
"It's okay. If you want, we can make this our little secrets. If you know what I mean of course," she purred.
His eyes lit up at those words, and immediately, Holly knew that she was going to have fun with this. She moved towards his lap, sitting it and brushing her thighs right up against his crotch.
"You ever been with a mom before?"
"N-no. I haven't had a girlfriend in about three years, and even then it was a high school thing, so I'm a bit out of practice," he said.
"Oh don't you worry, I'll make sure you're in practice by the time I'm done with you," she told him with a smile on her face.
It was then she closed the distance between both of them, pressing her lips passionately to his own. He groaned, shocked by the sensation of all of this, and he quickly kissed her back. She deepened the kiss, taking control, and soon, she pushed her tongue out. He immediately met it as well, and to Holly's surprise, he started to fight for dominance to the kiss. It shocked her because she thought this man would just be compliant, but then, his hands

moved towards her hips, touching her curves there and getting towards her breasts. He touched them both, and she soon gasped, feeling everything start to tense up.
"Fuck," he said to her, his surprise obvious.
"You like it," she said.
He started to massage her breasts from over the shirt, touching her nipple slightly. That little ghosting was enough to drive her crazy, and everything immediately made her feel turned on and aroused. She started to move her hips against him, grinding her crotch there, and then, after a brief second, he kissed against her neck, touching the little spots there which turned her on.
'"Jesus," she said.
"What, surprised by my endeavors?" he teased.
"Yes. You're better than I thought. I want you inside me," she said.
The sudden forcefulness started to come forward, and she was turned on by the way he seemed to take perfect care of her. He then moved his tongue against the side of her neck, brushing against there. Holly let out an exhale in pleasure, enjoying the sensation of this, and it was then when he moved towards her shirt, fumbling with the buttons awkwardly. Holly smiled, moving her hands to her shirt, unbuttoning, and then pushing it off her body. She then shivered as she felt his hands move towards the cups of her breasts, touching her there and making her moan out loud. She then watched as he pinched her nipples, teasing her slightly, and she soon started to gasp, unsure of what to really do other than to accept the touch. He touched, pinched, and teased the nubs, lightly flicking his tongue over one at one point and letting his hand rub and pinch the other one. She shivered with delight at the sensation of this. But, it was when Jonathan started to push her down on the desk that she was surprised.
"What are you--"
She felt his lips and hands move up her legs, kissing her inner thigh and biting the flesh there. Holly shivered with delight, feeling like all of her emotions were at the forefront, and she was sensitive as all hell. She couldn't believe how perfect this guy was, how he was able to treat her so well.
She was shocked more than anything that he was single too since he was so good that she didn't even know how to react.
He then spread her legs apart, taking a whiff of her ripe pussy, smelling the desire that was leaking out of there. He moved his hands towards each side of her panties, slipping them off to reveal her pretty pink cunt. He spread her apart, letting his lisp invade her

pussy lips, licking the edges and teasing her to the point where she was completely turned on by everything.
"Fuck," she said, feeling her whole body react to this. He let his lips move towards her clit, flicking the area there with his tongue. He forced the area out of the sensitive hood, teasing and pleasuring her there and letting his lips do the talking with it. He started to move his tongue against there too, teasing it before moving towards her folds, letting his tongue move against there. After a moment, he pushed his tongue all the way in, letting it fuck her deep and letting her moan and gasp against him.
"Jesus fuck," she said, feeling like her entire body was on fire. He started to penetrate her deep, letting everything start to build up, and she felt as if everything was driving her to the point of madness. She loved everything about it, and she felt like she was in heaven. She was so close, but when he pushed his tongue up against that sensitive spot, she then tensed up, crying out loud and feeling everything start to drive her to the point of madness. She then came, feeling her juices come out of her body, and he licked up every single drop as if it was a nectar of life and he wanted every single droplet of it.
"That was amazing," she said.
He smiled at her, but he wasn't done yet. He spread her apart, letting his cock move all the way into her. Holly jolted and moaned at the sudden fullness, not sure what to do with herself for but a second. She hadn't felt this in a long time, and it felt so good. He started to thrust in deep, penetrating her and filling her up completely. The fullness was enough to drive her insane, and for Holly, she loved every single moment of this. She couldn't believe that he was this good, that his cock could pleasure her like this, that he was able to make her feel everything that she wanted to feel.
He started to penetrate in deeper and deeper, holding her hips and fucking her senseless. Holly could barely keep herself straight, for her eyes kept darting wildly, and everything was driving her to that point of madness. It was making her feel as if sanity was almost gone as if she had no idea what to do about any of it. He then started to fuck her harder and harder, making her moan with delight at everything that was happening, and it was then when, after a few more moments, Holly felt his hands against her clit. When he touched her there, Holly could feel the edge approaching, and she could feel her pussy clenching against his cock, which only prompted him to go harder.

He groaned, feeling it all drive him crazy, and then, after a few more thrusts, he tensed up, letting everything drive him to that point of madness, and it was then when he came, filling her up inside. That final little touch was enough to make her shiver, and she cried out, cumming once again.
She couldn't believe how good this felt. She normally didn't bother trying to get herself off like this. But, she was definitely enraptured by everything that transpired, and for a moment, she felt as if her body was about to fall asleep. He then moved back, smiling at her for a moment before he spoke.
"You good?"
"Better than good. That was definitely needed," she said.
"It was. Man, I've wanted to do that for a while, I just didn't want it to be weird," he admitted.
"I know. But, we both definitely are quite happy, that's for sure. Hopefully, he didn't hear us," Holly said.
"Doubt it, the kid is super obsessed with video games. When we are done with our studies, he's always talking about wanting to go upstairs and play Fortnite, so I think he's just playing some games right now," he said.
"I figured, but it never hurts to ask," she said.
"Yeah well, don't worry about him. In fact, hopefully, I got your mind off the fact that he's been a bit neglectful with studies," he said with a purr.
She smiled and nodded.
"You did that and then some. It's been a long time since I've been able to indulge in that. Years actually. Haven't been able to do that since my ex, and even then, he was nowhere near as good as you were," Holly admitted.
Her ex could never make her cum, let alone from penetration, but Jonathan here with his eight-inch cock could make her do that and then some. Jonathan simply smiled, happy to be of service to her.
"Well, I'm glad to help. If you ever need that kind of help again, just let me know. I'm always ready to stick around for a little bit of overtime," he told her with a wink.
Holly blushed, but then he got himself together, heading out of the office. Holly got herself together as well, and sure enough, Jonathan was right about Steven. Steven was in the bedroom, playing his video games, and not really caring about much else. Holly was just happy his grades were better, and she was happy he had such a studly tutor as well.

Holly definitely wouldn't mind learning again and again from this man, and she definitely wouldn’t mind experiencing once more what she did get to experience with Jonathan back in the office, and maybe next time, it would be in a different place that both of them would love to indulge at.

The Milf Teacher

Carrie looked at the grades, noticing that of course, Derek was at the bottom of the class once again. She was a college professor, and most of the kids that were here were in her class so they could move to other subjects, but it just felt like Derek didn't even care about that. Of course, Derek was a smart kid, he just was doing terrible in her class.

Carrie had to do something.

She didn't have to get home to her daughter early anymore, for her daughter had sports, and if anything, Carrie's sister could pick her up from school. Her daughter was 10, and Carrie knew that the child was definitely getting older and more independent. It was hard being a teacher and a single mom, but she got the help she could get.

After that class that day, Carrie looked at everyone, but as they were leaving, she spoke.

"Derek, I need to talk to you," she said.

He stuck around, and for a moment, Carrie had to admit that he was a cutie. With golden blonde hair and beautiful blue eyes, he was quite a looker, and it was no wonder that the other students liked him. She knew that he was popular, and he certainly was one of the guys girls were enthralled with, but he never seemed to want a girlfriend.

When everyone left, Carrie closed the door, locking it and looking at Derek. She thought about how to approach this. In truth, she wanted him, and she thought that he was a cutie. The first time they locked eyes, she could feel a slight jolt. She knew that he was one of the older college kids, at 21, but she knew that this was ground she had to tread lightly.

"So Derek, you failed a test. Again," she said.

"I'm sorry, I've just been kind of distracted," he said.

Carrie patted the seat across from her desk. Derek moved there, sitting down and looking at her.

"I'm not in trouble am I?"

"Depends. If you and I can come to an agreement, we'll make this work, and you'll be off the hook," she said.

"Okay," he replied, blushing madly.

She thought it was the most adorable thing, and for a moment, she was completely enthralled.
"So, why are you having so much trouble in school Derek? Or my class that is," she said.
He averted his eyes, and she looked at him with a serious glance.
"It's a little embarrassing," he admitted.
"Come on, just tell me. I swear, I'm not going to make fun of you or tell any of the girls," she said.
He blushed, but then, after trying his hardest to look away, he finally spoke.
"It's because I may have a small crush on you," he finally said with the tiniest voice.
For a moment, Carrie didn't know how to react. She thought it was both adorable, and slightly odd.
"So you like me?"
"I do, but you're a teacher and like...I feel kind of stupid. I really wanted to tell you, but I didn't know what to do," he said.
Carrie smiled.
"Well, I guess that makes two of us. I do like you too. I mean, you're quite the looker, and I enjoy younger men. Luckily, my daughter has my sister picking her up, so I can stick around for a little bit," she said with a purr.
"W-what do you mean," he said.
Carrie had an idea. She then took a deep breath, a seductive smile that made him look at her with worry was on her face.
"If you want, we can have a little bit of fun. It seems that you're a bit needy, and I can take care of you. You take care of me, I take care of you, I'll be able to magically change the grade. How does that sound," she said.
She moved towards him, and he gulped. She sat in his lap, letting her fingers dance against the very edge of his crotch, and she could see the obvious tent in his pants.
"Y-you mean like sex?" he said.
"Course. What else did you think I meant?" she said with a teasing smile.
She could tell that he was debating on this. Carrie knew hat it was risky behavior, but she wanted him as well. Finally, after a brief moment, he took a deep breath and nodded.
"Please. I'll do it," he said.
"Very good. You know a good deal when you see one. If you make me feel good, I can just...magically wipe away those bad grades. You're a good student otherwise, so I figured either you weren't

good with this subject, or you were just doing it for attention," she said.
She started to hike up her skirt, revealing her panties, and then, she undid her blouse, taking it off her body. His eyes widened at the sight, biting his lips in shock as he looked at her. She could tell that this was the first time he ever saw a girl like this.
"What's the matter? Cat got your tongue?"
"Sorry it's just...I've never seen a girl like this. Despite my reputation as one of the hottest guys in school, I've never been with a girl," he said.
"Fortunately your first time is with someone who can make you feel really good," she said, letting her hands ghost against her thighs. His eyes widened, and soon, she moved towards his lips, giving him a deep, passionate kiss.
He immediately responded, kissing her back and making Carrie moan. She was surprised by how needy this man was. Maybe he did want her this badly. She immediately responded to this, kissing him with a passion that she enjoyed, and he wanted her just as much. He started to rut against her, and soon, he pushed her down on the desk. Carrie was surprised, mostly because guys weren't this forceful, but she liked it.
He climbed on top, hovering over her body, giving her another passion-filled kiss. She immediately responded, letting her tongue mingle with his own, and she quickly found him kissing down her neck, leaving gentle touches so that she didn't have marks. He started to move towards her shirt, and after awkwardly fumbling with this, Carrie watched as he pulled her shirt apart, grasping her large breasts and touching them. Carrie moaned, surprised by everything. In truth, she felt as if she was in heaven. His touches were perfect, and he soon grasped her breasts, playing with them and lightly thumbing the nipples slightly. She groaned, excited about everything that was happening, and enjoying it all.
He started to play with them a little bit more, moaning in pleasure at the sensations that were there. He pulled one of her breasts from the confines of her bra, and when he sucked on it, she shivered with delight. But then, Carrie moved forward, pushing him back down into his seat. She pulled his cock out from the confines of his pants, looking at him with a smoldering look.
"Why don't I give this little guy a bit of attention," she said with a purr, lightly stroking him. She watched as he started to moan, wincing slightly as she teased him. She smiled with delight, watching as he shivered when she pushed her mouth to the tip of his

cock. She flicked her tongue there, inciting a moan from Derek as she played with the tip, progressively taking more and more of his cock down her throat. He shivered, moaning in pleasure as she took him in deeper, loving the way he reacted to everything that was transpiring. She watched as he groaned, excited about everything that was happening, and soon, she took him all the way down her throat, feeling a gag as she felt the veiny member touch the very edge of her mouth. She shivered as she started to move up and down against there, shocked that her gag reflex wasn't getting the best of her. He began to moan, arching his back and shivering with delight as she continued this. She watched as he held her head, jerking her up and down, and Carrie struggled to relax, moaning in pleasure as he continued these actions. After a bit, he then started to pull back, looking at her with lust-ridden eyes. The darkened look made her shiver, and soon he looked to the desk.

"Get on there," he said with a smoldering voice.

Carrie didn't need to be told twice. She laid there on her back, her legs spread and her pussy glistening wet. She looked at him with a small smile, and soon, he spread her legs apart, diving into there with his cock. When he finally got all the way in, she tensed up, moaning in pleasure as he filled her.

He was big, and she couldn't even get all of him inside of her. When he started to press in and out, fucking her mercilessly and with passion, she began to cry. She shivered with delight, every single fiber of muscle in her body sensitive to the touch because of how amazing this felt, and soon, he started to fuck her faster and faster. He grabbed her hips, ramming into the desk, and she could feel his cock pressing against every single one of the areas that was there. She was so close, she could already feel him getting her to that point, but then, he pressed a finger against her clit while he braced her with his other hand, fucking her raw and mercilessly, and it was then when she started to realize just how desperate and needy she was.

As she felt him do this, he fucked her hard, hitting that one spot that she loved more than anything else. As he did this, she began to scream, feeling her orgasm immediately overtake her body. She tried very hard to muffle it, and it was when he pushed his hand to her lips, holding the scream back did she let it out. She felt her body cum hard, her orgasm immediately overtake her body, and everything begin to change there. She looked at him, seeing him also tense up. He then pulled out, cumming against her stomach with little strings.

She shivered as she felt the hot liquid fall there, but she was glad he didn't try to cum inside. It felt so good though, so amazing, that she didn't want this to be the end. After he finished, he fell back into the chair, and for a long time, Carrie didn't move. She did grab some tissues to clean the cum off her body, and she managed to straighten out her outfit, looking at him with a devilish smile. This was perfect, the moment she'd been waiting for, and as he sat there, spent as much as she was but also satisfied, she struggled to find the words, unsure of where to go with this.
"How are you doing?" she inquired.
"Good. I don't really have many words right now. That was just...wow. Amazing," he admitted.
"I could say the same thing. It was magical, really. I feel happy about everything that just transpired," she admitted to him.
"That makes two of us, that's for sure," he replied.
"Well, I do suggest we try this again sometime in the future if that's what you want," she said.
"Yeah, but maybe not here at school. I feel like we are already pushing the limits here," he said.
That's right. Most of the teachers were gone, and she knew that the kids were too. If someone were to walk in, they'd be royally screwed.
"Well, hopefully, we can finish things up here before then. So, since you held up your own end of the bargain, I can hold up mine, if that's what you'd like," she told him with a smile.
He looked at her with surprised eyes, but he quickly nodded.
'I'd like that," he said.
"Well good. You'll be seeing a couple grade changes very soon," she purred.
She then got herself together, heading towards the desk and then putting the information in. She knew that it was risky because an administrator could go in at any time and see these, but in truth, Carrie was someone who always kept her end of the bargain. She looked over at Derek, who seemed worried, but she simply smiled.
"Relax, I'm not going to betray you. I'm putting in the information currently," she admitted.
"T-thanks," he said to her.
"You're very welcome. I don't go back on my words," she said to him.
"I didn't think so. Thanks," he told her.
After it was all said and done, she submitted the work, looking at him with a devilish glance.

"Well, I think it's safe to say that you're off the hook for now. You got lucky, and I think you should probably head back. Don't tell anyone about this, and you'll be fine," she said.
"Thank you," he replied.
She watched as he got up, scurrying out of there, and for a moment, she sat there with a smile on her face. For Carrie, she couldn't believe she let the guy get away with this, but it also fulfilled the need that she had within her body, a raging need that was quelled for now. She would definitely have him come back eventually, and she would make sure that next time would be just as fun as this time.

The New Babysitter

Nichole came home after a long day at the office. She saw the familiar light that was on in her living room, and she smiled to herself. She knew immediately that Timothy was still here, and it sent a small fire down her loins.

For Nichole, hiring Timothy wasn't just a good thing for herself, she knew for him it was great too. Nichole needed a babysitter for her son Kevin, who was six but still needed someone around. She heard of the horror stories of kids getting kidnapped, and that was the last thing she wanted when it came to taking care of her son. She met Timothy, and after a lot of extensive interviews, she chose him.

He seemed happy with the job, not because he got paid well, but she could see the subtle looks that he would give to her, and it would make her flush crimson in response. Nichole hadn't been with a man in forever, and she did crave that touch sometimes.

She thought about what to do tonight. Kevin was probably already asleep as usual, so Timothy would be awake and alone, probably just watching TV while he waited for her. Nichole opened the door, seeing Timothy there, and she greeted him with a wry smile.

"Hey there Timothy. How was he?" she inquired.

"Fine as usual Nichole. He went to bed about an hour ago, and won't be waking up anytime soon," Timothy said.

Nichole smiled, putting the contents in her hand down. She sauntered over to Timothy, smiling at him.

"It seems like you've been taking care of him quite well. I appreciate it, you know," she said.

She could see the blush on Timothy's face as she leaned over, and she could see that his eyes widened as he stared at her ample cleavage which threatened to come out.

"I-it's nothing," he said.

"Oh come now, you know it's not nothing. You're enjoying this, and I don't think it's because I pay you a lot of money. I think you like it for...other reasons," she said.

The way he turned his head away, flushing red told Nichole everything. She was right, and soon, she moved towards his body, letting her hands skirt against his legs. He hissed, breathing out slightly, and she knew that it was her turn to attack.

"So Timothy, do you have a girlfriend?" she asked.
"No. Casey and I broke up a while ago. I've been a little distracted anyways with making money to have a girlfriend," he said.
"Oh, well that's good. I actually haven't been seeing anyone either. My workaholic personality, plus taking care of my son has left me unable to really pursue anything serious. But, I don't mind having a bit of fun," she said with a purr, letting her hands ghost against his thighs, just barely touching the obvious member between his legs.
"I-I see," he said. He was unable to contain himself, and she could see him getting hard from this.
"So, what do you say? Want to take care of a few things? Consider this an extra little bonus for you," she purred, moving closer and turning his face to face her own.
She could see the desperation in his eyes, along with the doubt.
"But what about Kevin?"
"He would sleep through an earthquake. You'll be fine. Trust me," she told him.
She could feel him getting harder just from the way she used her words. She loved teasing men like this. There was something so damn satisfying about all of this, and as he breathed in, she could tell his head was spinning, and he was doubtful of everything.
"B-but this won't cause anything weird to happen, right?" he asked.
"Not at all. This can be our little secret. I take care of you, you take care of me. Besides, it's probably been forever since you've gotten some. I can barely remember the last time I did," she said with a smile.
He gulped, but then, she brushed his lips over her own, and he immediately responded, groaning in response to everything that was happening. He kissed her back, causing her to smile devilishly at the sensation of everything that was happening. She began to push her body so that she was straddling him, kissing him with a passionate, needy nature. She'd been horny and desperate, and she wanted nothing more than to make this man feel amazing. He did respond to her actions, kissing her back, and she immediately groaned at the sensation of this.
There was something just so hot about all that was happening, and as she kissed him, she felt that urge to have more of him grow. They were quiet about it, but she then brushed her lips down his neck, causing him to let out a small gasp of shock. For Nichole, this was the fun she'd been waiting for.
What most men didn't know, was that she was very dominant in personality. While she didn't mind a guy taking control, she liked it

when they responded to her whims. That's why, her hands were already at his shirt, pulling it off, and she started to kiss and bite down on his neck. At first, she did it softly, causing him to let out a small gasp, but then, she bit down a bit harder, making sure to leave a mark.
"You okay with me taking care of you?" she said.
"Y-yes," he said.
She smiled, seeing the way his eyes seemed to glance over her body. She could tell that he liked being babied. He probably did have a little mommy kink himself.
She continued to kiss down his neck towards his pecs, which were nice and defined. She took a nipple into his mouth, lightly kissing and teasing it, and he soon let out a gasp. She smiled, letting her tongue circle around there.
"Someone has sensitive nipples," she said.
She lightly pinched them, and she saw him bite his lip, groaning in pleasure. He was quiet, but she thought that it was utterly adorable that he was submitting himself to her like this. She could tell that he liked her being in control, so she continued this, letting her tongue work wonders against each of the little nubs.
She then moved downwards, getting towards his inner thighs and lightly rubbing and massaging them. The look on his face was that of desperation, and she could see that his eyes were practically begging for her.
"Please. I need it," he whispered.
She smiled, and then, she moved towards the fly of his pants, undoing it along with the zipper. She shucked them off his body, taking his cock out, and flicking her tongue over the tip. She knew what men liked, so she started to suck on his cock, moving up and down and watching as his eyes started to roll back and dilate, his breathing growing heavy and his cock getting harder.
He was hypersensitive, and she wondered if it was because he hadn't gotten any in so long. She could feel the throbbing of her pussy in her panties, the need for this cock to plunge into her. But, she wanted to tease him a bit more. She undid the buttons on her shirt, smiling at him as she pulled the top area apart. She pulled her breasts out from underneath the cups, exposing her large breasts and perky nipples.
"Fuck," he said.
She then wrapped her breasts around there, teasing the sides of his cock. She drooled on it to provide lubrication, and that was enough

to make him almost cum right there. But, she stopped it. He groaned, but then, she smiled.
"Not yet. You're not allowed to cum until I say so," she said.
He groaned, and she loved seeing him fall into the trap of her desires. She then pushed her breasts up and down against his shaft, pushing them about and watching as he sat there, completely immersed in everything that was happening, unable to do much else. She could tell that he was at the mercy of her hands and motions, and she soon began to move her breasts up and down there faster and faster, letting her mouth take part of the cock as she did this. The motions that she created were enough to drive him mad, but then, she moved her lips downwards, taking one of the balls into her mouth and watching with rapt attention as he started to thrust up.
"Jesus fuck," he said.
"You're enjoying this, aren't you," she teased.
"Please let me cum," he said.
"Not yet. You're not allowed to until you get me off," Nichole said.
He looked at her, desperation in his eyes, but then, she moved towards his legs once again, straddling them, but this time, she shifted her panties to the side, plunging her pussy down on his aching cock.
He shivered with delight as she started to ride him, at first slow, but then a bit faster and faster. She watched as his eyes dilated once more, and even just the small, succulent pace was enough to make this man go tongue-tied. She started to thrust up and down on this faster and faster, watching with excited eyes as he continued to moan against her body, his body relishing in everything that was happening.
She then started to move faster and faster against there, watching him as he started to grasp at her hips, pushing her up and down. He drove his cock right into one of the spots that she knew she liked being penetrated, and then, she started to gasp, holding back her moans. He started to react, thrusting in as deep as he could, and Nichole enjoyed watching the desire in his eyes, the need that he had grown more and more as she started to thrust faster.
"That's right, you like this, don't you. Come on, make me cum," she said.
His hands moved to two different places and so did his mouth. One of them moved towards her breasts, which were roughly pinched, and he began to suckle on her other breast with his mouth. The

other hand, moved towards her clit, playing with it as she continued to ride, and his hips continued to thrust deeper and deeper.

She was close. Nichole loved being stuffed by the huge cock, and he seemed satisfied. After a brief moment, she felt the desire grow, the urge to cum started to flood forward, and she knew that she would definitely be at that point in a brief second.

Sure enough, after thrusting against that one spot, combined with all of the other ministrations, she moved his lips to her own, kissing him passionately to hide the moans that came out of her mouth as she came. He then groaned, pushing in deep as he tensed up, filling her pussy with his warm seed.

She then pulled back, looking at him with delight, and then, she spoke.

"That was just...wow," she said to him.

"Indeed. You're happy though, right?"

"I haven't been fucked that hard in a very long time Timothy. You certainly did the job quite well," she replied.

She got her clothes back on, and she watched as Timothy stared at her. She then smiled back at him, giving a teasing glance.

"What, got something to say?" she inquired.

"No it's just...what does this mean for us?" he said.

"What it means is, if you want to maybe do it again and have another round on that cock of yours, then we can most certainly do that," she said.

He let out a gasp, but then he nodded.

"I would love that. After all, I do have a thing for Milfs," he admitted.

"Well good, because I like to have fun with younger men. Hopefully, school doesn't kick your ass too much," she said.

"Nah, college is kind of easy minus the work. It's finding a good job in the meanwhile that's hard," he said.

"Well remember that you'll always have a job here with me, and you might get a nice little bonus in your paycheck next time," Nichole told him with a small grin.

He smiled back, knowing immediately what that meant.

"I can't wait for that. Anyways, it's late, I should be going," he said.

"I should get ready for bed too. But, I had fun, and I'd love to do that again if you're ever so willing to indulge in this with me," she replied.

He nodded, grabbing his keys and heading out, and for a moment, Nichole didn't know what to think. That was the best fuck that she had in a long time, but she feared what might happen if they continued this. Was it right? Was she doing the right thing?

She believed so, but she also knew that she was being risky with this. However, it did help, for she finally got off, and she got the fuck she'd been craving for a while. Timothy was fun, and she certainly enjoyed indulging in that younger man tonight, that's for sure. She would see where this went, and hopefully, it would generate some great things.

The Fun with the Son's Friend

Brandi saw her son Devin with the friend that she knew of. His name was Clayton or something, and when Brandi saw the young man, immediately a sizzling need was there. Devin was in college, so naturally, this was one of his friends from classes, but the moment Devin brought his friend over, immediately Brandi knew she had to get into that.

With brown hair, big, blue eyes and a muscular body, she could feel her body ache for him. She was older, about 40 or so, and she wondered if there was any way to to get a younger man in bed with her. He primarily hung around Devin, but Brandi could see the small glances he stole at her, and she could feel her body ache for more as she did that.

Brandi wanted him. She craved the idea of this man, but she feared what might happen if she overstepped her boundaries. She wondered what he would say if she did. On the one hand, Devin normally didn't care what she did, but usually, he was always with his friends, and the friends were never alone. It didn't bother her in the past, but with Clayton, she craved him.

One night, Brandi sat alone in bed. Clayton was staying over and hanging out with Devin, but as she thought about the fact that he was here, her body craved the touch. She laid in bed, her hands at her pussy and breasts, playing with them and moaning softly. She closed her eyes, imagining the feeling of Clayton against her body, eating out her ripe pussy, fucking her mercilessly.

What Brandi didn't realize, was that the door was slightly open, and when she touched herself, she didn't even realize Clayton was there. She fingered herself, moaning slightly, but then, she heard a sound.

"Ms. Baxter?" the voice said.

Immediately, Brandi covered herself, blushing at the fact that Clayton was here. The guy she lusted after but could never get alone saw her playing with herself, moaning in pleasure at the sensations she'd been experiencing.

"Oh fuck that door wasn't closed," she said.

"It's fine but uh...I thought I heard my name," he said.

She looked at the hunky man, staring him up and down. Her son did know how to pick hot friends. Of course, she felt completely exposed at the fact that he looked at her like this, and then, after a brief second, she finally figured out how to speak once again.

"I-It's not what you think it looks like," she admitted.

"I mean, I heard my name. You were...masturbating to me weren't you?"

The blush that was on her face was the obvious answer. She thought that he would leave, and she would never see him again.

"And what if I was? You're probably never going to come over again, are you?" she said.

However, what happened next shocked her to the core. Instead of leaving and telling her son that she was weird, or leaving the house and not staying over, he closed the door and locked it. He took off his shirt, his defined, ripped chest making her salivate suddenly. He looked at her with darkened eyes, and then, his voice rumbled at a low tone.

"I can help satisfy those desires, and this can be our little secret," he said.

"You think so?" she asked.

"Oh yeah. Devin is out cold. He's not getting up. Besides I...I kind of wanted to try this for a long time. I honestly came over more often than not cause I wanted to see you," he admitted.

The blush that was present on her face said it all, but then, she uncovered herself, smiling.

"Well, you have that opportunity," she replied.

He leaned over, capturing her lips in a passionate kiss, and she immediately kissed him back, moaning against his lips. This felt exactly like how she wanted it, but it was obvious that her pleasure was the focal element of everything tonight. As he kissed her, she felt her body ache for more, a deep need that only grew more so.

He pulled away, gasping in pleasure at the sensation of his lips against her own. He then looked at her with a dark, lustful gaze, and then, he moved down her body. He gave her soft, gentle kisses that made her shiver, and when he got to her breasts, he touched them slightly, causing her to let out a sudden gasp, and she soon felt him move his hands against each of the nipples.

"I've never seen tits this big before," he said, grabbing them and playing with them. The touch was enough to set her on fire, and Brandi was trying her best to keep quiet. The last thing she wanted was for her son to find out about them, so she needed to keep herself together. But the touches he bestowed upon her, the way his fingers danced against her nipples, the little touch against the tips, was enough to drive her mad, and she loved everything about this.

He moved towards the other edge of the nipple that his hands weren't on, capturing it against his mouth, and playing with both of them as he looked at her.
The stare that he gave to her was enough to drive her mad. She let out a huff of air, feeling her body ache for more, and as he did this, she could feel the desperation growing against her body, the aching need that seemed to only grow even more than ever before.
Everything about this was a huge turn on, and he was making her feel the effects of what he was doing even more so. He then moved down her body, kissing and touching her curves until he got to the area between her legs. He took a deep breath, inhaling her scent and looking up at her with dark eyes.
"You smell delicious," he said.
Those words were enough to drive her crazy, and she started to push her soaked pussy up. He immediately kissed her inner thighs, teasing her as he trailed his lips all the way up to the sensitive warmth that was there. She could tell he wanted to tease her, to play with her, and he seemed enthralled by the state in which she was in.
"I've never been with a mom before," he said.
"Well, hopefully, I'm good enough for you," she said with a smile.
"Oh you will be," he replied.
He started to lick the sides of her pussy, teasing the folds there, and It was better than what she imagined. He danced his lips and tongue against every single nook and cranny of her pussy, making her shiver with delight as he took care of her. He then started to push his tongue against her clit, teasing the very edges of this and making her shiver and cry out loud. She moaned with delight, feeling everything drive her to the point of madness, and as he did this, she knew that there was no way she could hold herself back. She bit her lip as he trailed his tongue against every single sensitive area, sucking on her clit before he spread her pussy lips apart, diving into there and tonguing her deep. With that alone, she felt her eyes widen, her breathing grow ragged and rampant, and she knew that she was close. When he flicked his tongue up, she then cried out slightly, using the pillow to mask her cries as she felt her orgasm come forward.
He pulled back, licking the release off his lips and looking at her. She shivered, smiling at her and looking at him with a lustful need.
"God I want more," she said.
Her hunger for cock was larger than she thought. She pushed him over towards the bed, laying him down and getting towards his pants. He gasped in surprise as she pulled them off his body,

revealing the obvious bulge that was there. He was bigger than she thought, and as she pulled his boxers down, she felt like a kid opening up a Christmas present.

A Christmas present that was going to plunge into her pussy sooner or later.

She then moved her tongue against the sides, swirling it about against the head, and he lightly groaned. She could see the desire in his eyes, and she wanted to have a taste. Beads of precum exuded from there, and she could tell by the way that he was quivering that this was certainly his first time. She took the very edge of this into her mouth, pushing her body against there and taking him all the way in. She looked at him, watching as his eyes widened as she let his cock dance against the edge of her throat.

She hadn't deep-throated a dick in a long time, but she was a natural at it. His hands moved towards her head, pushing it down further. She gagged, but that didn't mean much for her, for she felt like she was definitely enjoying this more and more than she thought. She definitely wanted to see just where this might go.

After teasing it for a bit, she sat back, spreading her legs apart and looking at him with a need. She played with her pussy, an invitation for him to plunge into it, fucking her senseless.

He took that invitation, and soon, he spread her apart, looking at Brandi with a look of lust. Brandi simply smiled there, playing with her pussy as she looked at him. After a brief second, he pushed in deep, grabbing her hips and letting her legs move towards his shoulders. She locked herself into there, forcing him to stay inside, and for Brandi, she felt delighted when she saw the slightly pained look on his face, the shock that he was trapped against her legs making her feel the excitement.

He started to move in and out of her, and she smiled with delight at the sensation of this. She certainly loved watching him as he began to press downward, fucking her mercilessly and without stopping. The sounds of their breathing were enough to turn them both on, and she clung to him, feeling him plunge deep into her. She enjoyed this, watching with delight as he continued this. After a bit, she then watched as he pushed her legs up further, giving him better leverage to fuck her.

The sounds of their breathing and slight groans were the only things that could be heard. But, when he was getting close, Brandi felt his hands against her clit, rubbing her.

"I want to cum together," he said.

She agreed with that, and then, after a brief moment, he then pushed against there, sliding all the way in and moaning with delight. She gasped as well, feeling the sudden influx of pleasure from her other orgasm, and she soon began to shiver, thrusting her hips up and down, losing everything about this, and it was then when, after a moment or so, she felt the high of this, and then, she relaxed. He pulled out of her as he started to soften, staying by her side initially for a moment before taking a deep breath, experiencing the pleasure of it all and then speaking.

"Guess it was fine that I came to your room then. I don't regret following what I heard," he said to her.

"I don't either," she replied after catching her breath.

He put his clothes back on, taking a moment to look at Brandi for a second. He then smiled to himself.

"You know, you're definitely hotter than the girl I lost my virginity to. And fucked better as well," he said.

"Well, I'm glad that you enjoyed it. You know, I wouldn't mind having that same type of fun again, if you wanted to that is," she said with a purr.

"I'll think about it. But of course, we'd have to do it whenever he's not around. Then again, Devin does sleep soundly, so I think we can make do," he told her.

"I think so too," she replied.

The two of them looked at one another for a second, both of them knowing that this wouldn't be the last time they got to experience this sort of thing together. But, they would have to keep it on the down low.

For Clayton, finally getting to fuck his best friend's mom had been something that he wanted for a long time. He did fap to her a few times, and he wondered if there was anything about it he could do. But now, now that he got a chance to experience this, he certainly wouldn't mind doing it again. Of course, he wondered if they would have a chance. But, he knew where to find her, and he could always get Devin super drunk so that he'd pass out early and have a little bit of fun.

Brandi didn't regret it either. She thirsted for young cock, and this was the type of cock she'd been craving. She wouldn't mind doing it again, and she knew that Clayton came over a lot. They could continue to have their fun together, and experience the pleasure that they both wanted to enjoy. She was definitely ready for action, and she wanted nothing more than to create a fun time once again with him.

They would have one another again, and more often than not, they would figure out a way to see each other, and mess around under the radar of Devin.

The Milf Businesswoman

Ellie watched as the new intern came in. She smiled to herself, knowing that this man was hot as hell, and the perfect catch. She knew he was personally chosen by her HR department, so he was worth their money, but she could see that he was more than just good at his job. He was attractive, and Ellie rarely went for employees, but being the owner of her company, she had a desire for an attractive young man, and this one definitely caught her eye.

"Hello there, you must be nick," she said.

"I am," he replied with a flush, staring at her curvy body.

"I'm Ellie. I'm your boss. I hope you can help me grow this company," she said with a purr.

"I'll do my best. I'm going to be working directly under you, right?"

"Correct. Let's make some magic," she replied, giving him a teasing smile.

The first couple weeks consisted of the usual awkwardness, where Ellie would tease the young intern, and he would blush and get embarrassed, which she thought was super cute. But, she noticed he didn't shy away from her affections, and in turn, he would actually appreciate them and want to get to know her better. Of course, they rarely had time alone, so Ellie couldn't make her move completely, but, one night after everyone left, they were alone in the office, working together.

"Say, Nick, you like to stay late a lot. Why is that?" she asked, breaking the silence.

"Oh, it's just...I like getting the work done," he said.

"You don't have a girlfriend to go home to?" she asked the young guy.

The brunette flushed, adjusting his glasses and shaking his head.

"No, I'm a bit awkward you see, and most girls want a guy whose super confident and out there," he said.

"I think you're a great man, and quite a cutie too," she replied.

He looked at her, and she smiled at him.

"What about you? You're like, super attractive and stuff," he said.

"Yeah well, I'm a businesswoman with a daughter. She's in her teens, so I don't have to play momma bird as much, but since I am

divorced, I usually dedicate the time that I have to her, or my work so it's been rough," he said.
"You have a child? Wow, I never thought that you did. You're like super pretty I didn't expect it," he said.
"Why thank you. You're pretty cute yourself," she said.
She moved towards him lightly tapping her fingers against his arms and thighs. She could see him growing nervous, her overbearing personality enticing him.
"Well, we are alone currently. It's nice to have that. Plus, I kind of noticed you kept looking at me, staring at me and everything," she said.
"S-sorry it's just you're so pretty," he admitted.
"I think it's more than I'm just pretty. I think you want something," she said.
He blushed, but then he nodded.
"I-I do. I want you," he said.
"Well, if you'd like, we can have a fun little arrangement together, just you and me. Don't let anyone else know about this, or I'll fire you on the spot. But, we can keep this our little secret," she said wth a purr.
He blushed, and she could tell that he wanted it, but he was quite nervous. The fact that he was so tense and nervous was honestly quite adorable. She didn't expect him to be like that.
"I-I wouldn't mind that," he said.
"Good, then that makes two of us. We can have our own little adventure," she told him.
She moved forward, pressing her lips to his own, watching as his eyes widened at her sudden actions. She didn't like to beat around the bush. She knew that he wanted her, and Ellie wasn't going to let this man get away. The two of them let their lips touch and collide with one another, a dance that only the two of them knew, and she enjoyed every moment of this. She watched as he pulled back, flushing red as he stared at her.
"T-that was...nice," he said.
"Just nice? I take it you've never been with a woman before?" she asked.
He then turned redder and then nodded.
"I kind of focused mostly on school, and most people avoided me because I was a little awkward," he said.
"Well, I enjoy awkward boys, so I'm going to make you feel nice and welcome," she said.

It was then when she moved her hands towards his crotch, lightly teasing it, and he soon looked at her with a shocked expression as she teased him through the fabric. Shit, this guy really was a virgin, and her Milf pussy would be the first one he would get to experience.
He moved his hands up as she kissed him and fondled him, touching her breasts. He tried to undo the buttons, but he was bad at it, and she giggled, undoing it for him.
"It's alright. They're a little weird," she replied.
He gasped as he stared at her luscious breasts. They were big, but not too big, and as he touched them and played with them against his hands, she let out a small moan of pleasure. He started to lightly pinch the nipples, teasing them slightly, and he soon started to watch as she gasped in response. He looked at her with a lustful need, and she smiled back.
"Play with them all you want," she instructed with a devilish smile.
He didn't need to be told twice, for he began to dote her breasts, playing with them again and again, watching as she let out a small gasp and moan of desire. She loved every single moment of this, and she could tell that he was enjoying it just as much. She then started to watch as he suckled on her breasts, pinching them in tandem with this. She moaned, feeling taken care of, but then, he pulled back.
"You want more?" she asked.
She wanted to make sure that he wanted this, and then he nodded.
"Yes," he said.
She smiled, and soon, she pulled his cock out of his pants, undoing the zipper and the button like it was nothing. She looked at him with a smile as she took his shaft, moving her hands up and down on it and watching with delight as he began to look at her with a lustful expression, easily overwhelmed by what was going on. She began to tease him a bit more and more, watching with excitement as he continued to push his cock up, meeting her hands.
Ellie then replaced her hands with her mouth, taking him down her throat and moving her lips up and down against his shaft. He groaned, excited about everything, and Ellie smiled with satisfaction as she took him all the way in, only gagging slightly. She missed deep throating, and it was obvious that this guy enjoyed it just as much. She began to move her lips up and down against there with satisfactory motions, enjoying the sensation of teasing this man completely.

He seemed to enjoy it, and she could taste the precum that was coming out of his cock. But, she didn't want him to cum yet. In fact, she wanted to give him the time of his life. It was when she pulled away and moved to her desk that she gave him a dark look, spreading her legs apart to reveal her shaven pussy.

"I hoped that you would take the bait. I didn't wear underwear today," she said.

He looked at her with widened eyes, shock plastered on his face. He wanted to taste it, and she spread her legs while she sat on the desk, her pussy begging to be teased. He moved forward, pushing his tongue against the very tip of it, touching her clit and hearing the little whimper of satisfaction.

He loved the smell and taste of it, and he lapped at her like a dog in heat practically begging for more. She enjoyed seeing this, loving the way he took care of her, and for Ellie, she knew that Nick wasn't going to stop. He pushed her thighs so that they enclosed around him, letting his tongue work its magic and moving about. She shivered with delight, enjoying every single touch, and she knew that it was only a matter of time before her release would happen.

As if on cue, he pushed his tongue in, moving it right up against the top, and when it hit that one spot, she immediately cried out, happy that everyone in the office already left. She pushed his head in between her legs, begging him to continue, and it was then, she felt the sudden onslaught of her orgasm start to immediately hit her. She then pushed her hips up, letting her pussy rut against his mouth as she came.

He pulled back, shocked by how forceful she was, but he loved it.

"I need to be inside you right now," he said, desperation obvious in his voice.

She was surprised by his words, but she immediately got up, pushing her hands and arms onto the desk and sticking her backside out for hm to see.

"Put it in then," she purred, seeing the delight on his face.

He spread her apart, plunging straight into her, and it was then when she immediately felt how full she was. He took her all the way in, shocked by the sudden fullness, and it was then when he started to penetrate her deep. She shivered, enjoying every single moment of it, but she could practically feel her vision going blurry the moment his cock penetrated her deep. She was still high off her orgasm, but she loved the sensitivity of her wet cunt against his hard cock. He started to penetrate her a bit faster, and after a bit, she turned to him with a devilish smile.

"You can be a bit rougher with me, I'm not going to break," she teased.
It was then when he moaned, and soon, he started to penetrate her hard, feeling everything inside her body. She loved how he was hitting that one spot, filling her up completely. He knew how to work his cock despite never doing this before, and it created a rapturous desire within her. For Ellie, she missed the feeling of a dick inside of her, completely eking everything out of her, and she definitely longed for more of this. Her pussy craved cock, and as he penetrated her insides, hitting that one spot, she could practically feel the urge to cum start to overtake her.
"Harder, please," she begged, her body aching to be fucked so hard she couldn't think straight.
He obliged her, fucking her mercilessly, his thrusts never ending and making her immediately lust for more of this. She screamed out, and it was then that, after a couple of thrusts, she immediately tensed up, feeling as if all of her parts were all overwhelmed by the feeling of her orgasm.
She really didn't know what happened next, for her vision went white, and she had the best goddamn orgasm she had ever felt. Her pussy clenched against him, and for Nick, he tried so hard to hold on. But, his cock was about ready to explode, and he was surprised at how long he held on. It was probably due to the fact that he had masturbated a lot, but he was at his wit's end. This pussy was godlike, and she knew that he was right at the end too.
With one last push, he groaned, spilling his load straight into her. For Ellie, she sat there, completely shocked by how good she felt and overwhelmed by the sheer amount of pleasure that she felt at this present moment. Everything felt amazing, it felt so good, and it was then when, after a brief moment or so, he pulled out, and she felt her legs give out for just a moment.
Ellie couldn't believe how good that felt. After a brief second, she felt a hand extend to her own, pulling her up and bringing her over to the couch. She laid there, basking in the shock and force of her orgasm, one of the best she ever had, if not the best. She looked over at him, and she smiled excitedly.
"That was...the best goddamn thing," she said.
"It really was. Fuck. I never thought my first time would be so good," he admitted.
"I'm glad I could provide an excellent first time for you," she said.
He turned, giving her a kiss and then smiling.
"I think you definitely enjoyed it too."

"Yeah well, most guys never fuck me that good, and you're honestly the first so I definitely am grateful for that," she replied.
"Good. I'm glad too," he said to her.
For a moment, the two of them just stayed like that, and she didn't want to move whatsoever. When he finally got up, he looked at her and then at the clock.
"It's super late. I should get going," he said.
"I should too. So much fr getting the extra work done," she said.
"I lied. I really don't actually stay here just to do work, I like to stay around here with you," he admitted.
She smiled back. "Well, perhaps we could continue this fun little arrangement again at some point," she replied.
"I'd love that," he said.
He turned and walked away, leaving Ellie to sit there and bask in her orgasm. It was one of the best she ever had, and she definitely didn't regret making a move on the hot young intern, that's for sure.

feeling of his lips, and despite the fact that Toby did have a great job, a beautiful look to him, and a body that made her melt, she knew that he liked it when she took control.
And taking control she did. She brought him over to the bed, kissing him passionately. She was surprised when he quickly responded back, their tongues mingling and moving against one another both of them realizing just how much they enjoy each other. For Amanda, she loved everything about it, and she did realize that this was indeed the beginning of a future, one that she was desperately ready to take on. She pulled back, looking at him and tracing his cheeks, smiling.
"You ever been with a Milf before?" she said.
"No, but I want to," he said.
"Well, ask, and you shall deserve," she said with a smile on her face. She then started to move her lips against him once again, and he quickly moaned, kissing her back. She shivered with delight at the sensation of his lips, her body grinding against his own. She didn't even know if they would actually make it past the first date, but she certainly was going to get the excitement and the happiness that she deserved, and the life that truly mattered.
For Amanda, she started to move her lips down his neck, causing him to let out a small moan of pleasure. She smiled to herself, lightly nibbling on the skin there, watching with delight as he began to moan in pleasure. She then started to bite down there, leaving a mark for him to remember her by.
She usually rarely did that but there was something so fun about the fact that she was able to do this to him that she wasted no time in playing with him.
She moved down his body, playing with his nipples, and she could tell that Toby was at the mercy of her actions. She smiled to herself, enjoying the way she got to tease this man, knowing full well that he enjoyed it just as much as she did. Each and every single touch, everything that she did, was driving him crazy, and she surely would love to continue to do this.
But, as she was about to undo his shirt, he flipped her over, pinning her down and kissing her passionately. He rutted his cock against her slit, which was exposed due to her skirt hiking up, and for Amanda, her pussy was already leaking juices and begging for more from him. He started to lightly push his hands towards her breasts, cupping the orbs there and lightly playing with them. She shivered, groaning out loud and in pleasure, and with every single touch, every single motion, she could feel her entire body just begging for

more. Everything was making her super excited, and as he danced his fingers right against the tips of her nipples, she shivered, crying out loud and with delight, and she moved her pussy up, immediately rutting against him once again.
The desire for him started to grow even more so within her, and as he started to push his hands down her curvy body, he admired her figure. The two of them wanted each other just for tonight, and they'd figure out where to go from there once this was over, but for now, Amanda just wanted his cock in her pussy, for she knew that he was big and thick, and she was dripping just waiting for more.
He then moved towards her slit, spreading her pussy lips apart and thrusting a finger in. He rubbed her clit, smiling at her with a devilish grin as she began to moan and gasp at everything he was doing. His touches were exact, so perfect, and her body was only growing more and more aroused with time. Everything seemed so perfect, and Amanda just wanted him to continue his efforts. He was definitely happy with the way he was making her cry out, and as he slipped another finger into her, he lightly brushed up against a spot, making her cry out and buck her hips up.
That was her g-spot. Most men couldn't find it, and she never felt this good. But, Toby knew exactly where to penetrate her, exactly where he needed to touch her, and everything was making her lust for more of a touch. She looked at him, her eyes dilating and her pussy throbbing with delight as he continued to thrust into her, and soon, after a few moments, he pushed up again, and started to rub and pinch her clit in tandem.
"Fuck," she screamed out loud, the sudden urge to cum invading her mouth. She then tensed up, feeling her hips thrust up and thrash, and then, the sudden urge to release immediately overtook her. She came hard, her body feeling the effects of everything that just transpired, and when she looked at him, he smiled at her with a small grin of excitement.
"Seems like you had fun," he said.
"I did, but I'm going to return the favor," she said with a purr.
He was pushed on the bed, her hands immediately at his pants, practically ripping them off his body. He gasped at the sudden coolness that came with her actions, surprised at how desperate she was. She then pulled his cock out of the confines of his pants, stroking it a little bit, and it was that alone that made him groan, his entire body immediately bucking slightly in response.
"Someone is enjoying this," she said.

In truth, she hadn't gotten a guy off in a long time, and she could tell by the blush on Toby's face, he hadn't done this in a while either.
"It's been a little while for me too," he said.
"Well, let me take care of you then," she told him with a purr.
She then started to move her hands up and down, taking the tip of his cock into her mouth, and that was when she saw the man buckle, sitting there and shivering as she took the tip of his cock into her mouth. She moved her tongue about in circles and in lines, watching with delight as he began to groan and hold her there. He pushed his hands to each side of her head, lightly motioning for her to move up and down. She couldn't believe that he was so determined to keep her there, and while she normally wasn't used to this, she definitely felt the excitement that came from this. She loved the way that he was acting, and the way he treated her, and she knew that he was definitely losing his mind with every single touch.
After a moment though, she noticed that he was about to cum. She didn't want that yet. She wanted him deep within her pussy, fucking her to oblivion. She pulled back, smiling at him as she laid down, spreading her legs apart and keeping her knees up. She looked at him with a small blush, smiling at him for but a moment before speaking.
"You want in?" she said.
He looked at it like a puppy that was just thrown a bone. He didn't need to be told twice as he climbed over to her, pushing his cock all the way inside almost immediately, he pounded straight into her, not stopping whatsoever, and for Amanda, she simply shivered with delight, watching with excitement as he started to move his cock deep within her, thrusting in and out and enjoying everything about this. Every single touch penetrated her sensitive walls, and his cock was so big and thick that the fullness of it was something that she enjoyed and craved. She then started to feel everything overwhelm her, and as she began to feel him move deeper and deeper, she knew for a fact that it was only a matter of time before she could feel everything start to change within her.
She wanted more, her entire body practically begging for him to get deeper, and soon, she wrapped her legs around his body, holding him there as he started to fuck her mercilessly. He didn't want to stop, and she practically held him there, forcing him to stick around. Her tight pussy was begging for him to get in deep, and judging from the look in his eyes, the expression that showcased he was getting there, she knew for a fact that he was getting pretty close as well.

She wanted him inside her, and she would keep him there. But, he skillfully moved his hand up, rubbing her clit, and she soon felt her own physical urge to climax once again overtake her. It was like a drug, something she got a taste of but practically begged for more. It was then when, after a few more thrusts, she knew that the end was coming, and she knew that he was getting there too.

The kisses and the thrusts that they shared were amazing, and she knew for a fact that he was enjoying this just as much as she was. After a few more thrusts, she tensed up, feeling everything in her body practically pushed over the edge, and it was then that, after a brief moment or so, she cried out.

He groaned, pushing deep into her, and she felt his hot cum spill into her pussy, and she definitely enjoyed the hot warmth as it slid into her. Her tight pussy practically eked everything out of him, and she watched with delight as he groaned, finishing up for a brief moment before he slipped away. He looked at her, and she smiled at him. Both of them didn't say much for a second, trying to get their bearings together.

"Well that went differently than how I imagined our first date would go, but I'm definitely not disappointed," he said.

"I imagined you wouldn't be. After all, it's not every day you get to fuck a hot Milf," she said.

"Yeah, and I know that we had a great conversation earlier too. You're honestly impressive Amanda, and I mean...i really like you. Would you mind perhaps going on another date sometime in the future? Maybe sometime next week," he said.

Amanda smiled. She didn't expect a second date out of this at all. She figured this was just a romp, but in truth, she was quite happy with the way things were going, and she definitely wouldn't say no to another fun time together.

"I would love that actually," she said with a smile.

"Well good, because I would love to take you up on this once again, and perhaps, we can have a little fun at my own place," he said to her.

"Sure, I'd love that," she replied.

She looked at him, and he gave her a kiss. He didn't leave though, and Amanda was quite surprised by that. She felt like he would probably just leave after he got what he wanted, but he didn't. Rather, he stayed there, spending time with her, and appreciating her body. The two of them did end up going for another round, and at the end of the night, the two of them laid in bed together, happy and satisfied.

For Amanda, she knew that this was not what she was expecting, and she thought that this would be a one-time thing, but as he laid there with her, this younger man caught her attention, and she wanted nothing more than to spend time with him once again. Her pussy craved the next experience, and she wanted nothing more than to have this once again with him. When they parted ways the next day, she knew that he would be coming back, and he would come to see her once again.

"I'll make sure that we have even more fun the next time," she said with a purr.

As she bade farewell, she smiled to herself, understanding how nice and amazing the experience with him truly was.

Daycare Milf Fun

Jackie walked the last of the children from the daycare out to their parents. She usually met some of the moms, who were fortunate to have her as the instructor for their kids. Most of the time, their conversations involved them thanking her for taking care of their child, and dealing with their little brat.

But, the last parent that was there was a young man.

He was in his twenties, with glasses and brown hair, and Jackie immediately looked at him with delight.

"Why hello there," she said.

"Hey, I'm here to pick up my niece Katie. I'm Travis, Katrina's brother. She needs me to pick her up for the next week or so, cause Katrina is out of town," he said.

Jackie was focused on Travis more than the fact that Katrina was gone.

"Well, that's totally fine. Katie and my daughter Olivia get along pretty well, so I'm happy to take care of her," she said.

"Great, thanks," he said.

The next week went by the same, with Travis picking up the kid, both of them making small talk and flirting, and then Travis leaving. She wanted to ask him for his number, but she feared that it might be a bit awkward.

One night, after Jackie dropped Olivia off at home to get ready for dinner with her mother, Jackie heard the sound of footsteps near her office. It was after hours at the daycare, so she looked at the doorway with confusion.

"Whose there," she asked out loud.

The door opened, and then, Travis appeared.

"Oh. Hi there," she said.

She realized that she hadn't seen Travis n a week. Katrina went back to picking her daughter up, but they never talked about him. Jackie wondered if Katrina knew about the small crush. But then, Travis closed the door.

"I hope I'm not intruding, but Katrina was feeling better so she's been picking up Katie. And I never gave you my number," he said.

"That's fine. I'm sorry, I didn't want it to be awkward," Jackie admitted.

She noticed Travis eying her hot Milf body, staring at her luscious curves, and then, he bit his lip. For a moment, Jackie smiled at Travis, and then she spoke.

"Want to stay here for a bit? I already dropped Olivia off at home. I was just getting some work done," she said.

"That would be nice," he admitted.

He then moved towards the other chair, looking at her with needy eyes, she smiled back at him, both of them trying to awkwardly approach this subject.

"So uh, you are quite a pretty lady. Do you have a husband?" he asked.

"No. never did. I raised Olivia on my own. No thanks to my shitty ex," Jackie said.

"I see. I haven't really found anyone either and... I have to say, you're pretty amazing. You run this entire daycare, and it seems like you have a lot going on. Seems stressful," Travis said.

In truth, Jackie was very stressed out. She wouldn't mind a little bit of relief, and when she looked at Travis's delicious body, she shivered with delight.

"I mean, I wouldn't mind the extra little help with overcoming the stress that I have. It can be quite rough," she said.

He was looking at her body, eying the slight cleavage her shirt created. Jackie didn't expect to be turned on by the way he stared at her, but as he moved forward, cupping her shin and looking at her, she felt her pussy wetten with delight at the idea of this.

"You know, I could help with that. We can keep this our little secret," he said.

She moaned against his lips almost involuntarily, shivering with delight. It had been so long since she was touched like this, and the stresses of life were sometimes hard to deal with. Suddenly, she pressed her lips to his own, kissing him passionately and without a goddamn care in the world. He moaned, immediately kissing her back, and she gasped at the sensation of this, overwhelmed by the sheer force of his lips, and the touch he provided. She craved this, and he soon moved his hand to her pants, undoing them and pulling them off.

Jackie knew that it was taboo to do this at work, but nobody was around, and her body was horny and desperate. She did let her mom know that she'd be home late, so she probably wouldn't see her daughter anyways. No matter, she didn't really care about much else at this point besides the feeling of his lips, and the quivering need her pussy had.

He slipped her onto the desk, holding her there as he kissed her. He clung to her, and then, he started to trail small, sensual kisses against her body. She groaned, but not before he moved his hands to her shirt, pulling it off her body and revealing her large, supple breasts.

"Wow," he said.

He grasped them, holding the large mounds there, and soon, Jackie shivered with delight. His cold hands against her sensitive its were making her want nothing more than to just lose herself at this point. She groaned, gasping in pleasure as he started to play with her tits a little bit more, smiling as she immediately reacted to everything that was happening.

He was so good with his touches that it was driving her to the point of craziness. She shivered as he continued to pinch and tease them, playing with her large nipples and teasing the areolas. He was so gentle but at the same time rough enough that it made her crave more. She shivered with delight, relishing in the feeling of this, her body aching for more from his touch.

He then took the time to move his hands downwards, moving one of them to her pussy and rubbing her there. Her panties were already sopping wet, a huge desire for his cock already at the forefront of her mind. She craved it, her body aching for it, and she knew now more than ever she desired the feeling of him inside her.

He then pushed his lips to one of her nipples, playing with them as he rubbed her against his hands. Her panties were getting wetter and wetter, making the foreboding squish sounds that she knew and loved. Everything about this was making her body ache for more, her pussy craving the feeling of the touch, but as soon as he did this, he pulled away, leaving a dull ache and a feeling of wanting more in her body.

He slipped his cock out of his pants, revealing the large and thick ember. He began stroking it, and for Jackie, she was amazed by how big and thick it was. She couldn't stop staring at it, and it was then when, she grasped her tits, wrapping them around the confines of his cock, and she soon started to move them up and down, watching with delight as he began to moan against her, and she soon started to move her hands against her breasts once more, letting everything bounce at a rhythm he enjoyed.

He held her there, and she soon started to take the tip of it into her mouth. He shivered, groaning with delight as she began to let her tongue flicker over the edges of this. Everything was driving him to

the point of madness, and she loved that she was able to take him to this point.
She then noticed he was pushing her head down a little bit, holding it there and making her gag. She loved everything about it, crying out with delight as he held her steadfast, gripping her head as she took more of his aching cock in. everything about this was too good, so perfect that she was loving everything about this, and she definitely was enjoying this just as much as he was. Everything happened for a reason, and as he held her there, letting his cock fill up her mouth, she could feel a slight gagging sensation, but just as soon as it happened, he pulled off, looking at her with delight.
"I need to be inside you," he said.
Those words along were enough to make her shiver with delight. She took off the last of her jeans, spreading her legs, and moving her underwear so that her glistening pussy lips were there, begging for him. He reached down, taking her clit into his mouth and lightly sucking on it, letting his tongue drape out and tease her folds. Everything about this made her want nothing more than to continue, and she knew for a fact that with everything that had been going on, she was definitely enthralled by this. It was so perfect, the teasing so masterful, that it was only a matter of time when she felt her own climax come. But, she pushed him away, a desire to have him all the way inside of her immediately driving her forward.
"No, I need you inside me," she said.
He smiled, spreading her lips and practically ripping her panties off of her. He grasped her hips, holding them there as he pressed his cock inside, immediately filling her up.
She was shocked at just how big he was, his whole cock immediately engulfing every single inch of her pussy. She shivered with delight as he started to move in and out of her, taking it slow with the thrusts initially, but then growing as well. He began to thrust in deeper and deeper, feeling her cling to him with every single moment. He arched her hips a little bit so that he could hit that one spot that he knew that she loved, and she definitely enjoyed everything about this. It was all driving her to the point of madness, and she knew that he was getting to that point as well.
After a few more thrusts, she could tell that he was getting close, and she was getting to that limit as well. She didn't want it to end though. The aching desire for cock, the fact that she was actually being satisfied by this man, everything was making her need grow within her. After a few more thrusts though, he then penetrated her deep, hitting that one spot that she knew that she loved getting

penetrated, and that, combined with the feeling of his hand against her clit, sent shivers down her spine, and it was then when she cried out, feeling the sudden urge to cum immediately envelope over her.
She came hard, realizing that she was definitely at her limit. She felt the force of it all drive her to the point of insanity, and it was then that, he groaned as he penetrated her a couple more times, shivering as he spilled his seed into her.
For a moment, neither of them moved. For Jackie, this was the first time in forever she'd been satisfied. She pulled out, sitting on the desk and catching her breath. He looked at her with a devilish grin, and she smiled back.
"You enjoy that?"
"Yeah, more than I thought I would. I guess I needed it," she said.
"Well, if you ever need something like that again, you should know where to find me," he said with a teasing smile.
"Oh yes. Maybe next time we can at least get a little dinner or something first before we smash," she said.
"I wouldn't mind that," he said with a teasing smile.
He then moved out of the way, allowing her to get her clothes back on once again. They walked out together, and while Jackie wished that she could tell him that he could come with her, they would need to take this slow. It was a fun little romp, and it helped with he growing frustrations, but she didn't know what this would mean for the both of them.
In truth, she would just need to wait and see.

Nerd Grown Up

For Stephanie, she never thought that she would see her childhood friend after all this time. But, when she went to the banquet for her work, she saw a familiar brunette there, with glasses she could see from a mile away.

"David?" she asked.

He turned around, seeing his former childhood friend look at her with that same smile that he had.

"Steph!" he said.

The two embraced, talking animatedly with one another about their lives. Stephanie realized that David grew up. In the past, she never ever thought about him in a romantic manner because he was so needy, but puberty hit him like a freight train, and after so long, she definitely was amazed.

"Wait, you have a kid now?" he said.

"Yeah. Daisy is her name. She's seven," Stephanie said.

"Wow, you definitely don't look like it," he said, eying her curvy and luscious body. Her breasts and ass had grown since she had her daughter, but Stephanie took care of herself, getting her body in shape for whatever.

"You've cleaned up too. You've become really cute," she said with a purr.

It was his turn to blush.

"Thanks. Do you want to maybe...take this somewhere more private.' he said.

Stephanie wanted that. In truth, she was only here on behalf of her boss, because she liked these types of events, and plus, she would get paid more. Stephanie was being taken care of by a sitter, so she had all the time in the world to flirt with her childhood friend who grew up to be a total fucking hottie.

They went to one of the private rooms up there, and Stephanie locked it, looking over at David who seemed to have his eyes on her. The two sat down, reminiscing about their past, and it was then when David spoke.

"man, if only I wasn't such a total nerd back in high school, I would've totally hit you up," he said.

"Yeah well, you grew up, and the two of us were in a weird place. But, we're different now. We work for partner companies, I have a kid and well...you got really hot," she said.

He looked at her, biting his lip as he stared at her, and then, he spoke.

"You got pretty hot too, I have to admit," he said.

"Aww, that's pretty cute. Seems like someone has a crush, she said.

There was silence, and immediately Stephanie wondered if she said the wrong thing. But, it was shortly after that he spoke, blushing furiously.

"Actually, I've had a crush on you for a very long time," he said.

Stephanie then felt her jaw drop. She couldn't believe it. He seemed to ignore her back in high school, focused way more on hitting the books than anything, and Stephanie got herself embroiled with a dumbass boyfriend that got her knocked up only to shortly leave her after high school.

"Yeah well, I'm a bit of a mess, so I don't really know if you want to deal with that," she admitted.

"But you're a hot mess, and I very much want to," he replied.

She could see from the way that he looked at her that he wanted this just as much as she did. She started to learn in, pressing her lips to his own and kissing him passionately.

She wondered if this was fate, or maybe if this was something the both of them just wanted to do for one another, but as she kissed him, the raging desire that grew within her started to come forward. She wanted him, and she craved his touch. Everything about this was something that sat in the back of her mind, creating that lofty need that grew within her.

He started kissing her back, letting her take control of the kiss. Despite the fact that her childhood friend went from nerdy to hot, he still had that social awkwardness to him that she found quite attracted when she thought about it. She started to press her tongue to his lips, and he soon kissed her back, enjoying the sensation of her lips against his own. The tension, the passion, the desire that they both shared, all of this was driving her mad, and she craved the feeling of his lips and his body. She wanted his cock inside her, and she knew that this nerdy stud would certainly entertain her needs.

He then moved a little bit, letting his body move on top of her. They were on the couch, but seeing the desire in his eyes, and the way his body overtook her, it turned Stephanie on even more. David then moved his hands to the back of her dress, undoing it and slipping it off. There, he saw her luscious breasts, which were bigger than he remembered.

"You got big," he said.

"Yeah. I know. It happens after you have a kid," she said.

"Well, you still look fucking amazing in my eyes," he said with a purr.

He took one of the nipples into his mouth, playing with the other one. Stephanie laid back, groaning in satisfaction at the way that he played with them. He was gentle, but e didn't act like he was handling a bomb or anything like some dudes. Instead, he applied the perfect amount of pleasure, and she immediately embraced it, enjoying everything about his actions.

He continued to dote her for a little bit before he started to place his focus on other areas. He looked at her, making sure that this was what she wanted, and she immediately smiled.

"Go ahead," she told him.

He eagerly hiked her skirt up, revealing a small piece of black silk fabric. It was the thong she decided to wear because she didn't want her underwear line showing, but of course, it meant other implications for what they were doing currently. He started to move his hands up, taking the contents off her body, revealing her shaven pussy. Her pink pussy lips were practically begging for him, and he could smell the desire that she exuded off of there, groaning in delight. He loved everything about this, and he knew for a fact that she was enjoying this just as much.

He slipped a finger into her, lightly thrusting in and out, and she whimpered with delight. He continued to tease her, letting his lips move towards her clit, touching the very tip of it softly before he started to flick his tongue over it. She shivered, loving everything about this, and he soon continued the actions, watching with delight as she enjoyed everything about this. She could tell that he was loving this too, completely surprised by how she was willing to have him take care of her. In truth, this was a dream for David, and for Stephanie, she certainly wasn't complaining at all. In fact, she wanted more from him, and she desired everything that this man bestowed to her.

He then started to suck on her clit, moving his hands up and inserting two fingers into her. She cried out, shocked by everything that was going on, and she wanted nothing more than for her to feel all of this. He brushed the bundle of nerves within her, and then suddenly, she cried out, shivering with delight as she felt the urge to cum started to overtake her.

She then felt his hands move back, lightly licking the juices off of there, and she immediately looked at him he was blushing, his cock huge in his pants. He was already popping a tent, and with gentle hands, Stephanie started to undo his pants, pulling them off to reveal his cock. He stroked his member with soft hands, and he started to lose his composure, letting one of his hands rest on the couch in order to brace himself. Stephanie pulled him closer, pressing her breasts around his cock, and she decided to give him a titfuck. His eyes practically rolled to the back of his head as she did this, and she smiled as she saw the man lose himself against the amazing feeling of her hands around her breasts, jerking off his cock.

She decided to add a bit more to the foray though. She then licked her lips, letting the tip of his cock move towards her tongue. She watched as he cried out, immediately losing control of himself with everything that was happening. She loved seeing him shiver with delight, cry out loud and practically shiver against her body. She loved seeing all of this, and it was obvious that he was near his limit. But, she didn't want the fun to stop. With a pop, she moved off his cock and smiled at him, and soon, she spread her legs apart, pushing her pussy lips open to ask for him to enter.

"Come on in," she said with a purr.

He looked at her, and then, he pushed his cock against her, holding her backside to brace himself as he thrust into her. The feeling of his large member penetrating into her drove her mad. He was better than she thought. She was honestly quite surprised that he actually had the experience to back up his movements, but she won't complain, for he knew exactly where to hit, and all of the good spots that she loved being penetrated in.

He continued mercilessly for a bit, holding her there and fucking her hard. She could feel him hitting close to that spot, but after adjusting her hips, he immediately penetrated there, and for a second, Stephenie didn't know how much of her composure she could maintain. Everything about this was so good. She never expected David to be so killer in the sack. He moved his lips to one of her breasts, sucking on the nipple while one of his hands moved towards where her clit was, playing with it while he fucked her mercilessly. She wanted to continue this, but she could feel her own personal urge to cum starting to overwhelm her. What she didn't know, was that David was already at his limit, and he was near the end.

She immediately screamed out, clenching against his cock, and she could feel the sudden force of her orgasm start to overtake her. She felt her body cum hard, but when he got to his limit, she pulled out of there, letting her lips encircle against there. She wanted to taste him, and he seemed completely fine with that.

With a shiver, he pushed her head all the way down, making her gag on his cock as he came into her mouth. Cum flooded her orifice, and she was immediately shocked at just how much this could take. She was gobbling it up like it was her last meal, and as she looked at him, she sucked out every single drop. His sensitive cock was getting stimulated by her mouth, and after a small groan, she pulled away, and she smiled at him.

As much as she wanted him to cum inside her, that would've been a bad move, cause she wasn't on birth control and she didn't know if it was a dangerous day or not. She would rather not have to deal with that oopsie, but it was obvious that David didn't care. In fact, he simply sat on the couch, trying to come back to his senses, but it was obvious that he had one of the greatest orgasms he's had. For Stephanie, she enjoyed it. It had been a long time since she was able to cum by someone else's hand or body other than her own. She missed the feeling of intimacy in many different aspects, but even she was struggling to find the right words.

For a long time, neither of them spoke. She loved the feeling of their silence, for they both knew they could be comfortable with one another. After a brief moment though, David turned to her with glassy eyes, smiling warmly.

"That was better than I ever dreamed it would be," he said.

"Same here. Well, I never thought I would get to have sex with my former childhood friend, but I'm not complaining," she said.

"Yeah, I'm not either. I realized from this as well that you're better than I fantasized," he admitted.

"I've never fantasized about this till now, but I'm definitely happy with the results," she said.

He gave her a kiss, and she looked at him with a smile.

"You loved that, didn't you?"

"I've had a crush on you for a while Stephanie, I was just too much of a wuss to admit it," he said.

"Well, you have now, and I mean, if you want to see where this might go, then be my guest. But, let's take it slow. I'm a little worried about going fast with anything currently," she said.

"I know. We can take it slow, just the two of us. I want you in my life Stephanie, and I'm glad that we are reunited again," he replied.

Stephanie was glad about that too. In truth, she normally didn't think that she would meet up with childhood friends and they would become bangable, but David was the nerd grown up, and although she never thought about it before, she would definitely be thinking about this again very soon.

Horny Milf in the Library

Jessica didn't know how much more of this she could take. Her breathing was growing ragged, and her pussy was definitely aching for a release. She started to touch herself from underneath the desk, looking at the young, black-haired college student that was there.

That was the object of her needs, a man named Allen. He came in here a lot and was an awkward, but really cute college kid that strove to get the degree he desired in his field. For Jessica, she loved working with him, providing the help that he desired for her projects. But, he was also really cute, and behind the little flirty glances, she could tell that he desired her just as much as she desired him.

He came over to the desk, and Jessica realized most of the library was dead. That's why her fingers wouldn't stop moving. He looked at her with a wry smile before speaking.

"Say uh Jessica, could you help me out," he said.

Jessica smiled. She definitely could, but she was two fingers deep, and she would need a little bit of help too. She couldn't wait till she got home, for she knew that her daughter Caitlyn would bother her with something, and she was mostly alone here, so she definitely would need to finish up fast and then head out.

"Sure, what is it?" she asked.

"I'm trying to find this book, and I can't seem to find it. Could you assist me?" he inquired.

Jessica was so close, her pussy sopping with delight, and her face slightly flushed. But, she got up, her curvy hips swaying as she walked past the desk and over to Allen.

"Sure, let's go find it," she said.

"It's in the chemistry section, I know this," he said.

She nodded, her body feeling the ache. She needed to go back and take care of this. They walked past the first few shelves, and she wondered if he noticed. He didn't seem to, but maybe he was just being nice. She then moved towards the chemistry section, which was all the way in the back, and then she looked at him.

"Alright, here we are. What do you--"

Before she could respond any further, she felt his lips against her own. He kissed her passionately, rutting his crotch against her own. She kissed him back, feeling the outright desire as she felt his lips immediately entangle with her own. She loved everything about this, and she knew that he did as well.

The two of them stayed like that, kissing one another and enjoying the sensation of their lips mingling with her own. He reached down, pushing his hands between her legs, and she lightly bit his lip. He pulled back, smirking at her.

"I knew you were wet. I could tell that you needed a small release. Why don't we have some fun," he said.

She realized by this point that he totally wasn't looking for a book. In fact, that was just some bullshit excuse to get her back here. Oh well, not like she was complaining. She smiled a devilish grin, looking at him with delight.

"I'd enjoy that," she said to him.

She then kissed him once more, the two of them staying like this. He ground his hips against her crotch, and as much as she like this, she knew that she had to be quick. The last thing that they needed was someone walking in on them. She turned her attention towards the cock that was practically aching to get out of his pants.

She slipped downwards, looking at him with a teasing little smile, before she undid his pants, pulling his cock out from the confines. He let out the smallest breath of relief as she started stroking him to hardness, watching as he bit his lip, enjoying everything that she was doing. She continued to tease the tip of it, letting her tongue flick along the edges, and she could see the delight in the other man's eyes as she did this. She started to take him deeper into her mouth, watching as he held her head there. She sucked him off, trying her best to stay quiet.

Luckily, the library was dead at this hour, so she didn't have to worry about others coming in. but, she knew for a fact that if they weren't careful, it could mean a whole lot of trouble for them. If she did get caught, she would most certainly be fired, and that wouldn't be good. But, the thrill of getting caught was why she took his cock into her mouth deeper and deeper, and he started to exhale with delight. She could feel him gagging her, which was a bit jarring, but she enjoyed the sensation, her whole body aching for more. She wanted to feel his cock inside of her, but she also wanted to tease him a little bit.

When she pulled away, she stroked him, taking one of his balls into her mouth, and she soon heard him exhale suddenly. He bit his lip,

trying to contain his moans, and she knew that he was getting close too. She then pulled off, grasping one of the shelves on the end, hiking up her skirt slightly and pushing her panties to the side, as if to practically beg for entrance from him.
He smiled, holding her hips and entering into her. This was better than she thought it would be. The way that his cock penetrated her sent shivers down her spine, and she started to exhale slightly. The only sounds that were made in this area were that sounds of him fucking her, and the small exhale that came from her mouth. She prepared herself for this day, knowing full well that she would have to be quiet, lest they would get caught.
He moved his hands upwards towards where her shirt was, taking both of his hands and moving towards her tits. He pinched them lightly, and she immediately felt that urge to cry out. He began to pound in deeper, watching her and seeing the way that her face contorted into that of pleasure. She watched with delight as he moved in deep, and she definitely could feel everything within her core.
The feeling of his hands on her perky tits delighted her. She loved it when guys played with them, and while they weren't huge, they were very sensitive, and she definitely loved the feeling of this.
However, as he continued to fondle and fuck her, she heard something in the distance. It was the sound of two students walking around.
"Shit, be quiet," she whispered to him.
He didn't stop fucking her though, which surprised her. She knew for a fact that he was doing this relentlessly, and she wasn't going to stop anytime soon. She noticed that he was holding her hips steadily, fucking her mercilessly. But, she could hear the students as they walked past.
"Do you think it's in the science section?"
"Perhaps. Maybe we should go check," the other replied.
Shit. If they came down this aisle, they would totally see him fucking her. But, she couldn't stop. She loved the feeling of everything that was happening. He then spread her further apart, plunging into her, hitting that one spot that would make her scream out otherwise, but she bit her lip so that neither of them would get caught.
The girls started walking down each of the aisles that were there. She hoped more than anything they would skip the chemistry section. They were working on a science project probably, so it probably would be one of these aisles and not all of them. But, for Jessica, she didn't want the luck of the draw to not be in her favor,

and she could hear both of them coming down each and every single one of the aisles, threatening to come to where she was.
They were right next to the aisle that they were in. The biology section. She gritted her teeth, knowing that if they came down this aisle, they would be so fucked, both literally and figuratively. They stayed there for a second, and she could practically feel the eyes darting about, looking for something.
"Oh, here we go!" one of them said.
"Great, let's see," the other one replied.
They were over there looking at the books now, and she could see it vaguely out of the corner of one of the shelves. Fuck, she hoped that they wouldn't look up. They stayed there for what seemed to be forever looking at the contents of said book before they closed it and then one of them spoke.
"This is totally it. Let's go take a few notes and then check out," one of them said.
"Okay," the other replied.
They walked out of the aisles, and immediately, Jessica breathed a sigh of relief. There was that danger of getting caught, but it also created a thrill that she enjoyed more than anything else. She then felt him start to ram it into her, hitting that spot, and she had to bite her lip once more, feeling the sudden urge to cum start to press forward. She wanted to, but she feared the ending of this.
But, she knew that this quickie was just that, a quickie. He moved his hands down, pressing against her clit and playing with it, and then, she let out a small, choked moan, cumming hard against him. She then felt her pussy tighten against him, and he groaned, thrusting in deep once more before she felt him groan as he spilled the rest of his seed into her. She shivered as she felt the content drip down her body, filling her pussy, and then, just as quickly as it happened, he pulled back, zipping himself up.
She straightened her panties, looking at him as she fixed her shirt. But then, she heard the sound of footsteps, and she immediately tensed up. She looked over to see the two students from before walking right down the aisle.
"Oh, there she is!" One of them said.
"We would like to check out," the other added.
Jessica smiled at them, and then, she walked forward.
"That's totally fine, we can do that now," she said.
Neither of these girls knew about what happened in the library, and she planned to keep it like that. She didn't need anyone else prying into her life. She walked with the two girls over to the checkout

counter, taking care of each of the transactions that were there. When the two of them left, she looked at the clock, realizing that she only had about 15 minutes until closing. She smiled to herself, realizing that she managed to get some dick while on the job, and she could tell from the way that Allen looked at her, this wouldn't be the end.

When she locked up, she felt a presence behind her. Allen started to rub her there, teasing her clit and pushing into her, feeling the cum that he pushed into her moments before.

"You're a naughty little slut, doing it in the library like that," he said.

She moaned, letting his hands work his magic, and she could feel the heat rising once again. She loved the feeling of his hands rubbing her there, the way that his fingers deftly played with her while hitting all of those spots. She leaned against the wall, letting out a few more breaths before she felt the urge to cum. She then released, cumming against his hands and watching as he pulled his fingers away, smiling to himself as he looked at her.

"Want to go another round?" he asked.

She thought about saying no, since she may have to head home soon, but then, she smiled at him and nodded.

"Course. After all, I'm just helping you find the books that you need for your project, and this is just some 'after hours' help that I can provide for you," she said.

He grinned, pulling her hand over to one of the shelves that were there.

"Then I suggest that we do it in a more popular section for some more fun," he said.

She didn't need to refuse this, for her pussy craved the attention, and her body ached for more of him. When he slammed her against the wall, thrusting into her, Jessica craved all of this. She didn't even realize that her body wanted this so damn badly, but as he fucked her mercilessly, she desired more.

Allen seemed to crave the Milf pussy, and when they were finished, he looked at her once more with a smile.

"I will definitely be meeting up with you again for some more private fun," he said.

"I can't wait for that then," she purred.

The two parted ways, and for Jessica, she knew for a fact that he was serious about this. He craved more of her pussy, and she wanted his dick too. The two of them would get one another off, and she would continue to have her fun in the library. It was nice to finally have the college student, and he seemed happy to fuck her too. But, she needed to head home, to take care of her daughter and get back to reality, so when they finished, the bade adieu for now, and she told him that she couldn't wait for the next time.

The Milf's Repairman

Hannah hated that she needed to wait around for the repairman, but she needed her dishwasher fixed, and this guy seemed to know what he was doing. She took the day off, and after dropping off her daughter Clara at school, she sat around. Hopefully, this guy would come soon and make it worth her time.

She hated when things would break. They were ultimately a waste of time, and she didn't like waiting around. But, after about an hour, she heard a knock at the door. She walked over, and as she opened the door, her eyes practically boggled out of her head.

In front of her was an attractive blonde with big, blue eyes. He was totally the repairman judging from his uniform, and for Hannah, she loved seeing the way his eyes widened at the sight of her.

"Oh, you're the one I'm supposed to help with fixing the dishwasher," he said.

"Yes, I am. I'm Hannah."

"Caleb," the young guy replied.

They shook hands, and she could see the guy staring at her assets, her low-cut shirt showing off cleavage and her thick thighs just barely contained in the leggings she wore. She smiled to herself, showing him inside and then closing the door. She then showed him over to the dishwasher, and as he got started with it, he certainly seemed to know what he was doing. That was a big turn on for Hannah, and she could feel herself touching herself from the confines of her leggings.

"Ahh, I see there's a small leak here, and I--"

As he turned around, he saw the look of desire on her face.

"You're so smart. I couldn't have done this myself. I'm just a businesswoman who takes care of my kid," she said.

"Well, that's still something worthwhile. You're quite pretty, and you have nice...assets," he said.

"Oh really now. Someone likes them it seems," she said.

"I do," he replied with an awkward groan. He went back to working on it, and after a few minutes, he was done.

"There we go. You're all set," he said.

But, what he didn't realize, was that her hands were against his chest, pulling him back so that her breasts were on each side of his head. He gasped, and she smiled to herself.

"Aww, it seems you deserve another little reward, that I would love to provide to you," he said.

She could see the obvious boner in his pants, and as he got up, he smiled.

"Really now? Do you reward all of your repairmen like this?" he teased.

"Just the ones I like," she told him with a grin.

He then moved his body so that he was against the counter, the dishwasher already repaired and forgotten. She wouldn't mind giving him that little extra bonus.

Caleb didn't expect any of this. But, he wasn't going to say no to this horny Milf, one that seemed practically ready to jump on his cock.

She then pulled his pants down, smiling devilishly until she got them to his ankles. She pulled his cock out, stroking it to full hardness, and she soon kissed the tip of it. He then moaned, feeling everything go blank as she started to play with the tip, pressing her lips to it and swirling her tongue against the head of his aching cock. He then started to roan, feeling everything tense up, and she smiled to herself, loving the way that he was reacting to everything that she was doing. She took him into her mouth, getting about halfway down and then moving up and down against there. She smiled with delight as he stood there, groaning and breathing out loud as she did this.

She loved watching this man lose composure like this. There was something so hot about it, and she knew for a fact that she was getting excited too. It had been so long since she got fucked, since she didn't really want to date men, and her late husband died about five years ago. She definitely wanted to have a little bit of fun without the extra stress of a relationship, that's for sure. And, as she continued to dote and tease this man's cock, he groaned out loud, holding her head there as he started to fuck her mouth vigorously. She gasped, feeling his cock immediately flood her mouth, the sudden urge to take it in deeper and try not to gag immediately overwhelming her.

She continued to suck him off for what seemed to be forever, but then, he pulled back, looking at her with serious eyes.

"Please, use your tits," he said.

She smiled, indulging in his words. She slipped her shirt off, revealing her luscious breasts. Her perky nipples were already hard, and as she wrapped her tits around his cock, she began to move them up and down, watching with delight as he began to threw his head back, gasping.

“motherfucker,” he said to himself.

She loved watching this man lose all semblance of control. She began to lick the tip of it with her tongue, letting her tits move up and down against the shaft. She then reached over with one of her free hands, letting them play with his balls, and it was then when he started to let out the cutest gasps, watching with delight as she continued to do this.

Everything was driving him to the point of madness. Everything seemed to hit that edge, but, as quickly as he got there, she pulled back and smiled.

"Not yet. We get to have a bit of fun first,” she said to him.

He groaned, excited but also frustrated. He then pushed her onto the dining room table, taking off the leggings and panties that she wore like it was nothing. He spread her apart, digging into her pussy with his lips and tongue, tasting every part of her. He began with flicking his tongue against the clit, causing her to let out a small garbled sound of pleasure. She was surprised at how good he ate women out. Most men could rarely get her super excited, but he seemed to be almost like a professional at this. He began to let his tongue trail against her clit, and he sucked on it, causing her to let out a cry. He dipped his tongue into her, pressing it in deep and flicking it over the very roof of her pussy. She shivered with delight, crying out loud and feeling everything start to tense up. She definitely loved everything about it, and as he continued to touch her, she could feel her looming orgasm start to come up.

She missed this feeling, the feeling of a man getting her off. While the vibrator that she had was nice, this wasn’t the same thing. He took her so carefully and meticulously into her mouth that she shivered, tensing her legs up and crying out loud, feeling everything grow needier and her body hornier than before. She then screamed out loud, tensing up for a second as she came into his mouth. She felt everything go blank for a second as he swallowed her juices, licking his lips with delight. As he pulled back, he smiled at her, excited about everything.

"You like it?”

"I loved it,” she replied, feeling a blush on her face.

She thought that he was done, but then, he spread her legs apart, pushing his cock deep into her pussy. He fucked her against the table, the small sounds of pleasure that she uttered echoing through the room. He got so deep, deeper than she thought they ever would get, and she could feel his thick cock inside of her, fitting perfectly and without any problems. He smiled to himself as he saw the clear desperation in her eyes, the need for more growing within her. Everything was driving her to the point of madness, the excitement only grew as he continued to do this.

He then held her hips, fucking her faster and faster. She draped her legs against his back, holding him there as he fucked her mercilessly. But, what she didn't realize, was that he was going to pick her up, which he did, and then, he thrust it deep into her, causing her to let out a cry of shock, and also of pleasure.

He was hitting that spot that most men weren't good at hitting. She felt her eyes roll towards the back of her head, everything driving her crazy, and it was then when, after a few more thrusts, she could feel her next orgasm coming. But then, he seemed to see it himself, and he achingly slowed down at this point, causing her to let out a groan of frustration.

"Not yet," he said with a purr against her ear, licking the shell of it. The erotic gesture was enough to make her moan, and soon, he let her down. But then, he looked towards the counter and smiled.

"Spread those cheeks apart against the counter," he said with a purr. She moved over there, bracing the counter and looking at him. He then pushed his cock into her from behind, and she could feel it brushing against that spot that she enjoyed being penetrated against once again, feeling her eyes practically roll to the back of her head once more. He began to thrust in deep, groaning as he felt his cock get inside of her, and her insides practically hugging him. She gasped herself, feeling how it was hitting the spot in a different way, and she could feel her breathing growing ragged and her body aching for more from this man. He started to brush against her faster and faster, getting in deep and enjoying the sensation of fucking her mercilessly and raw. She gasped at everything that happened, and she definitely needed to cum soon. She could feel the raw need growing within her body, and as he pushed against there again, it was like a jolt to her body.

She cried out, excited about everything as it started to happen. He then pushed in once more, and she let out a garbled sound, crying out loud as she felt the sudden urge push through her. She grasped the couch, screaming out loud as she came hard, tightening her pussy against him, feeling the sheer force of it all drive her forward. She could feel her eyes going blank, everything changing within her, and her body craving more.

He then groaned, feeling how tight her pussy was against him, how he practically was being pulled in, and then, he groaned, his cock throbbing before he spilled himself all the way inside of her. She gasped at the hot liquid as it hit her insides, making her groan loudly and in pleasure. It was so satisfying to have a cock inside of her, and the fact that he made her feel good while he fucked her was something that she enjoyed. She missed this feeling, and everything about this made her feel just so good inside she didn't have any other words.

He pulled out, causing her to fall to the floor. It was tough to even get up, and as he looked at her, he smiled.

"You good?" he asked.

"Yeah. I feel utterly fucking amazing," she admitted.

Hannah didn't know how to get up. Her legs felt like jelly and her orgasm was definitely better than she thought. But, Caleb grasped her body, bringing her over to the living room and settling her on the couch.

"You seem like you had a fun time," he said with a purr.

"Yeah, and I'd do it again if you ever wanted to. I definitely like you repairing my stuff, and of course, checking my own pipes too," she told him with a purr.

She couldn't believe that she still had the energy to flirt, but then he smiled at her, acknowledging her actions.

"Well, I can certainly make that happen once again, you can just call on me, and I'll be over right away," he said.

"That would be nice. Also, your check is on the dining room table. I'd get it for you but...I'm a little tired," she said.

"I know. You just get some rest," he said.

He gave her a kiss on the lips before he went to get his check, heading towards the truck and then leaving. For Hannah, she didn't really know what else to do at this point besides basking in her orgasm, which was one of the best things she experienced. She couldn't believe it was so good, and that a guy could make her feel like that. But, for Hannah, she knew that she would need to go back to reality sooner or later, which sucked, but she definitely enjoyed the fun that she got to have.

She got herself together, getting ready to pick her daughter up from school later on. She did get a little bit of work done, but nothing of value. Her mind was on other things, the fucking that she experienced and the hot guy who serviced her. She certainly would be calling on his services again, and she hoped more than anything

that she could get him over for another fun little repair that led to more fun for the both of them as a result.
That was the goal, and Hannah would definitely take him up on his offer again.

www.ingramcontent.com/pod-product-compliance
Ingram Content Group UK Ltd.
Pitfield, Milton Keynes, MK11 3LW, UK
UKHW011358241125
9154UKWH00028B/264

9 781951 339623